ALSO BY CRESSIDA COWELL

P9-ELS-171

How to Train Your Dragon

How to Train Your Dragon
How to Be a Pirate
How to Speak Dragonese
How to Cheat a Dragon's Curse
How to Twist a Dragon's Tale
A Hero's Guide to Deadly Dragons
How to Ride a Dragon's Storm
How to Break a Dragon's Heart
How to Steal a Dragon's Sword
How to Seize a Dragon's Jewel
How to Betray a Dragon's Hero
How to Fight a Dragon's Fury

The Complete Book of Dragons: A Guide to Dragon Species
A Journal for Heroes

The Wizards of Once

The Wizards of Once
Twice Magic
Knock Three Times

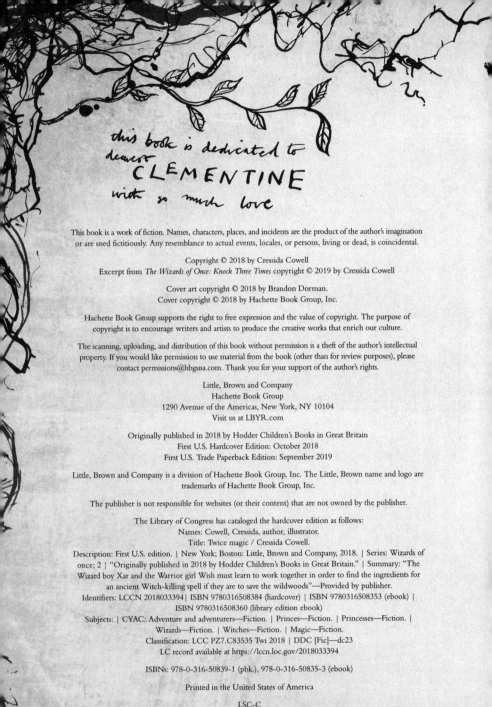

this book is dedicated to dearest
CLEMENTINE
with so much love

This book is a work of fiction. Names, characters, places, and incidents are the product of the author's imagination or are used fictitiously. Any resemblance to actual events, locales, or persons, living or dead, is coincidental.

Copyright © 2018 by Cressida Cowell
Excerpt from *The Wizards of Once: Knock Three Times* copyright © 2019 by Cressida Cowell

Cover art copyright © 2018 by Brandon Dorman.
Cover copyright © 2018 by Hachette Book Group, Inc.

Hachette Book Group supports the right to free expression and the value of copyright. The purpose of copyright is to encourage writers and artists to produce the creative works that enrich our culture.

The scanning, uploading, and distribution of this book without permission is a theft of the author's intellectual property. If you would like permission to use material from the book (other than for review purposes), please contact permissions@hbgusa.com. Thank you for your support of the author's rights.

Little, Brown and Company
Hachette Book Group
1290 Avenue of the Americas, New York, NY 10104
Visit us at LBYR.com

Originally published in 2018 by Hodder Children's Books in Great Britain
First U.S. Hardcover Edition: October 2018
First U.S. Trade Paperback Edition: September 2019

Little, Brown and Company is a division of Hachette Book Group, Inc. The Little, Brown name and logo are trademarks of Hachette Book Group, Inc.

The publisher is not responsible for websites (or their content) that are not owned by the publisher.

The Library of Congress has cataloged the hardcover edition as follows:
Names: Cowell, Cressida, author, illustrator.
Title: Twice magic / Cressida Cowell.
Description: First U.S. edition. | New York; Boston: Little, Brown and Company, 2018. | Series: Wizards of once; 2 ¦ "Originally published in 2018 by Hodder Children's Books in Great Britain." | Summary: "The Wizard boy Xar and the Warrior girl Wish must learn to work together in order to find the ingredients for an ancient Witch-killing spell if they are to save the wildwoods"—Provided by publisher.
Identifiers: LCCN 2018033394| ISBN 9780316508384 (hardcover) | ISBN 9780316508353 (ebook) | ISBN 9780316508360 (library edition ebook)
Subjects: | CYAC: Adventure and adventurers—Fiction. | Princes—Fiction. | Princesses—Fiction. | Wizards—Fiction. | Witches—Fiction. | Magic—Fiction.
Classification: LCC PZ7.C83535 Twi 2018 | DDC [Fic]—dc23
LC record available at https://lccn.loc.gov/2018033394

ISBNs: 978-0-316-50839-1 (pbk.), 978-0-316-50835-3 (ebook)

Printed in the United States of America

LSC-C

10 9 8 7 6 5 4 3 2 1

THE WIZARDS OF ONCE

TWICE MAGIC

written and illustrated by

CRESSIDA COWELL

Little, Brown and Company

New York Boston

This is a story
with two heroes.

The girl, Wish, is a Warrior,
BUT she has a strange and powerful
Magic-that-works-on-iron.

The boy, Xar, is a Wizard,
but he has a Witch-stain on his
hand that may be impossible to remove...

QUERED
TERRITORIES
Warrior Capital
THIS WAY
The Sweet Track
WARRIOR
EMPIRE
Iron Warrior Fort
HE
QUEENDOM
of
SYCHORAX
Queen Sychorax's New Wall (built on the remains of the LAST Wall...)
LD
WOODS
Ragged Ri..

Twice there was Magic...

Prologue

Imagine an age of giants.

It was a long, long time ago, in a British Isles so old it did not know it was the British Isles yet, when the country was all wildwoods, and there were two types of humans fighting in the woodlands.

The WIZARDS, who had lived in this forest for as long as memory, and were as Magic as the wood itself, and rode on the back of the giant snowcats. And the WARRIORS, who hunted the Magic down with bright swords and fire, so they could build their forts and their fields and their new modern world.

The Warriors were winning, for their weapons were made of IRON...

...and IRON was the only thing that Magic would not work on.

This is the story of a young boy Wizard and a young girl Warrior, who were both cheerful and hopeful and full of good ideas, but they had been taught since birth to hate each other like poison. It is the tale of how they met, and learned to be friends and to see things from each other's point of view, and it really wants to be a HAPPY story...but unfortunately in the course of their last joyful adventure...

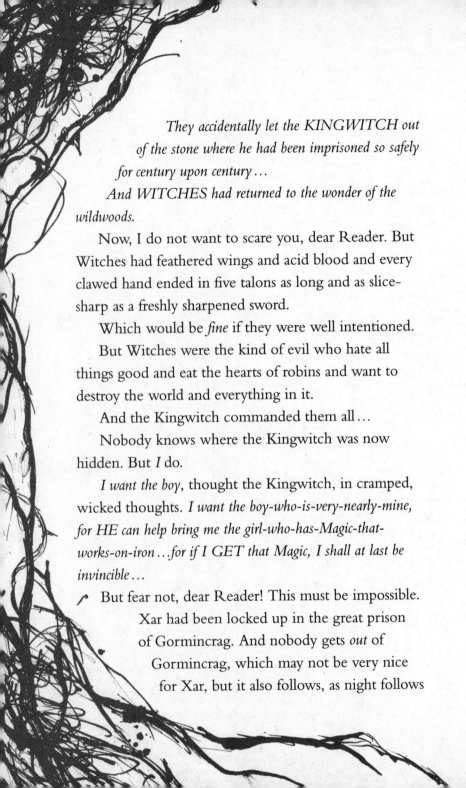

They accidentally let the KINGWITCH out
of the stone where he had been imprisoned so safely
for century upon century...

And WITCHES had returned to the wonder of the
wildwoods.

Now, I do not want to scare you, dear Reader. But
Witches had feathered wings and acid blood and every
clawed hand ended in five talons as long and as slice-
sharp as a freshly sharpened sword.

Which would be *fine* if they were well intentioned.

But Witches were the kind of evil who hate all
things good and eat the hearts of robins and want to
destroy the world and everything in it.

And the Kingwitch commanded them all...

Nobody knows where the Kingwitch was now
hidden. But *I* do.

I want the boy, thought the Kingwitch, in cramped,
wicked thoughts. *I want the boy-who-is-very-nearly-mine,*
for HE can help bring me the girl-who-has-Magic-that-
works-on-iron...for if I GET that Magic, I shall at last be
invincible...

But fear not, dear Reader! This must be impossible.
Xar had been locked up in the great prison
of Gormincrag. And nobody gets *out* of
Gormincrag, which may not be very nice
for Xar, but it also follows, as night follows

day, that the Kingwitch and his Witches cannot get *in*.

And as for Wish, why Wish's scary mother, the great Warrior queen Sychorax, has built a gigantic Wall across the entire western edge of her kingdom, a Wall so high that even a Longstepper High-Walker giant couldn't see over it on tiptoes, to protect her people from the attacks of the Witches.

So our heroes can't possibly meet each other, or the Kingwitch, in a story as short as this one.

It was extremely unlikely that they would ever have met in the first place.

It happened ONCE.

Surely it couldn't happen TWICE?

I am a character
in this story...
who sees everything,
knows everything.
I will not tell you
who I am.

Have You GUESSED yet?

Follow the ink path of the
story.

(Don't get lost.
These woods are DANGEROUS.)

GORMINCRAG
PRISON

Gormincrag prison is surrounded
by a sunken forest in a sea
filled with Bladderbones, Bloody
Bones and Daggerfins —
there are swimming skulls of
the battleneat.

NOBODY gets out of the terrible prison of GORMINCRAG →

Sea of ↙ Skulls

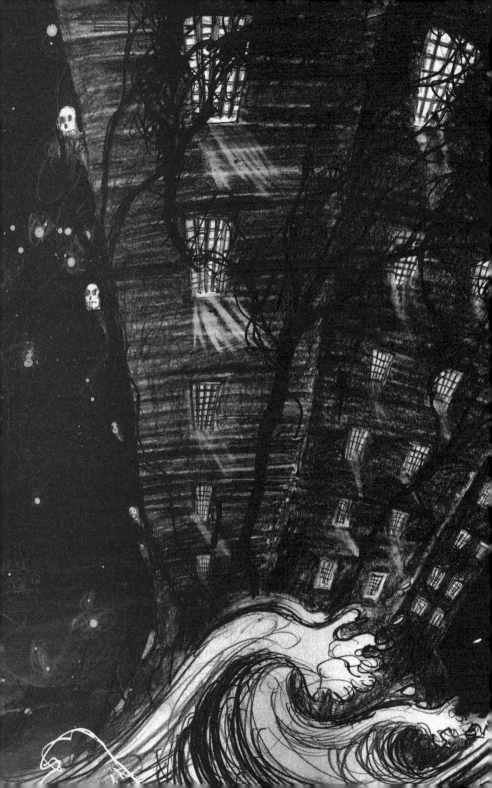

1. Escape from Gormincrag is Impossible

It was a quarter past midnight, four weeks before Midwinter's End Eve, and a thirteen-year-old boy was dangling precariously from a disintegrating homemade rope hanging from outside the darkest tower of Gormincrag, the Rehabilitation Center for the Re-Education of Dark Magic and Wicked Wizards.

(That, by the way, is a long and fancy name for a jail, and not just any old jail, the most secure and impregnable jail in the wildwoods.)

The boy's name was Xar (which is pronounced "Zar"—I don't know why, spelling is weird) and he really, really, *really* should not have been there.

He was supposed to be INSIDE the prison, not OUTSIDE it, dangling fifty feet above sea level from one of the windows. That's one of the most important rules about prisons, and Xar really should have known that.

But Xar was not the kind of boy who followed the rules.

Xar *acted* first and *thought* later, and this was exactly what had led him to be put in the Gormincrag Rehabilitation Center in the first place, and given him

the reputation of being the naughtiest, wildest boy born into the Wizard kingdom in about four generations.

See if you think that reputation is justified...

In the past week, for example, Xar had:

Put what was supposed to be sleeping potion into the Rogrebreath guards' wine, but it turned out to be cursing potion instead...glued the bottoms of the entire Drood High Command to their chairs in the hope that it would give him time for a quick getaway—but forgot to glue the chairs to the floor, so the Droods just ran after him with chairs stuck to their bottoms...treated himself to some stolen invisibility potion, but unfortunately it had only made his HEAD disappear, giving the Drood in charge of Reprogramming a terrible shock because he imagined on visiting Xar's cell that the prison had been invaded by headless GHOSTS...

None of these disobedient things had been *intentional*, exactly. They had all just happened by accident, in the course of him trying to escape, for even though Xar was a happy-go-lucky cheerful sort of person, two months of imprisonment had given even *his* high spirits a bit of a battering, and his quiff of hair had drooped a little under the pressure, and he had been feeling, at times, a little desperate.

Gormincrag was well known to be impossible to escape from, but Xar never let a little thing like impossibility put him off. So although to an outsider his present predicament might have looked pretty bad, Xar was remarkably pleased with himself for a person who was hanging on to a crumbling rope swaying violently above seas known to be infested with such dreadful monsters as Blunderbouths, Daggerfins, and Bloody Barbeards.

His wide-awake eyes were bright with excitement and hope.

"You see!" Xar whispered triumphantly to his

squeezjoos

companions. "What did I tell you? We're doing brilliantly! We've *nearly* escaped already!"

And Xar was right: They had really done a very good job to get this far.

The Gormincrag Rehabilitation Center for the Re-Education of Dark Magic and Wicked Wizards had been designed to imprison some of the most terrifying monsters in the entire Magic world. Bogeymen. Ogres of all sizes and savageries. Jack o' Kents, Bugbears, Kelpies, Grim Annises, you name it, and even, once upon a time, dare I say it, WITCHES, who were once extinct, and had recently reemerged in that part of the wildwoods.

NO ONE, no Dark-sprite, no Rogrebreath however large and terrifying, no Wicked Wizard of spells the most fiendish, had EVER escaped from Gormincrag before. People had tried of course, and the legends of brave but failed escape attempts from Gormincrag were

Bumbleboozle

told from sprite to sprite across the years. But no one had ever successfully made it out of there alive.

Even if, by some extraordinary chance, you made it beyond the prison perimeter without the skulls screaming, the grim towers of Gormincrag were built on seven islands set in a sea called prettily "the Sea of Skulls," and the treacherous waves would get you, or those vicious merfolk, the Bloody Barbeards, would swim out of their holes in the Drowned Forest on the seafloor and get you, and bring you back.

As the son of a King Enchanter, and a boy with a great deal of personal charisma, Xar had quite a few followers.

At the moment he was accompanied by five sprites (Tiffinstorm, Timeloss, Hinkypunk, Ariel, and Mustardthought)—and these were beautiful, fierce-looking creatures, resembling a cross between a very small human and an angry insect, and three hairy fairies, (Squeezjoos, Bumbleboozle, and the baby), smaller, more beelike animals, who were too young to have climbed into their cocoons and metamorphosed into proper adult sprites yet.

Sprites can light up like stars in the night-time, but these ones did not want to be detected at the moment, so they had subdued the light of their little bodies to the very dimmest of glows.

The Baby

11

These sprites all belonged to Xar, and loyally, quietly, invisibly, they had sneaked in to Gormincrag to try and help him escape.

"Yous right, Master!" Squeezjoos, one of the hairy fairies, whispered back. Squeezjoos was a tiny little six-legged creature, larger than a bumblebee but still so small he could fit into your hand, and he was buzzing excitedly around Xar's head. "Yous ALWAYS right! That'ss why youss the leader and you never leads uss into any trouble! Oo! What's this fasscintressting cave?"

This "fasscintressting cave" was in fact a large skull with its mouth open. Squeezjoos buzzed in to investigate and the mouth snapped shut with an ominous clang and the eyeholes squeezed tight closed as if they still had lids on them. "Helloooo?" buzzed Squeezjoos in anxious echoes from within. "Helloooo? I think I iss stuck!"

The sprites nearly fell out of the air they were laughing so much, but Xar intervened in quick alarm, hissing, "Don't go over the boundary of the battlements anybody! There's a Magic force field around this castle, and it's fine getting IN, but you can't get across it to get OUT!"

At some considerable danger to himself, because the skull was just out of reach, and he had to tie the end of the rope to his ankle and dangle upside down to get his

13

I can't look...

hands on it, Xar then
very, very carefully
and delicately released
the mouth bone of the
skull so that Squeezjoos
could buzz out triumphantly
squeaking, "I is fine! Don't worry
everyone! I is FINE!"

And then Xar swung
himself back onto a
safer ledge again and
explained to his interested
companions that those
skulls were the screaming
kind, and they were one
of the final defenses of
Gormincrag.

I is FINE!

If you put one fingertip beyond the perimeter of the prison, the skulls would open up their mouths and scream bloodcurdling yells, which would wake the guards of Gormincrag and bring them down upon you.

This was typical of Xar. Although he had spent his entire young life leading his followers into considerable trouble, to do him justice, he always tried his hardest to get them OUT of it, even if it put him personally in great peril.

Xar was also accompanied by a talking raven—who had his wings over his eyes, such was his horror at the whole dangling-upside-down-and-rescuing-hairy-fairies-from-screaming-skulls episode—and a seven-and-a-half-foot Loner Raving Fangmouth werewolf called Lonesome, who made anxious grunting noises when Xar mentioned the Gormincrag guards.

Xar had met Lonesome in the prison, and while it is not really advisable to make friends with Loner Raving Fangmouth werewolves, neither Xar nor the werewolf had a lot of choice in the matter. They both wanted to escape.

The werewolf gave a smothered howl of discontent.

"What is the werewolf saying?" asked the raven.

The talking raven was called Caliburn, and he would have been a handsome bird, but unfortunately it was his job to keep Xar out of trouble, and the worry and general impossibility of this hopeless mission meant his feathers kept falling out.

"I think he's saying, why are we heading in *this* direction?" said Xar.

Xar was the only one of them who had been taught werewolf language, but Xar wasn't great at concentrating in class, and the problem with werewolves is they do mumble their words, so sometimes you could mistake a grunt for a gurgle, or an *oooarrghh* for an *eerrggagh*, and completely misunderstand what they were talking about.

"We're going *this* way," explained Xar, "because we're just going to drop into the Drood Commander's Room…It's an important step in our escape…"

The werewolf gave a smothered howl of horror and waved his shaggy paws around with such alarm that he nearly fell off the rope.

"You shouldn't be escaping! And we shouldn't be helping you!" said Caliburn in a flurry of anxiety. "But surely if we *are* helping you to escape, the idea would be to do it *quietly*? Crusher and the animals are waiting for us down at the bottom of the western battlements…"

(Crusher was a Longstepper High-Walker giant, and he and the wolves, the snowcats, and the bear were also Xar's companions.)

"We should be joining Crusher and the others!"

16

Caliburn pointed out. "Hopping over the back of the wall, without telling anyone, not presenting ourselves to the head of the prison for a nice little chat and a cup of herbal tea!"

"Yes, well, that's why no one has ever gotten out of this armpit of a jail before," said Xar. "How many times have YOU tried to escape from here, Lonesome?"

The werewolf mumbled something that might have been "twenty-three"...

"You see?" said Xar. "Trust me, everyone! I have a plan that could just be the cunning-est, most brilliant, and daring escape plan in the entire *history* of the wildwoods..."

Xar had a lot of good qualities, but modesty wasn't one of them.

Inch by inch, the little party crept down the ropes, landed on the windowsill outside the Drood Commander's Room, and peered inside.

The room might have been the shape of a star, or a circle, or a pentagon, who knew? For the walls had a habit of moving around while you were looking at them, and the floor looked like the sea, and the ceiling might have been the sky. It was enough to make you feel a little bit sick just to look at it.

The only still point in the room was a gigantic desk.

Three Wizards were sitting around the desk, talking.

17

One of the Wizards was the Drood Commander of Gormincrag, and Xar pointed to the spelling staff the Drood Commander was holding.

"That's the reason we're here..." whispered Xar. *"Because the Drood Commander's spelling staff controls everything in this castle."*

"Ohhh no...oh noo..." whispered Caliburn the raven, in a frenzy of alarm. "Don't tell me that your plan is to steal the Staff-That-Commands-the-Castle?"

Xar nodded. That was indeed his plan.

"It'sss brilliant! Is brilliant!" squeaked Squeezjoos, buzzing around in such an overexcited fashion that he was very nearly sick.

"Sssshhhhhhhh..." everyone else whispered back.

The werewolf gave a small grunt that might have been approval. It was quite a good plan actually. At least, it was something the werewolf had never tried before.

But as Xar peered into the room, the shaggy weight of the werewolf's fur on his shoulder, he started so violently he nearly fell off the windowsill.

For he suddenly recognized the other Wizards who were talking to the Drood Commander of Gormincrag.

"*My father...*and my *brother...*" whispered Xar.

It was indeed Xar's father, the Great Wizard Enchanter, Encanzo the Magnificent, King of Wizards, and Xar's older brother, Looter.

Xar could feel a mixture of fear and shame rising within him, starting with a queasy flip of his stomach and then bubbling up into a hot flush of shame.

When Xar had been arrested by the Drood Guards, Encanzo and Looter had been traveling on a mission to the Witch Mountains, to find out how bad the threat from the Witches was.

So they did not yet know why Xar was in here…and Xar really, really didn't want them to find that out…

Xar could just about hear what the Wizards were saying, if he leaned in through the window.

"Your Droods have crept into my kingdom while I was away and have stolen my son from me!" raged Encanzo. "I demand that you release him this instant!"

Xar's father, Encanzo, was a tall, immensely powerful Wizard, of such Magic strength that it was curiously difficult to look at him. His outline was blurred by Magic, shifting, moving, and great steaming clouds of enchantment drifted off his head as he spoke. He was looking a little weary, for he was at his wit's end, trying to lead his people in the fight against the Witches.

The Drood Commander was taller still, a rake of a man, spitefully thin, and with eyebrows so long he had braided them. He had grown so old in the forest that there was something of the tree about him. His fingers

had bent and twisted into twigs, and his face was as
green and wrinkled as ancient bark.

The Drood Commander was well
intentioned, but he was convinced that he
was right about absolutely everything,
and everyone else was absolutely wrong.
Over time that can make you bitter
rather than gentle, for whatever
we are tends to concentrate as
we get older, and it had distilled
him into a pungent, poisonous
drink indeed. Angry, judgmental
little eyes glittered
in his tree-bark
wrinkled face, and
his clawlike hands
closed jealously over
his spelling staff.

"I am not keeping
Xar here for my
own amusement!"
snapped the Drood
Commander. "Your
wretched son has
completely disrupted
my prison!

The Drood Commander

IS SO FUNNY!

He has:

> *For no reason whatsoever, cut off some tail hair of the Great Howling Hairy Hindogre while it was sleeping in its cell, and the Great Howling Hairy Hindogre is still howling in fury five days later, keeping everyone in the western tower of the prison awake all night...*"

"Ah," said Encanzo thoughtfully. "Is that the distant moaning sound I can hear?"

"That *wasn't* for no reason!" objected Xar in a whisper to his companions. "I needed that hair so I could escape in an absolutely foolproof Bigfoot-soldier-with-a-beard disguise..."

"*Nobody'sss* going to think you're old enough to have a beard, Xar!" objected Caliburn. "And Bigfoot soldiers are at least six feet tall!"

"That *was* a slight flaw in the foolproof plan," admitted Xar.

It wasn't the only flaw. When their winter coats

tee hee he hee!

come in, Howling Hairy Hindogres are an attractive shade of midnight blue, and Xar had been caught within about five minutes because the Drood Guards agreed with Caliburn that there was no such thing as a five-foot-tall Bigfoot with a bright blue beard.

The Drood Commander was really getting going now, with a long list of Xar's offenses:

"... put itching powder in the underwear of my guards on patrol ... stolen a prison guard's cape and hood and dropped it in the vampire-dog pit ... dropped the stinky socks of a Rogrebreath guard into the breakfast porridge so that it tasted disgustingly of rotten eggs ..."

"Accidents ... all accidents and misunderstandings ..." whispered Xar from the window.

"And then, out of sheer wanton mischief," the Drood Commander ended, "he glued the behinds of Drood High Command to their chairs while they sat quietly and peacefully eating their dinner! Indefensible, inexplicable, inexcusable behavior!"

This last incident had particularly upset the Drood Commander, for he was a man of great dignity, and he had not liked having to visit the Sanatorium with a chair stuck firmly to his bottom. He had draped a cloak over it, but it was quite a large chair and the Rogrebreaths, still stuffed to the tips of their hairy ears with cursing potion, had made quite a few personal remarks that still stung when the Drood Commander remembered them.

"That was quite funny," admitted Xar, smiling at the memory of it, "but that was an accident too! They shouldn't have locked me up if they didn't want me to try and escape!"

"All of these things you are describing are just disobediences," said Xar's father, Encanzo, with relief. "Annoying, I grant you, and Xar ought to have grown out of such stuff, but there's nothing *wicked* in those things... He'll just be getting fed up with being in here, and I don't blame him, quite frankly..."

"I do have a prison to run," said the Drood, his lips pursing. "I cannot let your son completely disrupt it. He is here because he represents a severe threat to the entire Magic community," continued the Drood Commander, getting to his feet. "But I can show you he is safe. Come with me..."

All around the Drood Commander's Room were gigantic mirrors, and they were not normal mirrors. If you looked into those mirrors you could see into every single room in the castle. So at any point the Drood Commander of Gormincrag could know exactly what was going on, all around the prison.

The Drood Commander pointed at one of the mirrors, and the mirror clouded up, before gradually showing the view inside a small cell in the high security block.

"It's empty," said Encanzo the King Enchanter.

The cell was indeed, as Encanzo said, empty.

The Drood Commander stared at the empty cell in astonishment. "I don't understand it!" said the Drood Commander. "That is most definitely Xar's cell... Where on earth is he?"

"I thought you were supposed to be the most secure, maximum high-security prison in the wildwoods?" snapped Encanzo. "And you are telling me that you have somehow *misplaced* my thirteen-year-old son?"

"This is most unusual..." blustered the Drood Commander, blinking at all the mirrors so that they rapidly clouded up to reveal cell after cell, each one containing a captured rogre or Grim Annis or Venge-sprite...but absolutely no sign of Xar. "Of course there must be some perfectly reasonable explanation for all this...The Guards must have moved him without telling me..."

"Dear, oh dear..." purred Encanzo, "that's not very organized is it? Rather poor communication with your guards, I'd say...I repeat, Commander, *where is my son?*"

"Here I am," said a voice behind them.

Unfortunately, when the three Wizards stepped away from the Drood Commander's desk and stood in front

of the mirrors, they had
left their spelling staffs
lying on the desk behind
them, in full view of Xar,
who had an empty pouch just
the right size for a couple more
staffs.

So now when they all slo-o-owly
turned around...

...*there was Xar.*

He was accompanied by a seven-foot werewolf, standing by the desk. Above Xar's head buzzed his sprites and a very guilty-looking Caliburn.

There was a sprite word for the way that the Drood Commander and Encanzo and Looter were looking at Xar in that moment.

And the sprite word for it is "goggle-smarked." Absolutely "flabberwastedly, jiggerdroppingly goggle-smarked," to be precise.

Ariel

Squeezjoos

The Baby

Bumbleboozle

Xar's Sprites

Tiffinstorm

Mustardthought

Timeloss

Hinkypunk

2. Did I Mention That Escape from Gormincrag Is Impossible?

ello, Father," said Xar defiantly, annoyed to find himself trembling.

"Hello, Xar," said the Enchanter calmly. "We were just looking for you, and here you are…What are you doing?"

"I'm escaping," said Xar.

"Escape is impossible from Gormincrag!" blustered the Drood Commander.

Both Xar and the Enchanter ignored him.

"If you're escaping," said the Enchanter thoughtfully, "then what are you doing *here*? I would have thought that the Drood Commander's office is not the perfect place to come to if you want to make an escape."

"That's what *I* said!" said Caliburn in agreement.

"I suggest you put the staffs down," said the Enchanter, "and then we can talk reasonably. How are you? Are you all right?"

For Xar was looking shaken, and somewhat worn. His quiff of hair had drooped, and there was something a little desperate about his usual cheeky swagger. He looked like a thirteen-year-old boy who had gotten himself into a LOT of trouble.

"What have you Droods been doing to him?"

snapped Encanzo, turning to the Drood Commander. "How DARE you treat the son of a king in this way?"

"Ask the boy what he's done to be put in here," sneered the Drood Commander. "And then perhaps you will see why we acted as we did. Go on! Ask him!"

"Why did they put you in here, Xar?" said Encanzo calmly.

Xar would not answer his father's question.

He could not look his father in the eye. He could feel himself burning red with embarrassment.

"Aren't you going to tell your father the truth?" jeered the Drood Commander. "Are you…ashamed?"

Xar gripped the spelling staffs tighter. "Don't tell him!" pleaded Xar.

"He is here," shouted the Drood Commander, "because he has been using the Magic of a Witch!"

There was an uncomfortable silence.

"Is this true?" said the Enchanter, and it was every bit as bad as Xar had dreaded. He sounded so very, very disappointed.

Unfortunately, it was, indeed, completely true.

Wizards are not born with Magic, the Magic comes in when they are about twelve years old. Xar was thirteen, and his Magic still hadn't come in, and that was deeply embarrassing, particularly for a boy like Xar who had a lot of pride. The son of a King Enchanter to be a boy without Magic? Inconceivable!

So six months earlier, Xar had taken desperate steps to get hold of some Magic of his own.

Desperate, stupid, *dangerous* steps.

He had deliberately pricked his hand with Witchblood, so that the blood mixed with his own, and he was able to use the Magic of the Witch.

On his right hand there was a telltale green cross that marked where the Witchblood had gone in. He had managed to conceal this for a while, but the Droods had a way of knowing when people were using dark Magic, and they had taken Xar from his father's fort while Encanzo was away.

"That arm the boy is holding behind his back has a Witch-stain he has been using to perform banned Magic," said the Drood Commander. "I'm surprised," he continued, "that an all-powerful Enchanter like yourself did not notice your own son using dark Magic, right under your nose…"

How indeed had Xar's father not noticed?

Well, the truth is, sometimes parents do not want to believe the worst about their children, even if that worst is staring them right in the face.

"Show me your hand," said Encanzo, although one

look at Xar's guilty face let him know that the Drood
Commander was telling the truth.

Quickly, to get it over with, Xar brought his arm out
from behind his back, and took off the glove that he
wore to conceal the Witch-stain.

"It's not as bad as it looks," said Xar hopefully.

Encanzo stiffened with shock, his outline pulsing
with furious energy.

It was a gruesome sight.

The sprites hissed with horror when they saw it,
and little Squeezjoos stuck his tail between his legs,
crouching down and trembling in the air.

"Poor Xar..." whispered Squeezjoos.

The green of the Witch-stain had moved beyond
Xar's hand and up his wrist, and looked as if it
was spreading farther, like a creeping bruise, or ivy
slowly growing around and strangling a tender young
tree.

Poor Xar indeed.

He had been well punished for his one moment of
madness in a midnight wood.

"Of all the stupid things you have ever done, Xar,"
said Encanzo, bitingly, "this is undoubtedly the stupidest."

"I told you, Father!" jeered Looter. "A Wizard with
no Magic, who is using the Magic of a Witch! He's a
disgrace to our family! No wonder they locked him up!"

"It's hot as bad as it looks," said Xar.

Xar could feel himself going red with shame, and tears pricking away at the back of his eyelids.

"It was because my Magic should have come in!" explained Xar. "You don't know what it's like, Father, growing up without Magic when everyone else has it!"

"Oh, Xar..." said the Enchanter, shaking his head. He could feel himself getting angry. Why did Xar always put him in these situations? He had come to demand Xar's release, only to find his son had been put in jail for perfectly understandable reasons.

"Why didn't you tell me you had this Magic, and then I could have helped you try to get rid of it?" asked Encanzo, his brow descending like a thundercloud.

"And you, Caliburn? Ariel? Why did *no one* tell me about this?"

Caliburn looked even guiltier. "The boy trusts us," said Caliburn. "We cannot betray him."

"You made us Xar's advisorsss, not his jailersss..." hissed Ariel, moving protectively toward Xar's shoulder and showing his fangs in a snarl at the Enchanter.

It was Encanzo's turn to redden. "*I* did not jail him!"

"Well, thank goodness *we* jailed him!" said the Drood Commander. "The boy represents a severe threat to the entire Magic community, and until we can get rid of the dark Magic he has stolen, he cannot possibly be released."

"I promise I'll make everything right again."

"But why can't you help me *control* the Witchblood Magic?" said Xar. "I can command it, if you teach me...It's fine..."

"Witchblood Magic is almost impossible to control," said the Drood Commander. "Particularly for a boy like you, selfish and impulsive—"

"He's *thirteen*!" protested Encanzo. "Were *you* never young and a bit foolish, Commander? Did *you* never make a mistake, and regret it?"

"I was once young, but never foolish," said the Drood Commander, lips pursing.

Xar turned to his father.

"I'm sorry, Father, I didn't mean for this to happen. I'm sorry I got this dark Magic…I'm sorry I didn't tell you about it…I'm sorry for everything, I really, really am…" he said, hanging his head sadly, and he did mean that.

But Xar could never stay sad for long.

His face brightened, and he carried on eagerly, "But I promise you, I'll make everything right again! I'm going to make you SO PROUD of me!"

"I'm going to make you SO PROUD of me, Father!"

"I'm *already* proud of you!" said Encanzo, now seriously alarmed. "Exasperated sometimes…infuriated…but what are you planning to do now?"

"I'm going to make amends," said Xar. "I'm going to break out of here and destroy the Witches on my own, and *that* will get rid of the Witch-stain!"

There was a stunned silence. Encanzo tried not to laugh.

But Looter didn't try.

Looter was a lot bigger than Xar, and he was handsome and clever and smug and good at everything, including Magic.

"Oh, come ON, little brother!" Looter laughed. "You can't possibly do that!"

"Why not?" Xar asked belligerently.

"YOU? The boy of destiny?

HA! HA! HA!" scoffed Looter.

"Because you're just one small, stupid little kid!" scoffed Looter. "This is all part of Xar's silly idea that he is some kind of boy of destiny."

"I AM the boy of destiny!" cried Xar, punching the air.

Looter and the Drood Commander laughed even harder at that, and now even Encanzo joined in.

"Oh, *don't laugh*..." begged Caliburn, putting his wings over his eyes. "Think of Xar's dignity...Don't laugh, Encanzo!"

"It is a worthy ambition, Xar," said Encanzo, hastily recollecting himself, "and I'm impressed that you are truly sorry and want to make amends. It is

a sign that at last you are growing up. But trust me, I will make amends *for* you, and try and get rid of the Witches on your behalf. Just give me the staffs."

Calmly, Encanzo the Enchanter held out his hand.

Xar paused.

"So you will get rid of the Witches?" he asked warily.

"It could be impossible to do that entirely," admitted Encanzo. "But there may be other ways of removing that Witch-stain..."

"And you'll let me help?" Xar asked. "You'll get these Droods to set me free?"

"I'm sorry, Xar, but the Drood is right. Until we have gotten rid of that Witch-stain, you mustn't leave the safety of Gormincrag," said Encanzo. "The Droods are the greatest Wizards in the wildwoods, and if anyone can find a way of removing that Witch-stain, *they* can."

"I can *control* the Witch-stain, even if they can't remove it!" said Xar, backing away from his father. "Why are you so gloomy about everything? Why do you listen to this Drood here rather than me? *Caliburn* thinks I can get better. *Caliburn* believes in me."

"Caliburn and Ariel have shown themselves to be completely unworthy advisors!" snapped the Enchanter.

"They're better advisors than YOU!" roared Xar. "*You'll* NEVER get rid of the Witches, for you are too COWARDLY to fight Warriors or Witches with

40

the strength of our ancestors!"

The Enchanter lost his temper.

"You will stop this nonsense, Xar!" yelled the Enchanter. "You will stay here until the Witch-stain can be removed and you learn self-control and your place in this world. I am your father and I ORDER you to hand over those spelling staffs this instant!"

Xar backed away, his brows descending thunderously. "You don't trust me! You think I should be in jail! You think I am selfish! Well, I can be good! I can make amends! *I'LL SHOW YOU!*"

Encanzo realized his mistake. "No! I'm sorry, Xar, I do trust you, it's just that I think you need help. You can't do this on your own!"

But it was too late. The moment when Xar might have changed paths was lost.

The Drood Commander blinked, two swift blinks that brought out a bolt of Magic from his eyes, which went speeding toward his staff that Xar was holding.

There was instant pandemonium.

Don't perform Magic when you're angry, Xar!

Xar pointed
the staff at the
Drood Commander, and a great blast of
Magic came out of it, a blast so wild that it
stopped the Commander's Magic in its tracks.

Looter leaped forward to try to wrest the staff out of
Xar's hands, but Xar pointed the staff, keeping as calm
as possible and whispering the words of a freezing spell
that he vaguely remembered from one of his spelling
lessons.

After so many years of trying to perform Magic with
no results, Xar could not help his heart lifting in joyous

42

triumph as he felt the extraordinary tingling feeling, like pins and needles, in his right arm, that built and built, until the Magic came blasting out in a great satisfactory electric burst, hitting Looter in the stomach. Looter stopped, frozen, midaction, mouth open, arms stretched forward.

"You see!" said Xar, glowing with happy pride. *"I can do it!"*

But hardly had the confident words left his mouth, before the frozen Looter's nose melted and swelled, grew to twice its original size, and dripped violet-colored snot on the floor. Then Looter's

entire body shrunk into something small and furry that is hard to describe except to say no one had ever seen anything like it before.

WHOOPS. Um...,
I am
So sorry,
Looter.

"Oh!" said Xar in surprise. "I'm not sure what happened there..."

"*What have you done? Is this your idea of being good?*" raged Encanzo.

"It was an accident," said Xar, panting and shaking the staff, as if it were a bottle of potion that wasn't working and as if it were all the staff's fault, and not his.

Shaking the Staff-That-Commands-the-Castle wasn't a very good idea. Magic ricocheted madly around the room with such curving, bending ferocity that the Drood Commander's desk burst into flames.

The castle responded instantly to the flaming desk, for the building was equipped with the very latest in magical defenses. Rain poured out of the magical ceiling above with such intensity that, not only did it put out the fire, but the Wizards were drenched within seconds, stumbling about trying to see through the downpour and the clouds of smoke.

"Oh dear!" said Xar.

"Escape!" roared the werewolf, picking up Xar. (Actually he said, "Gruntsnar-ugh-rowarr," but that is what he meant.) The werewolf leaped up and out the window, followed by Xar's sprites and Caliburn, dropping feathers like dark rain.

"*I'll be good, Father, I promise!*" shouted Xar from the windowsill.

And then, "Shut!" cried Xar, waving the Staff-That-Commands-the-Castle.

The-Creature-that-Once-was-Looter

long (*)
dribbly
nose →

← 3 ears

hairy
bottom

And the window turned into wall behind them like the closing of an eye.

The Enchanter and the Drood Commander were too late with their next bolts of Magic. They rebounded harmlessly off the window-that-was-now-wall.

The two Wizards staggered toward the mirrors. The Drood Commander winked, and the mirrors flicked through views of the outside of the castle, until they could see in one of them Xar and the werewolf, hanging by a couple of homemade ropes from the exterior.

"They can't get away…Watch!" said the Drood Commander.

As Xar and the werewolf edged toward the outskirts of the castle, the skulls began to open their eyes. And as the tip of the Staff-That-Commands-the-Castle

got nearer to the barrier Xar had been so careful to avoid touching earlier, the skulls opened their mouths, and an unbearable screaming noise—like five hundred foxes cornered by dogs—came out of the toothy skinless grins. It was a noise so loud that they could see the sprites shaking in the air, their lights going on and off with the sound waves.

"There!" said the Drood Commander, pointing with satisfaction at the mirrors. "The Drood Guards are out."

Sure enough, you could see the winged forms of cockatrices flying up from the guardhouses situated within the castle walls. On the back of every cockatrice was a Drood Guard, each armed with an array of ominous-looking spelling staffs.

"We have a reaction time of under two minutes," said the Drood Commander with smug satisfaction.

"Do you?" said the Enchanter thoughtfully.

The little party of would-be escapees was panicking like mad as they peered over the battlements to where, far down below, Xar's loyal companions were waiting

for him, his giant, Crusher, and his snowcats, wolves, and bear. These had clung to Crusher's back as he swam across, braving the terrors of the Sea of Skulls in order to help Xar escape, for Xar may have had his faults, but he inspired great loyalty in his companions.

A sprite called the Once-sprite was sitting on a peregrine falcon, peering up at Xar, with his hand shielding his eyes. Behind him, one of the Witch feathers Xar had collected on his previous adventure was glowing with a weird, ominous light.

"Why'sss aren't they jumping?" asked the Once-sprite nervously, for he could smell a horribly familiar scent in the air, carried to his sensitive sprite nostrils on the wind and the mists of the seas they were standing in.

A deadly nightshade reek of rotten rat and choked-up corpse with a little bright stinging note of viper venom, as strong and as poisonous as the arsenic of an apothecary...

The smell of *Witches*...

Witches must be watching, and they were somewhere out there in that mist.

"Mmmfff?" replied Crusher absentmindedly in answer to the Once-sprite's question. Giants are big, and they tend to have BIG thoughts. Xar's giant was a Longstepper High-Walker giant, and they are the biggest thinkers of all.

Behind the Once-sprite, a Witch feather was glowing, with a strange, unnatural light...

"I wonder," said Crusher slowly, "if the fate of human beings is predetermined by the stars, or do they forge their own destiny? Is there really such a thing as 'luck'? And what *exactly* do we mean by the concept of 'free will'?"

Which were all interesting questions, but perhaps not *entirely* helpful right at that particular moment.

"They hassss to get a move on..." whispered the Once-sprite, peering nervously upward, then out into the mist, where he thought he might have seen wings or talons or the beak of a Witch. "We need to get out of here RIGHT NOW!"

"What are we going to dooooo?" moaned Caliburn, up on the battlements.

"Wings!" whispered Squeezjoos. "Why's doesn't humans beings have wings?"

"It's a design fault," admitted Xar, "and a nice idea, but I haven't really got time to evolve them, Squeezjoos. Don't worry... I have a plan!"

"I really, really hope it's a good one..." muttered Caliburn.

Xar shook the Staff-That-Commands-the-Castle, shouting the words of a spell.

And then he threw the spelling staff as hard as he could, so that it fell down, down in a great arc into

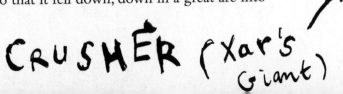

CRUSHER (Xar's Giant)

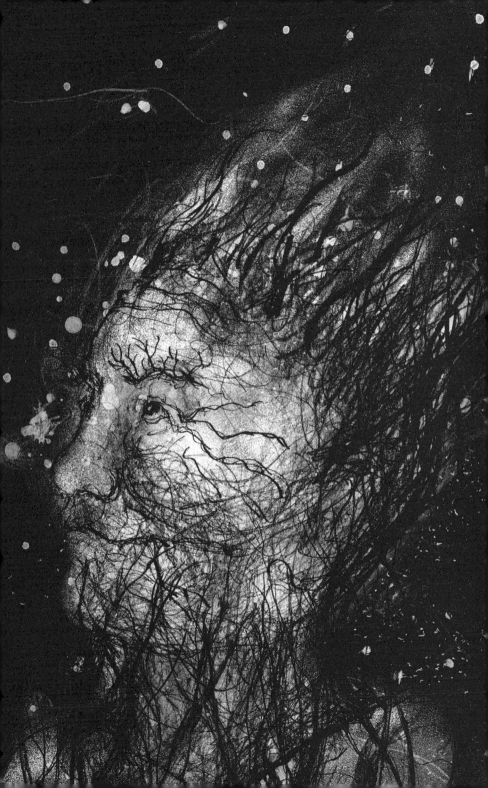

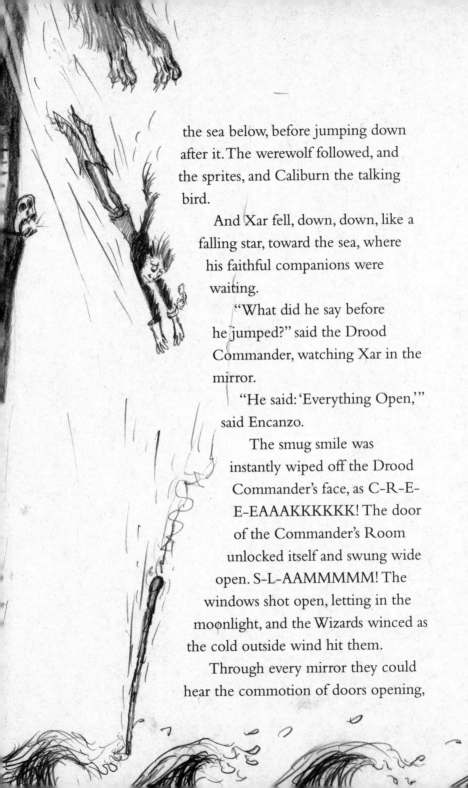

the sea below, before jumping down
after it. The werewolf followed, and
the sprites, and Caliburn the talking
bird.

And Xar fell, down, down, like a
falling star, toward the sea, where
his faithful companions were
waiting.

"What did he say before
he jumped?" said the Drood
Commander, watching Xar in the
mirror.

"He said: 'Everything Open,'"
said Encanzo.

The smug smile was
instantly wiped off the Drood
Commander's face, as C-R-E-
E-EAAAKKKKKK! The door
of the Commander's Room
unlocked itself and swung wide
open. S-L-AAMMMMM! The
windows shot open, letting in the
moonlight, and the Wizards winced as
the cold outside wind hit them.

Through every mirror they could
hear the commotion of doors opening,

portcullises rising, bars melting, invisible magical barriers dropping with electric hisses.

And then there was the sound of many, many pairs of running feet and opening wings.

"Oh by the steaming droppings of the Big-bottomed Bogburper!" swore the Drood Commander, his eyes popping with disbelief. "He's used the Staff-That-Commands-the-Castle to open all the doors so EVERYBODY can escape!!!!!!"

"Your guards are going to have their hands full *now*, Commander," said Encanzo drily. "We'll get to see how they deal with those Grim Annises, Rogrebreaths, and all those other terrible things you mentioned *now*. I suspect they might be so busy fighting with those particular villains that they may not have time to catch my son."

The Drood Commander shot him a filthy look. With a swirl of wet cloak he swooped out of the open door, shouting: "Jailbreak! CODE RED! WE HAVE MULTIPLE ESCAPE ATTEMPTS! SOMEONE FETCH ME MY COCKATRICE AND GET ME IT *NOW*!!!"

And Encanzo stood, watching in the mirror, as his son disappeared from view.

Then he sat down at the Drood Commander's desk.

"Mff!" said a small, insistent voice at Encanzo's

elbow. Sitting on the desk was the rather odd unknown creature that Xar had turned Looter into, a very unattractive little thing, slightly smaller than a rabbit, with a long dribbly nose and a high-pitched squeak.

"Yes, I'm sorry, Looter," said Encanzo. "I can't turn you back into human form until I find out exactly what Xar has turned you into...I'll look you up in my Spelling Book. In the meantime, you'll have to be patient I'm afraid. There are more important things at stake here. Xar is in real trouble..."

The Creature-That-Once-Was-Looter was not used to being anything other than the most important thing in his father's life. He looked panic-stricken, letting out a rather revolting jet-black liquid from his nostrils and then sitting down dejectedly in his own puddle.

"Maybe it serves us both right," said Encanzo with a sigh, desperately flicking his way through his Spelling Book, searching, searching, searching for a spell that could cure a Witch-stain. "Could you be a Winklefutt? No, too many ears...We were rather hard on the boy. We jeered at him, offended his dignity..."

There was a curious mixture of expressions on Encanzo's face. Now that his anger was retreating, he felt a reluctant pride in the sheer breathtaking cheek and ingenuity of his younger son. There are not many people who would have the brazen nerve to turn up in the Drood Commander's Room and steal his staff from him.

He was also feeling guilty, for Encanzo had not been able to prevent all this from happening.

But his dominant emotion was *fear*. For, despite everything, Encanzo loved his son, and he knew that Xar would now be in the most terrible danger.

Two ancient sprites settled gravely on Encanzo's shoulders.

He drummed his fingers with furious fright on the table in front of him. "That Witch-stain is not getting better…It is only a matter of time before we lose Xar entirely to the dark side. We HAVE to find a cure…" He sighed. "But firstly we have to find Xar himself, before his time runs out.

"Could I have prevented this?" said Encanzo to himself. "Caliburn was right…I should have listened to Xar. I should have reasoned with the boy, not hurt his pride."

But then Encanzo's face hardened. "But just because I am sorry for him does not mean that he isn't extremely dangerous. I fear the boy's faults are greater than his strengths, and we will all suffer for his mistakes."

Ah, being a parent is so much harder than it looks.

And just because you are old, does not mean that you do not make mistakes.

So that is the story of the Great Jailbreak of Gormincrag.
For the first time in a thousand years, not only was there
a successful escape attempt, but, indeed, the ENTIRE
PRISON POPULATION broke out in one single night.

The sprites would tell that story for many, many centuries
afterward. It was too good a tale not to tell. All of the escapees
were recaptured, of course. Apart from two.

A werewolf.

And Xar, son of Encanzo.

The first human being EVER to escape from the
rehabilitation center of Gormincrag did it by merely traveling across
the Sea of Skulls through the Drowned Forest on the back of his
snowcat, his animals and the werewolf swimming by his side.

"I am the boy of destiny!" said Xar as he struggled out
of the sea on the far shore. "And fate is on my side!" And he
vanished, glorious, wild, and jubilant, into the freedom of the
wildwoods.

But was Xar REALLY the master of his own destiny, and
did he really just escape through his cleverness and his luck?

I have to tell you that the Bloody Barbeards, the Daggerfins,
and the Blunderbouths that would have dragged Xar and his
companions to the bottom of the ocean were eliminated by a
talon between the ribs, an acid breath to the lungs, a whiff of
dark Magic in their ears, before they could attack.

The Witches got rid of them.

Xar and his companions
escaping underwater through the
Drowned Forest →

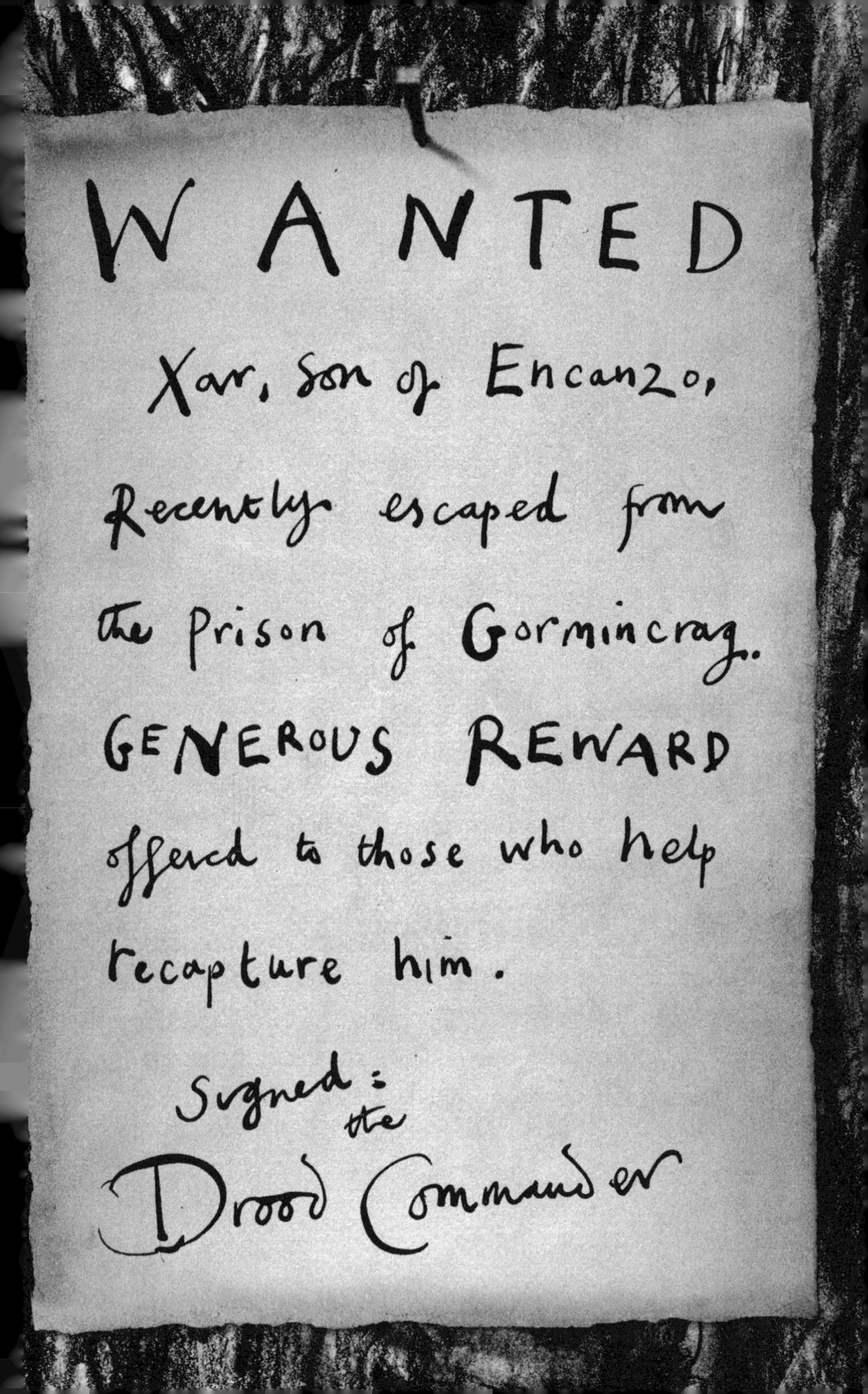

WANTED

Xar, son of Encanzo,

Recently escaped from

the prison of Gormincrag.

GENEROUS REWARD

offered to those who help

recapture him.

Signed:
the
Drood Commander

I am the Boy of Destiny!!

BUT WHY WOULD THE WITCHES WANT
XAR TO ESCAPE?

I told you that stories take you in unexpected directions.

I cannot apologize more, but we are only at the end of
Chapter TWO, and I have to take you back to the Kingwitch.
He is still suspended there, in that chamber that I told you
about, miles away, in the Witch Mountains.

Deep below those mountains, there were secret caverns where the Witches had been hanging in great dark cocoons, sleeping out the centuries. The cocoons had been cracking for some time. A limb poked out here, a feather there. A beak, a nose. And the Witches spread their dreadful wings, flew up and out of the caverns in numbers so huge they were impossible to count, and across the landscape to work their destruction.

The Kingwitch alone was frozen and unmoving. He sent out his troops to wage his War, but he had not moved, for he was waiting, and I fear he may have been conserving his energy for a greater battle that was to come. His great head, with those jaws that could unhinge to swallow a deer in one gulp, was drooping on his breast. He was hanging so high that, despite his immense size, if you walked into that chamber once built for giants you would not even know he was up there.

I would not be doing my duty as a storyteller if I did not warn you that the Kingwitch was up there, poised like a sword about to drop, hiding in the shadows.

But he was still a long, long way away from our heroes, dear Reader. And although Xar may have escaped from the prison of Gormincrag, our other hero Wish was still hidden behind her mother's Great Wall, way, way to the east in the Warrior territories. And as long as she stayed there, she was absolutely safe...

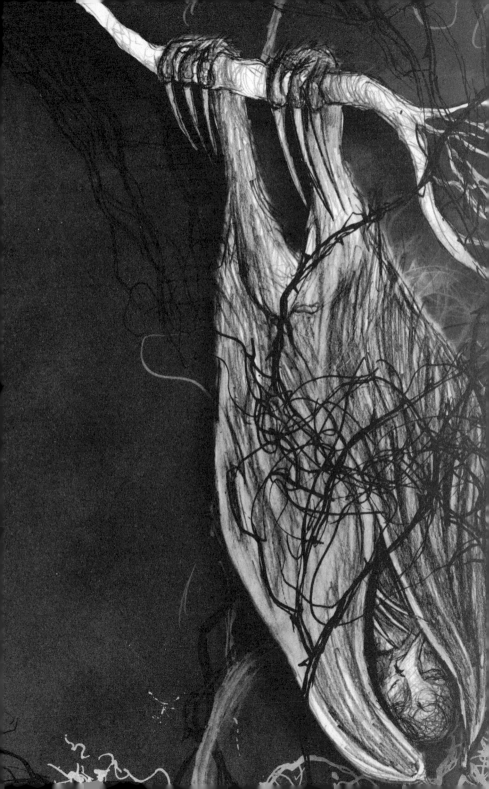

Queen Sychorax's
IRON WARRIOR FORT

The feathers fly on, and we have to follow. I told you these woods were DANGEROUS...

3. Inside the Punishment Cupboard

Two weeks after Xar made his spectacular escape from Gormincrag, a young Warrior princess called Wish was sitting inside a locked cupboard in the Tower of Education in Queen Sychorax's iron Warrior fort, when she made an important, and perhaps unfortunate, discovery.

Iron Warrior fort was the largest hill-fort you could possibly imagine, protected by seven great ditches cut into the hill, and the Great Wall Sychorax had recently rebuilt. It was constantly patrolled by Warriors looking out for Witches, who would shoot anything Magic that they saw on sight.

Like Xar, Wish was having imprisonment problems. That's right.

I *did* say she was sitting inside a locked cupboard.

Queen Sychorax, Wish's terrifying mother, was expecting visitors, and whenever Queen Sychorax had visitors she got Madam Dreadlock, Wish's tutor, to lock Wish and her bodyguard in the Punishment Cupboard of the schoolroom until after the visitors had left.

So Wish and her bodyguard had already been sitting in this locked, cramped cupboard for hours and hours and hours, and Wish had been whiling away the time by reading and writing stories.

Wish didn't really like small spaces, so she was keeping her spirits up by singing softly to herself as she read and wrote.

"*NO FEAR! That's the Warrior's marching song! NO FEAR! We sing it as we march along! NO FEAR!* 'Cause the Warriors' hearts are strong! Is a Warrior heart a-wailing, is a Warrior heart a-failing, is a Warrior heart a-railing? *NO FEAR!*"

Now, Wish wasn't entirely what you might expect from a Warrior princess. Warrior princesses were supposed to be like Wish's six older stepsisters, tall and tough and good at things like archery and shooting ogres with their arrows from a distance of thirty paces.

But Wish was small and sweet-natured and determined, with an eyepatch over one eye, and hair so disobediently flyaway that it looked as if it were being blown about by some personal independent wind.

But worse than that, she was MAGIC.

Wish had always been a little clumsy and forgetful, but when she turned thirteen her Magic had come in, and the problem had gotten worse. Objects she touched slipped through her hands like water or tingled with electricity when she put her fingers on them, clothes ripping, shoes coming loose, keys missing, needles wriggling to life in her hands, rugs inexplicably moving beneath her feet or curled up at the edges when she stepped on them...

Goodness knows HOW she was Magic, as she was a Warrior, but the fact remained that her eyepatch was hiding a Magic eye, and it wasn't any ordinary kind of Magic, it was Magic-that-works-on-iron.

And up until now, iron had been the only thing that Magic could not work on.

There was a spoon standing upright on one of Wish's shoulders.

It was a perfectly ordinary iron dinner spoon...

Except that he was *alive*.

Alive, and bending this way and

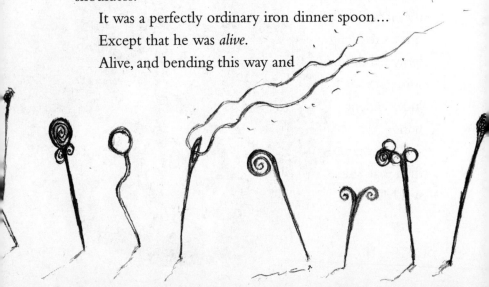

that, and dancing to the sound of Wish's singing, along with about thirty or so little iron pins, which were also swaying and jumping and regrouping to the rhythm. The spoon had a gentle glow coming from the bowl of his head that lit up the cupboard and the iron pins, and the book Wish was reading.

This was a Wizard's Spelling Book, and it was yet another enchanted object that Wish really, really should not have owned. It had once belonged to Xar, but Caliburn had given it to Wish in case Witches came after her in the future.

The Spelling Book is a complete guide to the entire magical world, so it is filled with recipes, potions, fairy stories, everything you might need to cope in a world of Magic.

It was in this book that Wish made her important, and perhaps unfortunate, discovery.

"Bodkin!" Wish exclaimed excitedly. "*Look!* I've found a SPELL TO GET RID OF WITCHES!"

Bodkin was an anxious, skinny boy about the

About

thirty

little

Enchanted

Pins...

same age as Wish. He was finding being the Assistant
Bodyguard to the princess really rather testing, because
he didn't like fighting very much, he had an unfortunate
tendency to fall asleep in situations of physical danger,
and trying to control the uncontrollable little princess
was an impossible task, because she seemed to have
absolutely no idea what rules were at all.

He too was reading—a book called *The Rules of
Warrior Bodyguarding: THE NEXT LEVEL*—but he put
the book aside, excited but a little wary, to look over
Wish's shoulder.

And there it was, in a section of the book entitled
"Write Your Own Story."

On the left-hand side of the page,
Wish had written down her
New Year's Resolutions:
"Noo Year's
Ressolushuns:

Noo Year's Ressolushuns
1. I will work hard at my
reeding and riteing and arithmatick
so I can be topp of the Klass.
2. I will mak a gud impreshun
on the teacher.

A Spell to G
Gather all ingredie
a living spoon.
Ingredeints
one: Grant's Last Bre
Castle Death

1. I wull work hard at my reeding and riteing and arithmatick so I can be topp of the klass. 2. I wull mak a gud impresshun on the teecher. 3. I wull impress my muther so she dus not think I am a Dissapointment."

And on the right-hand side of the page, Wish had written down in completely different beautiful curly writing, the words of a spell.

A Spell to Get Rid of Witches

Gather all ingredients and STIR with a living spoon.

Ingredients
One: Giant's Last Breath from Castle Death.
Two: Feathers from a Witch.
Three: Tears from a Frozen Queen.

But after "Three" the writing got a bit smudgy, as if the writer had suddenly been surprised in the middle of doing something.

"And do you want to know something *truly* extraordinary?" said Wish, eyes shining like stars.

Not really, thought Bodkin, who was beginning to get a very, very bad feeling about this.

"*I wasn't even looking for it!* I was just starting to write a story in this section of the book, because Caliburn gave me one of his feathers to do that with, and *suddenly the feather started writing all by itself!!!*"

"Oh dear..." said Bodkin, whose bad feeling was getting worse. "Are you sure it wasn't just *you* writing it? That's a bit spooky..."

"I'm certain!" said Wish. "It's not my writing, and it *definitely* isn't my spelling."

It was true.

Wish was very clever, but she had certain difficulties in the "reeding and riteing and arithmatick" departments. It may have been something to do with being Magic, but somehow all the letters and the numbers wandered about doing complicated alphabet dance exercises in her head, and they wouldn't stay still however hard she concentrated. It was very wearing.

Only that morning, her teacher, Madam Dreadlock, had been so exasperated with Wish's spelling that she

Madam Dreadlock was
not, perhaps, the most
sympathetic of teachers...

had made Wish write "I am a Fule" on a piece of paper
and hang it around her neck as a punishment.

But every single word on the page Wish was
showing Bodkin was spelled absolutely correctly.

"You're right," Bodkin confirmed. "That doesn't
look anything like your spelling..."

"Don't you see what this *means*?" said Wish, excitedly
waving her arms around. "The Witches have come back,
but now we have a spell to get rid of them! We HAVE
to get this spell to Xar, so he can give it to his father, and
then the Wizards can fight back against the Witches..."

Bodkin looked at her in horror. There were so

71

many things wrong with this plan that he didn't know where to start.

"Princess," said Bodkin, carefully, as if talking to a dangerous lunatic. "I hate to mention this, but we are sitting inside a locked cupboard, in a Warrior fort encircled by seven ditches, each one protected by your mother's guards, and Xar is somewhere out there, we have no idea where, on the *other* side of your mother's Great Wall. How are we going to get out of the cupboard? How will we get over the Wall? How would we find Xar?"

Wish frowned, thinking for a second. "We will go to my mother," said Wish, "and explain everything and ask for her help."

"Everything?" squeaked Bodkin. "We can't explain everything! What about your Magic, and the spoon and the pins and the Spelling Book? Look!"

There was a large notice attached to the inside of the cupboard door.

The notice read:

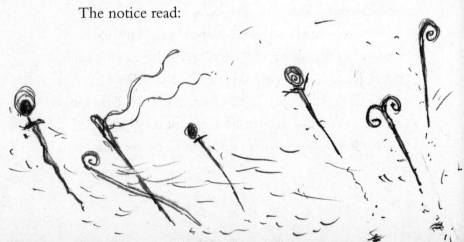

THE PUNISHMENT CUPBOARD WOULD
LIKE TO REMIND YOU THAT

ALL MAGIC IS BANNED IN THIS CASTLE.

NO SPRITES, NO SPELLING,
NO CURSING, NO CHARMING,
AND ABSOLUTELY
NO ENCHANTED OBJECTS.

By order of the queen, who will
most unfortunately remove your head
if you disobey.

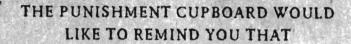

Queen Sycorax

"Right there! It says, quite clearly, **NO ENCHANTED OBJECTS**! It's against the rules!" Bodkin was a boy who really *believed* in the rules.

"The spoon isn't really an enchanted object," argued Wish. "Admittedly he's a little …*lively*… overexcitable perhaps …but he's only young; you have to make allowances. He can be quiet if he needs to be, can't you, spoon?"

Nodding Spoon ↓

The spoon nodded and very obligingly went rigid, falling flat on his face on Wish's shoulder and playing dead.

"Look!" said Wish proudly. "Just like a normal dinner spoon!"

"Normal dinner spoons don't nod! Normal dinner spoons don't pretend to be dead! He's quiet *now*, but mostly he's moving around all over the place!" said Bodkin, moving his arms wildly up in the air in his concern.

Wish thought for a moment.

And then eventually she said in a very small voice:

Spoon pretending to be dead... ↘

"Do you think if I told my mother I was Magic, she would be terribly disappointed?"

"Of COURSE she's going to be disappointed!" said Bodkin, so alarmed he spoke without thinking. "She's already so ashamed of you that she's locking you in Punishment Cupboards so that visitors can't meet you, and she doesn't even *know* about the Magic yet!"

Too late, Bodkin realized he had said the wrong thing.

Wish swallowed hard.

And then three large tears fell down her cheeks.

In her heart of hearts, Wish knew that she was a disappointment to her mother—she could see it in her mother's eyes when she looked at her. *She wishes I was more like my stepsisters*…But to hear it confirmed by another person made it even worse. "WHY doesn't my mother want me to meet visitors? WHY doesn't Madam Dreadlock like me, however hard I try? It's because I'm a bit weird, isn't it?" said Wish desolately.

My mother thinks I'm WEIRD, doesn't she?

Bodkin patted her on the back sympathetically. "Your mother doesn't know you like I do, Princess. You're going to be a brilliant Warrior one day, and you have loads of wonderful Warrior qualities. It's just going to take a little time..."

Wish wiped away the tears with the end of her sleeve, leaving big teary smudges on her cheeks.

"My mother is a magnificent person," said Wish fiercely, "but she shouldn't be ashamed of me, and I'm going to tell her that we need to get out there and help the Wizards!"

"But the Wizards are our enemies!" said Bodkin, a little hysterically.

"They're fellow human beings!" said Wish. "And Xar is our *friend*! My mother has built this Great Wall, to keep all us Warriors safe, but what about all those poor Wizards who she's left to fight the Witches all on their own?

"Sometimes, when I lie awake at night," said Wish, with big eyes, "I think I can hear, beyond the Wall, the sound of giants howling, as if they're being attacked by Witches...Don't you hear that, Bodkin? Are we supposed to just stay here, safe behind our Wall, and let that carry on?"

Oh dear, Bodkin *did* sometimes think he heard that. You see, this is the problem with meeting your enemies. Once you have met them, it's really quite difficult to carry on hating them in the way you absolutely ought to.

"*Xar* wouldn't let his father lock him up in cupboards when visitors came," said Wish mutinously. "*Xar*

My mother is WRONG, Bodkin!

stands up to his father when he thinks he is wrong. That is what *I* should be doing, not sitting around in dark horrible cupboards, too scared of my mother to stand up to her..."

"You're quite right to be scared of your mother!" said Bodkin, now thoroughly confused and beginning to panic. "Queen Sychorax is super scary! Scarier than Ghostshrieks! Scarier than Hellhounds! Scarier than an Ice Warlock in a really, really bad mood! Oh by the green gods...*what are you going to do*???"

"I'm going to break out of this stupid Punishment Cupboard, go down there, and tell my mother that we need to find Xar and his father and get this spell to them," said Wish. "There is good in my mother, she is firm but fair, and she will see my point and help us."

This was one of the most annoying things about Wish. She persisted in thinking the best of people even when they quite clearly did not deserve it.

"Your mother is not firm but fair!" objected Bodkin. "Your mother is a terrifying tyrant who locks people up in Punishment Cupboards for a really long time when they've done absolutely nothing at all!"

"Well, that's exactly my point," argued Wish. "She needs to understand that what she is doing is *wrong*."

"You don't tell terrifying tyrants they're wrong!" gibbered Bodkin. "You just do what they say! And I take

78

it back—there's probably some excellent reason for her keeping us in this cupboard…It's quite comfortable in here, don't you think? They've given us some food, so we won't starve…" There were indeed a couple of bowls of soup in there with them, and some bread. "And a bit of legroom…I can wriggle my toes! Quite cozy, wouldn't you say? Nice and warm for midwinter and *SAFE*! It's very safe in here…not many cobwebs…There's plenty of oxygen for two people…"

"It's a cupboard," said Wish. "We can't stay in a cupboard forever. And she's leaving us in here for longer and longer amounts of time…No, we're getting out."

"WE NEED TO STAY IN THE CUPBOARD, WISH!" said Bodkin in a strangled whisper.

But Wish knelt down and looked at the keyhole.

The Spelling Book had a handy alphabet at the beginning, and when Wish tapped her fingers on the letters to spell out "U-n-l-o-k-k-i-n-g L-o-k-k-s" the pages magically turned themselves to the "Spells for Unlocking" section in the book.*

Wish pushed up her eyepatch just a smidgeon (not too far—the Magic eye was horribly powerful), then muttered the words of the spell under her breath and the key on the other side of the door wriggled out of the lock and shot underneath the bottom of the door to their side of the cupboard, picking itself up off the floor and making them both a small bow.

The handle of the key formed the shape of a mouth, and the key said in a tiny, creaky, excitable little voice: "How can I help you?"

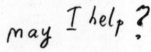

"It's speaking!" whispered Wish, delighted, for she had never made an enchanted object speak before.

"*Will . . . you . . . stop . . .*
BRINGING THINGS TO

*The Spelling Book didn't seem to mind a little creativity in spelling out words as long as you made a reasonable guess at them.

LIFE?????" whispered Bodkin through gritted teeth.

"You can help us unlock the door, key," said Wish, and the key bowed again, absolutely delighted, for there is nothing that enchanted objects enjoy more than doing the things they were created for. The key hopped up the door and unlocked their side of it with such overenthusiasm that there was a small explosion, and the wood of the door split in half.

"Whoops," said Wish as the half-broken door swung open.

"It's not too late to stay in the cupboard!" cried Bodkin as Wish scrambled out.

"Oh brother...she's not staying in the cupboard! I'm going to have to follow her..." groaned Bodkin, grabbing his weapons.

"She's exploded Madam Dreadlock's cupboard! She's left the schoolroom without permission!" moaned Bodkin, eyes wide open with horror as he stumbled out of the cupboard, through the schoolroom, and onto the battlements. "We're going to be in SUCH TROUBLE..."

Clank! Clank! Clank! Bodkin staggered after Wish, as fast as he could, given that he was wearing two sets of body armor.

"Wait…for…me…" puffed Bodkin.

Wish slowed down a little. "Oh! I'm so sorry, Bodkin. Am I going too fast for you? Wow, you're wearing a lot of armor…"

CLANK! CLANK!
CLANK!

It's important not to

Bodkin paused a second for breath. "You see, Wish, *this* is why Madam Dreadlock doesn't like you..." groaned Bodkin. "What about your New Year's Resolutions?"

It was true, Wish's New Year's Resolution number two, "mak a gud impresshun on the teecher," wasn't going so well, what with one thing and another.

"Bodkin," said Wish, "I'm sad that Madam Dreadlock doesn't like me, but there are some things that are more important than teachers and exploding cupboards. Look! Somewhere out there, over that Wall, Xar and the Wizards are in trouble, *and we can help them!*"

Bodkin swallowed hard.

"Oh dear, you're right, you're right, we have to help them...It's just that Witches are SO SCARY... And they're invisible until they attack so they could be anywhere!" whispered Bodkin with boggling eyes. He tried to look over his shoulder, but the weight of his helmet and body armor meant he had to shuffle his entire body around a hundred and eighty degrees. "I keep thinking they're here already...that we're being *followed*! That's why I'm wearing so much body armor!"

"Yes, it's probably better not to wear so much armor that you can't actually *move*, Bodkin," advised Wish.

"And your mother's busy...It won't be a good

Wear so much armor
that you can't MOVE.

moment…She's expecting visitors…I can see her already, up on the Royal Stage!" Bodkin pointed down, into the courtyard.

"My mother's ALWAYS busy! There's never a good moment. Don't worry, I've been practicing my Visitor Manners, Bodkin…" said Wish.

And she dashed off down the stairs.

Bodkin hopped unhappily from foot to foot, in an agony of anxiety. There was no stopping the little princess when she was in this kind of mood. He left the shield and the backpack behind because they were too heavy and slowing him down, and—*Clank! Clank! Clank!*—he staggered after Wish down the stairs.

"At the very least," begged Bodkin, catching up with Wish as she reached the bottom of the tower, because she'd lost one of her shoes and had to go back for it, "give me all the enchanted objects. You can't go on the Royal Stage with your pockets full of banned Magic things…I'll look after them while you're up there."

Wish did see Bodkin's point.

Wait… for… me…

She gave him the spoon, the Spelling Book, and all of the Enchanted Pins, who neatly pinned themselves all over Bodkin's shirt. And then she hurried off, pushing her way through the crowd toward the stage, practicing saying very firmly, "You are wrong, Mother, wrong. We have to help the Wizards!" and her Visitor Manners, just in case: "How do you do? What do *you* do?"

The Executioner, who was a kind man when he wasn't doing his job, helped her up onto the stage beside her sisters.

Wish's six older stepsisters were tidy, handsome Warrior girls, as muscled and hairy and unwelcoming as six well-groomed blond gorillas. When she scrambled up beside them, the sister nearest to her in age, Drama, gave her such a big shove in the stomach with her elbow that Wish nearly fell off the stage.

"What are *you* doing here, you weird little rat?" growled Drama. "Mother is ashamed of you. You're not fit to be seen by company."

CLANK!

Clank!

Clank!

Puff

Puff

puff

Queen
Sycorax

And the next oldest sister but one, Unforgiving, gave a great stamp on Wish's toe and added, with satisfaction, "Mother is going to be SO ANGRY ..."

It seemed they could be right.

The great queen Sychorax was sitting on a magnificent throne, right in the center of the courtyard. She was dressed in elaborately regal armor, with one black earring and one white.

Wish, already gasping for breath and hopping on one foot from her stepsisters' rather violent greeting, felt her stomach plunge with anxiety.

What had seemed such a good idea in the cupboard suddenly didn't seem such a good idea *now*.

Even to Wish's hopeful eyes, her mother didn't look firm but fair.

She looked absolutely hopping mad.

"What are *you* doing here, Wish?" hissed Queen Sychorax in the voice of a sweetly striking cobra. "How dare you disobey my orders?"

And then she gave Wish *That Look*.

In most people's eyes, Wish's mother, Queen Sychorax, was the most petrifying Warrior leader in the entire western wildwoods, known for her stern punishments, her short temper, and her dungeons of interminable depth.

In *Wish's* eyes, her mother was the most wonderful,

beautiful, splendid person in the entire world, and more than anything else in the world Wish longed to please her mother, get her golden approval.

Wish had meant to tell her mother she was wrong.

She meant to explain about the spell to get rid of Witches, and how they needed to get it to Xar and his father, and how they shouldn't be building Walls that left the Wizards and the poor Magic things to be attacked.

But when her mother gave her *That Look*, a Look of Deepest and Most Furious Disappointment, all the brave words Wish had been *intending* to say went completely out of her head.

She opened her mouth…and shut it again.

"I will deal with *you* later," snapped Queen Sychorax through gritted teeth.

It was too late for Wish to leave the stage.

For Queen Sychorax's visitors had already arrived, one of them stepping toward the throne in a curiously crabwise, menacing fashion.

"Be quiet, and don't draw attention to yourself!" Queen Sychorax ordered Wish. "Don't droop! Don't fidget! Don't move! Don't blink!"

"Oh! Yes, Mother, I won't cause any trouble, I promise..." said Wish miserably.

Queen Sychorax's visitor was a tall, alien figure of such alarming aspect that Wish felt a little sick and her hair began to move and stand up on the back of her neck, softly wriggling itself into a bird's nest of tangles as if each little individual hair had a life of its own.

"Who, or *what*, is *that*?" exclaimed Wish, in a kind of fascinated horror, desperately trying to flatten down her hair in the hope that no one would notice.

"Don't you know anything, you ignorant little ant?" demanded her stepsister Drama, trying to sound careless, even though she was extremely frightened herself. "*That* is the Witchsmeller."

We should have stayed in the cupboard! thought Bodkin, who had reached the Royal Stage and was peering up at the Witchsmeller. *We should have stayed in the cupboard!*

I should have
stayed in the Cupboard!

4. The Pointing Finger of the Witchsmeller

The Witchsmeller had a face that seemed to be entirely composed of nose. A nose that quivered and trembled sensitively at the tip, as if at any moment it might wander around to left and right like a pointing finger.

The Witchsmeller had bony fingers that quivered like the legs of a praying mantis, as if he could smell with his very fingers themselves.

Beards of dwarves hung from his cloak. Little skulls of poor sprites hung from his neck.

From his belt hung goblin hearts and the beards of elves and toenail clippings of famous giants he had killed (AFTER they gave themselves up, for the Witchsmeller did not think you needed to keep promises you made to giants).

He was a little annoyed at having to come so far out west to this godforsaken uncivilized jungle. He supposed the food would be terrible out here, but the emperor had insisted. He gave Queen Sychorax a very perfunctory bow.

"Ah, the pest controller," said Queen Sychorax, inclining her head.

"My name," said the Witchsmeller, stiffening somewhat, "is the Witchsmeller."

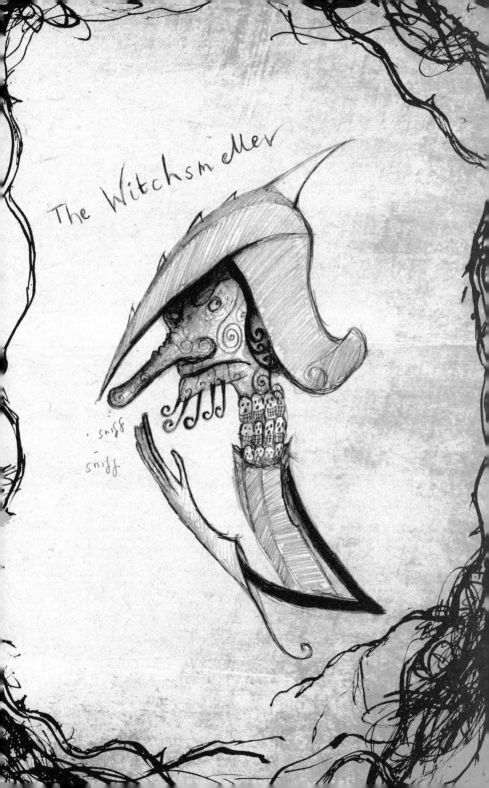

The Witchsmeller

sniff

sniff

"Excellent," said Queen Sychorax. "Welcome to iron Warrior fort. I have summoned you here to my queendom because we have made the unwelcome discovery that Witches are not extinct after all, and I need you to hunt some down for me."

Oh! thought Wish, cheering up a little. *So my mother ISN'T leaving the Wizards to fight the Witches on their own! But I'm not sure she's chosen the right person to help her...*

"You have come to the right person," said the Witchsmeller with a smile. He didn't quite like the word "summoned." Who did this backwater queen think she was?

"Let me explain my problem. This stone here used to be my Stone-That-Takes-Away-Magic," said Queen Sychorax.

She gestured to the back of the stage, where Wish realized for the first time, the stone had been carried up from the dungeon where it was normally kept. "And for many years I have successfully removed the Magic from many a giant and sprite. But about six months ago, the stone was found to contain a Kingwitch, who then escaped from the stone and as a result we have something of a Witch infestation in the western territories."

The Witchsmeller took a good look at the stone. There was a sword sticking out of the great jagged split that cracked the stone from side to side. The Witchsmeller tried to remove the sword from the cracked stone. It would not budge. The Witchsmeller made tut-tutting noises.

"I have built a Wall along the entire western edge of my kingdom to protect Warrior territories, but I need you and your troops to go out there and hunt down the Witches," said Queen Sychorax.

The Witchsmeller shook his head condescendingly. "Ah, Your Majesty, I am quite surprised that you used a Magic object like this stone in the first place. And you should have been KILLING the Magic, not removing it...The emperor would not be pleased. Such softness is not the Warrior way."

There was an uncomfortable murmur from Queen Sychorax's subjects, and they all took a step backward, as if moving away from the edge of a volcano that was about to blow.

Nobody spoke like that to Queen Sychorax.

Queen Sychorax's eyes sharpened to flinty arrows.

"Softness? *Softness????* *Not the Warrior way?* How dare you question my methods?" she said in a voice that could have frozen the very bone marrow of a lesser man. "I merely use Magic to destroy Magic, in a modern civilized manner. The ends justify the means. *I* am a great monarch and YOU are a mere common-or-garden *rodent-operative*. I have commanded you to go out and hunt Witches. So go out and do it!"

The Witchsmeller jumped as if he had been bitten.

He had never before met someone with quite the force of Queen Sychorax's personality. Mostly people cowered before him. He, the Witchsmeller, was the Terror of the Empire. He looked behind him at his soldiers, the emperor's crack Magic-hunting troops.

The sunlight glistened off their iron helmets, their bristling weaponry, their Magic-catching equipment.

"I believe *I* am the expert on Witches, Your Majesty," snapped the Witchsmeller. "Your problem is not the Witches out *there*, but the Witches here in this courtyard!"

Oh dear, oh dear, oh dear, oh dear! thought Wish. *This is DEFINITELY not the right person to help…*

"What on earth are you talking about?" snapped Queen Sychorax, out-snapping him by double. "I've told you, no Witches can get over my Wall!"

"YOU HAVE INVITED ME HERE LOOKING FOR WITCHES AND I INTEND TO FIND THEM!" shouted the Witchsmeller, pointing one quivering finger in the air.

He sidled forward and began to sniff at the nearest person, as if he were a dog.

"I smell *Witches*..." hissed the Witchsmeller, in a high, squeaky voice.

A murmer of horror went around the courtyard.

"Oh for goodness' sake," said Queen Sychorax with a sigh, thinking, *Oh no, just my luck, he's a nutcase*, and thoroughly regretting inviting this lunatic into her queendom in the first place.

Sniff

Sniff

Sniff

Sniff

She generally had perfect control of her subjects, but they were a superstitious lot, and she could see this might get out of hand.

"I smell WITCHES!" cried the Witchsmeller again, holding his shaking finger to the heavens in a voice of DOOM.

Mad as a box load of frogs. Nuttier than a tree full of squirrels...thought the queen.

"I can sniff out Magic, wherever it may be hiding," snarled the Witchsmeller. "I will move through the crowd and point at any person who is concealing Magic..."

Oh for goodness' sake...

Now there was a dreadful silence in the courtyard, and you did not need the nose of a Witchsmeller to detect the smell of fear.

Nerves and sweat.

Wish could feel herself getting very hot, and her clothes itching her neck and back.

"Murmuring mistletoe, you've never actually met a real *Witch*, have you, pest controller?"

said Queen Sychorax, drumming her fingers on the arms of her throne in great irritation. "You'd know it if you saw one…a big feathered thing with green blood and talons…"

"Those kind of Witches are extinct!" screamed the Witchsmeller. "I'm talking about the *modern* Witches!

sniff

The Witches in our midst!"

"You won't find any Magic here, pest controller," said Queen Sychorax, yawning. "I keep a very clean castle."

Wish tried to half hide behind her stepsister Drama, to make herself even smaller, so she would not be noticed. Her hair was so alarmingly frizzy and alive that she was having to hold it down forcibly with both arms. Maybe no one would notice.

Please don't let the finger land on me...

Please.

If that finger lands on me, I'm never going to be allowed out of that Punishment Cupboard EVER AGAIN...

My mother is going to be SO disappointed...

But that will be the least of my worries because I also may be DEAD...

And here the quivering nose was right behind her. *Sniff, sniff, sniff.*

The finger paused, she could almost feel it, the bony digit about to press itself into her back, like the spooky white bone of a chicken. It would happen in one second, two...

Wish could not bear it, the agony of suspense. She closed her one eye.

Please don't let the finger land on me.

Please.

The finger paused behind her—it was about to land on her, she knew it...

5. The Finger Lands on Wish... and Everything Gets a Bit Chaotic

The spooky chicken finger of the Witchsmeller landed right in the middle of Wish's back.

"Aha!" crowed the Witchsmeller triumphantly, swinging her around to face him. "A Witch!"

The crowd gave a moan of astonishment.

"How do you do?" gabbled Wish, rather desperately falling back on her Visitor Manners. "Welcome to Warrior Castle. Did you have a good trip? Very-pleasant-weather-for-the-time-of-year, I-do-hope-you-are-well and ... er ... what-do-YOU-do?"

The Witchsmeller blinked at her in amazement.

"I ... *hunt* ... *WITCHES* ..." he snarled.

You have to hand it to Queen Sychorax. She was absolutely cool as a cucumber in a crisis. She glided out of her throne in a graceful golden flash, and she laid a restraining hand on the Witchsmeller's arm. She even managed to sound a little bored.

"That is not a Witch, pest controller," said Queen Sychorax. "That is my daughter, Wish. She may be a bit

of an incompetent disgrace to her tribe, but she most
certainly is not a Witch."

"She couldn't possibly be the daughter of a Warrior
queen!" hissed the Witchsmeller. "She's very odd-
looking…"

"I think I know my own daughter," said the queen
witheringly. "Hair disgraceful, height poor, general
Warrior turnout utterly substandard—where are your
weapons, Wish?"

"I left them in the cupboard…" said Wish,
miserably looking down at her feet to avoid her
mother's scathing gaze.

"Spelling appalling, disobedience unspeakable, deportment tragic," continued Sychorax, brutal even by her own standards, for Sychorax was ANGRY. "Yes, it's definitely her."

"But this notice on her chest here says she's a *Fule*...What is a Fule?" spluttered the Witchsmeller suspiciously. "Is that some kind of weird western Magic being?"

"*You* are the fool, pest controller," said Queen Sychorax in her cold, reasoned voice. "Witches cannot hide themselves in people. I keep telling you, Witches are a very different thing altogether. Witches have green blood and feathered wings. They are not extinct, which is the reason I summoned you here in the first place."

The Witchsmeller had regained his composure. He held up his finger.

"THE FINGER IS NEVER WRONG!" shouted the Witchsmeller. "SEARCH THE FULE!"

Sychorax drew herself up to her full royal height.

"My daughter, however hopelessly unworthy, is of royal blood and a direct descendant of Grimshanks the Ogre-wrangler!" said Queen Sychorax. "You most certainly will not search her or I shall be complaining to the emperor personally! Wish will turn out her pockets on her own, won't you, Wish?"

Thank GOODNESS Bodkin had taken all those

enchanted objects off her, Wish thought. He was the best bodyguard in the world. And she really, really should start taking his advice.

Wish felt in her pockets, confident at least of finding nothing there, and turned a little white. She slowly drew out her hand, opened it, and there, sitting in the palm, was...

The Once-sprite.

And out of the other pocket, in terrified alarm, there buzzed...

Squeezjoos...who just had time to squeak at Wish: "I's ssorry, Wisssh!"

Wish blinked at him in astonishment. *What was he doing here anyway?????*

Out of nowhere a peregrine falcon dived down in a blurr of wings and hovered for a split second above Wish's hand. With impeccable timing (if Wish had been in the mood to admire it), the little Once-sprite hopped on the bird's back and Squeezjoos hung on to one of the falcon's claws, and they soared up, up, and away, Wish looking after them with her mouth open.

There was a nasty silence.

And then there was absolute chaos.

"She has sprites in her pockets!" screeched the Witchsmeller. "SHE'S A WITCH!"

"Is this your idea, Wish," said Queen Sychorax,

The Enchanted Spoon

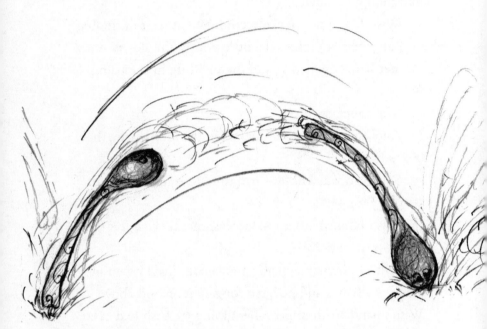

through teeth so gritted they were practically grinding, "of *not causing any trouble?*"

"I didn't know they were in there, honestly, Mother..." pleaded Wish with a very white face.

"SEIZE THE FULE!" screamed the lunatic Witchsmeller, drawing his sword.

"The princess may have a few sprites in her pockets," cried Queen Sychorax, incandescent with annoyance and drawing her own sword. "But that doesn't make the

to the Rescue!

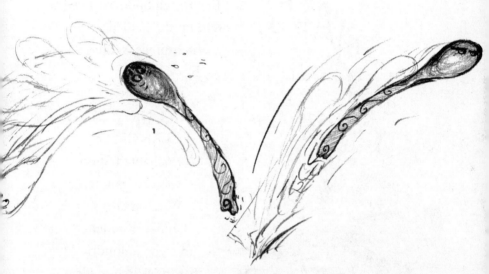

disobedient little excuse for a princess a *Witch*. Warriors!
DEFEND THE PRINCESS!"

And then she gave a start as...

CLANG! CLANG! CLANG! CLANG! CLANG!
Across the Royal Stage came the Enchanted Spoon,
rushing to Wish's rescue. He had a curious way of
propelling himself, like he was doing headstands, and
then jumping back onto his feet again, cartwheeling
from bowl to handle, and then back to bowl again.

CLANG!
CLANG!
CLANG!

"What is *that*???" hissed Queen Sychorax in disbelief. As quick as a whip, the Enchanted Spoon danced right up the baffled Witchsmeller's long black body.

CLANG! CLUNK! CLANG! CLANG! The Enchanted Spoon was clanging the Witchsmeller's helmet from left to right so loudly that the Witchsmeller dropped his sword and staggered, his ears ringing with the noise.

And, just as if things weren't confusing enough already...

"WITCH ATTACK!" screamed Bodkin as, with a strength born of fear, the Assistant Bodyguard managed, despite his two sets of armor, to clamber onto the Royal Stage.

For Bodkin, his mind full of Witches, had seen something that nobody else had noticed. The problem with invisible attackers is that you start seeing them everywhere. But this time Bodkin *knew* he was right.

There was a Witch's talon levitating in the air, heading in the direction of Wish and the Witchsmeller...

So Bodkin stormed the Royal Stage, screaming "WITCH! WITCH!" which, as you can imagine, didn't exactly calm the situation.

"WITCH, Wish! There's a Witch right behind you!" yelled Bodkin.

"SEIZE THE FULE!" screamed a whole crowd of Magic-hunters, storming the stage right behind Bodkin.

"DEFEND THE PRINCESS!" yelled the Warriors loyal to Queen Sychorax, storming the stage after them.

I told you it was chaos.

"AHA!" crowed the Witchsmeller in triumph, as eventually he managed to grab the thing that was attacking him and pull it off his head.

The spoon immediately stopped struggling and pretended to be dead.

The Witchsmeller blinked at the spoon in astonishment. "I'm being attacked...by a *spoon*?"

He leaned down and sniffed the spoon all over, the revolting tip of his nose snuffling up and down like it was a bloodhound's.

The spoon tried as hard as he could to be rigid. But eventually he couldn't quite bear it, the sniffing was so ticklish. Little ripples shook his sides like giggles, for one second, before he turned hard again.

The Witchsmeller blinked. Surely he hadn't seen that. A spoon couldn't move.

Tentatively he put the spoon in his mouth, because that is what you *do* with a spoon, after all. The minute the spoon touched his lips, the spoon struggled wildly, thrashing around from side to side, desperate to escape.

The Witchsmeller spat the spoon out in horror and screamed like he had been stung by a hornet: *"It's alive!!!!"*

It was hard to know who was the more revolted, the Witchsmeller or the spoon.

YUCKY.

The spoon leaped up,
rapped him sharply on
the sensitive end of his
nose, and hopped down
the Witchsmeller as fast
as he could hop, before
disappearing through the
nearest person's legs.

"Catch that spoon!!!!!!!"
yelled the Witchsmeller, holding
on to his nose.

*I wish I had a sword…*thought
Wish, looking desperately around her.

She was standing right next to the Enchanted Sword,
which was stuck fast in the Stone-That-No-Longer-
Took-Away-Magic.

So Wish reached out and took it.

Queen Sychorax watched Wish do this with her
royal mouth slightly ajar. Sychorax had spent the last *six
months* trying every trick in the book that she knew to
get that beastly Witch-killing sword out of the stone—
for with the return of the Witches to the forest, she
really, really needed it—and it would not budge.

Six months!

She'd had giants, Rogrebreaths, and strong men and
women from all over her queendom try to pull it out.

111

She'd even secretly tried *spelling* it out (for Queen Sychorax was a very tricky and unusual person, and she was not above using Magic to destroy Magic, as we have seen).

To no avail. Nothing had worked. And here was her odd, unsatisfactory little daughter just *reaching out and taking it!*

Queen Sychorax was reluctantly not only impressed but perhaps also a little confused. There were things going on here that Queen Sychorax did not perfectly understand, and Queen Sychorax absolutely hated that.

Wish wasn't normally all that good at swordfighting.

But the Enchanted Sword had the rather satisfactory effect of turning whoever was wielding it into the Best Swordfighter in the World, so Wish disarmed one, two, three Magic-hunters in a row. ("Nice work," said Queen Sychorax to herself, watching this.)

Wish then ran to help Bodkin, for he did now seem to be fighting what looked very like a Witch's talon that was floating in the air—clumsily, poor Bodkin, because, as Wish said earlier, it's very important not to wear so much armor that you find it difficult to *move*.

He couldn't turn his head to face the invisible opponent who he thought he was fighting; he had to turn his ENTIRE BODY three hundred and sixty degrees and shuffle around very, very slowly.

To make matters worse, Bodkin's impressive but completely blinding visor then came down, and he couldn't see a thing. The sword was so heavy that when he eventually managed to lift it and make a wild swipe at where he guessed his opponent might be, the weight of it carried him with it, and he lost his balance, and...

CLANG!

That was the sound of Bodkin's helmeted head hitting the floor.

Being a bodyguard is so much harder than it looks...

He immediately passed out, for Bodkin had a slight problem. He had a medical condition that caused him to fall asleep in situations of extreme danger.

"Bodkin! Wake up!" yelled Wish.

"Who? Where? What? How?" Bodkin sat up, holding his head.

"Iron Warrior fort! Possible Witch attack! Watch out! I think it's going to dive!" shouted Wish.

She was about to lunge with the Enchanted Sword toward where she thought the invisible assailant might be...

And then she checked herself just in time.

Could this be...?

6. And a Little More Chaotic Still

Indeed it could be.

The invisible assailant sl-o-o-owly became visible in front of Wish's eyes, as the iron of the soldiers surrounding him made whatever invisibility spell he was using wear off. It was the Wizard boy Xar, son of Encanzo.

"XAR!" exclaimed Wish, completely forgetting where they both were in her delight at seeing her old friend again. "But...but...what are you doing here?"

"I'm saving you, even though you've completely sabotaged my mission!" shouted Xar.

"That tricky wretch of a Wizard boy!" gasped Queen Sychorax.

Xar, you see, had gone to considerable trouble to get into iron Warrior fort. He needed his Spelling Book.

Caliburn had begged him not to involve Wish in all this trouble, but Xar had said he would just sneak in and take back the Spelling Book without her realizing. Everything had initially gone to plan. He had gotten through the Wall by the simple trick of approaching the gate wearing Queen Sychorax's hooded cloak, which he had stolen from her six months ago. Queen Sychorax made a habit of wearing these spectacular cloaks that didn't show her face, so she could come and go through her own Wall without people recognizing her. Xar passed through the gate unchallenged by the sentries, the sprites hidden underneath the folds of fabric.

It took a while for them to find Wish, creeping through the corridors of the fort, using invisibility spells and lurking in quiet corners.

When Wish and Bodkin had run out of the schoolroom, they had been followed by an invisible Xar and his sprites. Xar had tripped Wish up at the bottom of the stairs, so that the Once-sprite and Squeezjoos could search her pockets for the Spelling Book, but once they were in the courtyard, all the surrounding iron had turned them both visible, and by the time Wish had reached the Royal Stage it didn't seem a very good moment for the sprites to escape.

Tiffinstorm and Hinkypunk were all for leaving Wish to fend for herself when the Witchsmeller accused her of being a Witch.

But Xar was determined to stick to his resolution to be good. He couldn't abandon Wish...particularly when it was his sprites in her pockets that had gotten her into trouble.

So he made his invisible charge at the Witchsmeller... only to be tackled around the legs by Bodkin the bodyguard, who mistook Xar's drawn sword for the talon of a Witch.

But this was all news to Wish, who hadn't realized any of this was going on.

Saving me? Sabotaged his mission? What IS Xar talking about?

Blink! Blink! Blink! Blink! Blink! Blink! Out of nowhere, six sprites came blinking into visibility, and then—*Blink! Blink! Blink!*—three smaller lights of the hairy fairies.

Wish had been missing these sprites so badly, and at any other time she'd have been thrilled to see them, but right now...

"I have to say, I don't want to be unwelcoming, but this is a really, really bad moment for you to drop by," said Wish.

This was the understatement of the Iron Age.

The effect of a Wizard boy, a talking raven, six sprites, and three hairy fairies rapidly appearing in an iron Warrior fort full of blood-crazy Magic-hunters who have already been whipped into a Witch-finding frenzy by a barking mad Witchsmeller is a rather similar one to that of a large plump juicy chicken with ten dear little yellow fluffy baby chicks suddenly appearing in the middle of a pack of ravenous wolves who've had a bit of a lean streak lately.

"A WIZARD and its WITCH COMPANIONS!" shrieked the Witchsmeller.

(He really couldn't ever have seen a real Witch if he thought a Witch looked like Squeezjoos, but the other Magic-hunters weren't in a mood to be picky about their species identification so they all joined in joyfully.)

"GET THEM!" they cried.

Now, *this* was a crisis.

Queen Sychorax's Warriors might rush to stop the Magic-hunters from seizing their unsatisfactory little princess, but they weren't going to do the same for Xar. Indeed they might even join in. After meeting him six months ago, Xar wasn't exactly top of Queen Sychorax's Midwinter's End Eve present list.

Yes, it was most definitely a crisis.

But Wish, though she didn't look much like her mother, did in fact have a few things in common with Queen Sychorax.

She was rather good in a crisis. Cool. Collected. *Tricky*, if by tricky you mean clever.

In that split second when it became apparent that Xar might be killed if she didn't come up with a pretty nifty solution *right now*, Wish reviewed her options.

She was a bit hampered by the fact that no one had taught her how to use her Magic properly, so these choices were a little limited.

She could take her eyepatch off entirely.

That would make the castle fall down, which would create a diversion, but would also be dangerous and a little messy.

She could use the Spelling Book to do a spell of invisibility or transformation.

But Bodkin had the Spelling Book, and it would

119

take way too much time for him to retrieve it, carefully hidden as it was beneath many layers of body armor.

Or…she could cast a spell that she had seen someone do before, so she could copy it.

Wish thought back to six months ago, when Tiffinstorm had cast the spell that made Xar's bedroom door shrug out of its frame like an old man shrugging out of his jacket, and turned it into a flying door so that they could escape from Wizard fort.

She wriggled up her eyepatch, just a tiny, tiny smidgeon and looked up toward the Tower of Education. She imagined the door of the Punishment Cupboard (she knew that door well) gently shrugging out of its door frame in the same way as Xar's bedroom door had done. She spelled out the word that Tiffinstorm had said as she cast the spell: M–O–U–V–E…

Luckily, Magic did not seem to care about the exact positioning of the letters. Indeed, it seemed to positively LIKE creativity in the spelling department. It invigorated the Magic, like adding oxygen in some kind of chemical experiment.

As the Magic-hunters thundered toward them, swords drawn, shouting, "KILL THE WITCHES—"

BOOOOOOOM!!!!!!!!!!!!

Above their heads, the broken door of the Punishment Cupboard EXPLODED out of the top

window of the Tower of Education and rocketed at
breathtaking speed, neck-height across the courtyard.
Everybody had to stop charging toward Xar and the
sprites-misidentified-as-Witches and throw themselves
on the ground for fear of being decapitated.

The Witchsmeller rubbed his eyes and stared upward
at the door sailing up into the air and turning back
around again for another dive.

"What's that?" whispered the Witchsmeller in a
hollow voice of disbelief.

"It seems to be a door, sir," said his sergeant smartly.

"I know it's a door, *idiot!*" spat the Witchsmeller. "But
what is it doing flying through the air like a bird?"

The door came to a screeching, manic, hovering halt
in front of Xar and Wish.

"The Wizard boy's kidnapping me!" shouted Wish,
grabbing Xar by the arm and dragging him onto the
door. The sprites, already finding it difficult to fly
because of all the iron around, threw themselves down
on the door beside them.

Xar grinned. "Quick thinking, Princess."

Neither he nor the sprites could make this door fly
themselves, because the door had iron hinges and an
iron lock.

"How do I make it work?" panicked Wish. She'd
never driven a flying door before.

"Use the key!" advised Caliburn.

Without thinking, Wish put her hand on the key, and then moved her arm back sharply, as if she had been stung, as the head of the key moved like a mouth, asking: "Where would you like to go?" in its cozy, creaky, upbeat little voice.

"Up..." said Wish. "We want to go UP!"

She put her hand on the key again a little more cautiously this time and moved it gently upward, and the door went shrieking up into the air so wildly that all of them nearly fell off.

"We have to go back for Bodkin!" yelled Wish. "We can't leave him there—my mother is hopping mad, and she'll say it's all his fault for not looking after me!"

"HA!" said Xar. "Do we have to? He does kind of get in the way. If it wasn't for Bodkin interfering, I'd have SMOOSHED that horrible guy with the sniffing nose..."

"Er...I's thinks that Bodkin might have the Spelling Book, Boss," wheezed Squeezjoos. "It wasn't in Wisssh's pockets..."

"We go back for Bodkin!" said Xar, punching the air.

Wish slammed the Enchanted Key to the right and the door of the Punishment Cupboard veered violently around in a circle and made a great swooping dive back down again, sending everyone who was beginning to get up BACK onto their stomachs for the second time.

Xar and Wish both had to lean over and drag Bodkin onto the door, such was the heaviness of his armor.

"Nobody shoot, or the princess will die!" shouted Wish over the side of the door as it sailed up into the air, a little shakily because of Bodkin's weight, and swooped backward and forward over the crowd.

The only person still standing on the Royal Stage was Queen Sychorax. She would have DIED rather than throw herself on her stomach.

Nonetheless, she was rattled, really rattled.

The situation had gotten thoroughly out of hand.

She waved her sword up at the door shouting, not with her usual cool, for Queen Sychorax had lost her temper, "COME DOWN *IMMEDIATELY*, WISH! A Warrior princess does not fly about on the back of doors! A Warrior princess does not allow herself to get kidnapped!"

"Oh dear, she really *is* angry," said Wish, peering over the edge of the door. "I'm so glad we didn't leave you down there with her, Bodkin..."

"You're right, you don't ALLOW yourself to be kidnapped, Mother!" Wish shouted back down. "A kidnapping just happens..."

But Queen Sychorax was not fooled. She knew perfectly well who was kidnapping whom.

"DO NOT, ON ANY ACCOUNT, LEAVE THE SAFETY OF THIS FORT!" commanded Queen

Sychorax. "DO NOT, ON PAIN OF MY *MOST SEVERE DISPLEASURE*, GO OVER THAT WALL!"

Take the usual look of disappointment on Queen Sychorax's face when she looked at her daughter, then times that by about TEN, and you'll have an idea of what Queen Sychorax looked like as she gazed up at Wish and her disreputable companions lying on their stomachs on the back of the flying door.

"I'm so sorry, Mother!" said Wish guiltily. "Don't worry! I'll be right back, I promise I will!"

And then the door of the Punishment Cupboard sailed UP, UP, and away...

Over the battlements...

And on toward Queen Sychorax's Wall.

Queen Sychorax gave a sigh of fury and resignation. Maddening though her daughter might be, she really did not want her shot down.

She called up to the sentry on the Tower of Education. "Nobody shoot down the door! The princess is going over the Wall!"

And the astonished cry went up from sentry to sentry, and tower to tower, all along the fortifications and the battlements of Queen Sychorax's Great Wall.

"Orders of the queen! Nobody shoot down the door!"

The Wall of Queen Sychorax was supposed

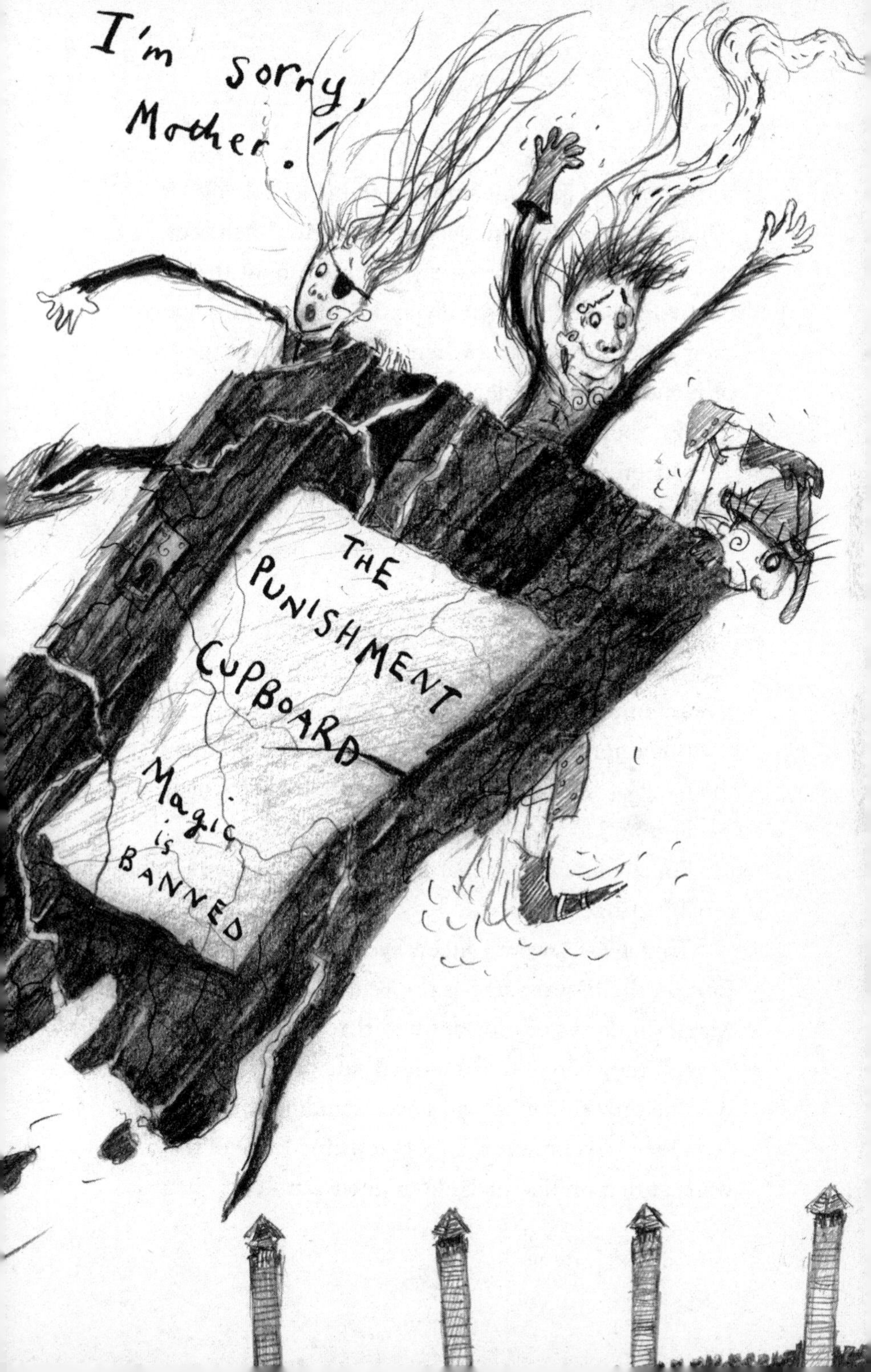
I'm sorry, Mother.
THE PUNISHMENT CUPBOARD
Magic is BANNED

to be impregnable, unclimbable, unbreachable by
Witches and everything Magic. The arrow-hands of
those sentries were absolutely *itching* to shoot that door
down as it sailed majestically and a little erratically over
their heads, particularly when Xar leaned over the side
of it and gave them all a cheeky wave.

But they were all far too scared to disobey orders.

Queen Sychorax watched it go. She closed her eyes
for a second as the door lurched wildly this way and
that, went into nosedives several times, before flying on,
on, over the forest.

With her clumsy little daughter in charge, it really
was going to be a miracle if they made it for more than
five minutes through that forest without crashing.

But among all the anger in Sychorax's face there was
the blink of an emotion much more unusual for her.

Fear.

For she knew now that her daughter was in real and
terrible danger.

Tap tap tap...went Queen Sychorax's furious little
foot on the Royal Stage as the Witchsmeller and his
Magic-hunters got cautiously to their feet, looking as
though they felt a little at a disadvantage, for the queen
was the only one who had stayed standing throughout.

Queen Sychorax's Warriors remained where they
were, curled up like hedgehogs, their arms over their

heads, for they knew that their queen was about to speak her mind and it was better to lie low until she had.

Queen Sychorax narrowed her eyes.

And then she *struck*, every single word a snakebite, dripping with poisonous sarcasm and contempt.

"I hold *you* entirely responsible for this mess, you miserable little pest controller!" flashed Queen Sychorax. "Thanks to *your* pathetic inability to follow orders and do your job, MY DAUGHTER has left the protection of MY castle and has been carried off into terrible danger! Because OUT THERE, beyond MY Wall, are REAL LIVE Witches, not that *you* would know one if it bit you on the nose, and those *real live Witches* are going to be chasing my daughter and trying to kill her! And this is *ALL...YOUR...FAULT!*"

The Witchsmeller's mouth opened and shut.

And then he drew himself up and put his finger in the air for full scariness. He trembled with indignation. He had never met a woman so dreadful in all his life. "None of this is *my* fault. It is *you* who is in big trouble, Queen Sychorax! You tried to cover up the fact that your daughter is an extremely dangerous 'FULE' and is fraternizing with evil Magic elements!"

"She was *kidnapped!*" said Queen Sychorax. "And there's no such thing as a 'FULE,' you unbalanced ignoramus!"

Shaking with fury, the Witchsmeller whirled around

to face his Magic-hunters in a swoop of cloak, the Sprite-heads around his neck rattling against the giants' toenails.

"AFTER THEM!" yelled the Witchsmeller. "MAGIC-HUNTERS, ONTO YOUR HORSES! FAIRY-CATCHERS, HAVE YOUR NETS READY! GIANT-KILLERS, SHARPEN YOUR AXES! WE WILL *HUNT...THEM...DOWN!*"

The Witchsmeller vaulted onto the back of his horse, and with terrible cries, the hunt poured out of the castle gates.

The Enchanted Door was so small in the distance now that it was beginning to disappear into that great dark greenness. After it raced the Magic-hunt, raving Dogwolves barking, as mad and out of control as if they had seen a fox, and the insane scream of the Witchsmeller at the front, his cloak flying behind him as they charged after the door and into the forest.

I don't know if *you* have ever seen a hunt in full cry, but it is a truly terrifying sight.

"That hunt is going to tear Wish to pieces when it catches up with her," said Drama with satisfaction.

"It most certainly will not," said Queen Sychorax grimly. "For *I* will reach the Witchsmeller first. Warriors!" She stamped on the Royal Stage, once, twice. "Up and on your feet! Saddle up my hunting horse! There's no time to lose! *We have a princess to catch!*"

7. On the Other Side of the Wall

s they approached Queen Sychorax's unbreachable, impregnable, invincible Wall, Xar let out a long crow of triumph.

"I did it!" cried Xar, punching the air.

"You mean, *we* did it!" Wish corrected him.

"Which way now?" asked the Enchanted Key chattily.

"I've never seen an enchanted object that talked before," said Xar.

"I don't know what I'm doing!" replied Wish, slightly hysterically. "I don't mean to bring things to life at all!"

Wish was struggling to keep control of the flying door. It had looked so easy when Xar did it six months ago. But somehow the door, when *she* was enchanting it, seemed to be going way too fast, and zigzagging out of control all over the place...

A bit like Wish's emotions.

Wish knew she should be feeling horrified, and anxious. She knew that Warrior princesses really shouldn't fly on the back of doors in the company of Wizards. She had tried so *hard* to be a Warrior princess, to concentrate on all the maths-work, and the sword-work, and the letter-work.

But the truth was, in her heart of hearts, she was absolutely fed up to the back teeth with trying to work out whether "i" went before "e" or what happened when you took "x" from "y," and whether she should be getting Madam Dreadlock's homework to the schoolroom or the stables because it was every second Thursday.

Of course she was scared and sad that her mother was going to be so disappointed, and so angry.

But part of her was just absolutely thrilled to be back in the adventure of it, soaring high, high, over the battlements…high, higher still to get over Queen Sychorax's Wall, the wind blowing her hair back. Oh my goodness, they were really going to get over it! Peering over the edge of the door, she could see the little figures of the Warrior sentries, shouting but not shooting up at them, way, way down below…

Her heart beat fast…They were over the Wall! The great forest stretched out for miles and miles like an enormous green carpet in every direction, full of excitement and possibilities of danger.

The peril was instant, for the out-of-control door

THE PUNISHMENT CUPBOARD

MAGIC IS BANNED

was sinking fast, and Bodkin pointed to the tiny
distant figures of the Magic-hunters, pouring
out of the gates of the fort. They had to get as
far away as possible if they were not going to be
caught very quickly.

"Bodkin!" ordered Wish. "Take off your armor!
It's weighing us down!"

And as Bodkin threw away breastplate after
breastplate, spears, swords, leg-protectors, arm-
protectors, and they fell down into the forest below,
the nose of the door lifted, and though it became
no slower—in fact it even sped up—it
became easier to control. Wish's heart
lifted too.

The Enchanted Door shot over the forest canopy as fast as a speeding arrow, and Wish thought joyfully, *They'll never catch us now! Or…not tonight, at least…*

They zoomed over the Ragged River, and on, on and beyond, out of Queen Sychorax's territory, out of the boringness of real life and Punishment Cupboards and horrible stepsisters, and into the drama and excitement of the Wizard wildwoods.

However, once they were away from Queen Sychorax's territory and flying above the forest, Wish's elation died. For there was something odd about the land she was looking down on, something different from the last time she had flown over it. Normally there was the friendly smoke of wandering giants moving slowly across the countryside, or the bonfires from the Wizard camps, or great swarms of chattering sprites migrating south, or north, depending on the season. Now there was not a breath of smoke, not a sound.

The forest was weirdly quiet, and worst of all were the sinister blackened circles cut into the woods, like a child had torn into them with a wicked pair of scissors.

"Oh my goodness…" whispered Wish. "This has all been done by…"

"Witches," said Xar, grimly finishing the sentence for her.

"I had no idea all this was going on!" said Wish.

It was a horrid thought, that while life was going on just exactly as normal in the Warrior territories, and they'd been doing their training and their maths-work just like they always did, terrible battles had been carried out on this side of the Wall.

"Yes, well, that's your mother all over," said Xar. "As long as you are safe, she doesn't care about us. She's left us to be exterminated."

"That's not entirely true," said Wish. "She hired the Witchsmeller and his Magic-hunters, didn't she?"

"If 'the Witchsmeller' is that guy with the sniffing nose and the weird pointing finger, do you really think he is going to improve the situation?" said Xar.

Wish had to agree, the Witchsmeller's arrival in the wildwoods could not be described as an improvement.

"No, it's all down to ME," said Xar moodily. "I AM the boy of destiny, after all."

Bodkin had shut his eyes at the word "Witches." Witches were all he needed to make him feel thoroughly sick, particularly because he'd now gotten rid of most of his armor. He was a reluctant flyer at the best of times, but as a first-time pilot, Wish was sending the door swooping up and down and swaying side to side in such a wild and uncontrolled manner that his stomach seemed to have been left behind somewhere back in the castle.

"Which way should I take it?" said Wish.

Xar pointed down to the right. "The snowcats and Crusher are waiting for us somewhere over in that direction," he said.

It was a bit of a bumpy landing.

When they got below the tree canopy, Wish had quite a lot of difficulty getting the door to slow down, and because she always got a tad confused between left and right, the door slalomed rather manically through the tree trunks until eventually she found a small clearing, and they slammed down into the ground with such energy that all three of them were catapulted off the door.

"Whoa," said Xar with reluctant respect, picking himself up and brushing himself off. "You are one crazy door-driver, Wish!"

And then he punched the air and shouted, "I DID it! Quest accomplished! Look at ME, O gods of the trees and water, and bow down in respect!"

"Oh yesssss, well done, Xar, well done!" squealed Squeezjoos excitedly. "You're brilliant, you really are!"

"I most certainly am," said Xar with a grin. "*One thirteen-year-old boy, flying very low, has achieved the impossible double! Breaking out of Gormincrag Prison AND getting over Queen Sychorax's supposedly unbreachable Wall ... not ONCE but TWICE!* I AM THE BOY OF DESTINY! FEEL MY POWER!!!!"

And then he threw back his head, and howled too.

"Urrr urr URRRR! Urr urr URRRRR!!!!!"

Wish and Bodkin, picking themselves up, and realizing the enormity of what had just happened, looked at the so-called boy of destiny very, very balefully indeed.

"Aren't you going to thank me for saving you?" said Xar, just to add insult to injury. "Or don't Warriors do thank-yous?"

The cheek of it!

"Ha! *HA!* You saved US??" exclaimed Wish in outrage, her hands on her hips. "WE saved *YOU!* If I hadn't enchanted that door, those Magic-hunters would have killed you! And now Bodkin and I are in big, big trouble!"

"Helping me out of there was the least you could do when all your relatives were attacking me!" said Xar. "You Warriors are not very friendly to your guests!"

"*Guests???* Guests are *invited!* Guests are *polite! Guests* don't sneak in invisibly and try to *steal* things off you!" said Wish. "I think the word you may be looking for is 'burglar,' not 'guest'..."

"That Spelling Book is mine!" howled Xar. "I need it for a very important quest! And talking of burglary, you Warriors know all about that, don't you, because you're the biggest burglars in the world, and you've been stealing this forest off us for as long as anyone can remember!"

"You can't steal a forest!" yelled Wish. "The forest belongs to everyone!"

"Try telling your mother that." Xar glowered.

"Your father is just as bad as my mother, I've seen him!" said Wish.

Wizard and Warrior stood nose to nose in the forest, bellowing insults and curses at each other, as their ancestors had done throughout history, ever since Warriors first invaded from across the seas, and the two sets of humans met in battle in the wildwoods centuries before.

Caliburn sighed.

However many lifetimes he lived, these humans never seemed to change. He'd hoped for better from these two, but maybe they were going to be just like the others...

But Xar wasn't feeling too pleased with his father, so he had to agree with

Wish's last remark. And Wish was feeling rather the same about her mother.

They both paused.

"We shouldn't be fighting, Xar," said Wish at last, sticking out her hand for him to shake. "I've been really worried about what happened to you, and I'm so glad you're safe. I thought we were friends..."

Xar didn't have all that many friends at the moment, what with one thing and another. And he rather liked Wish. Even if she *was* an enemy. He was even rather fond of the odd bodyguard who kept falling asleep. So after a while, he said, "Thank you for helping me out by enchanting that door." Xar shook her hand and grinned back. "And I like your style of door-driving."

Maybe there *was* hope for the humans after all.

"And it WASSSS really funny, wassssn't it?" hissed Tiffinstorm, blinking into life beside them. "The Witchsmeller, screeching like a sssscreech owl...'This spoon is alive! This spoon is alive!'"

Now the danger was over, it really was quite funny. Wish and Xar, the sprites, and even Bodkin were laughing at the memory of the Witchsmeller. The spoon did a brilliant impression of bonking him on the nose.

Even Caliburn's shoulders were shaking, before he remembered himself, and gave a little cough. "I'd just like

to gently remind you that you're supposed to
be meeting everyone else here, Xar..."

Xar stopped laughing.

"Oh yes! You're right, Caliburn." He whistled a
couple of times. "Now where ARE those snowcats?
And Crusher? I TOLD them not to wander off.

"Oh, there you are!" exclaimed Xar as, out of
the gloom of the forest, there burst three stunningly
beautiful lynxes, who padded over to Xar and greeted
him as enthusiastically as if they had been three
little kittens, knocking him over onto his back and
slathering his face with licks.

"Nighteye! Kingcat! Forestheart! Crusher!"
sang Wish delightedly, as with great crashing noises
the giant lumbered into the clearing, pushing the
trees aside, his head on a level with the topmost

Snowcats

branches. She hugged the snowcats, burying her face into the deep softness of their fur, and then ran to embrace the giant around the ankle. "Oh, I've MISSED you all..."

"And weezus missed you!!!" trilled Squeezjoos happily, flying into her hair and making a joyful little nest in it. "Ridunculous humungular being!"

"Ssssome of us have..." said Hinkypunk, and just to show that not ALL sprites were as soppy as Squeezjoos, he blew a little sprite-breath, which froze Wish's bangs to her forehead. "Nots *me* though... I hatesss Warriors..."

"And this is the Once-sprite," said Xar, pointing to the little sprite sitting on the back of a peregrine falcon that had landed on his shoulder. "He's a new member of my sprite team. Your wicked mother took his Magic away, but he's learning to live life without it, aren't you, Once-sprite? His wings don't work anymore, but he's learned to fly on the back of this peregrine falcon."

The Once-sprite was sprite-sized and sprite-shaped, but no bright light shone from his chest. His color had faded till you could hardly tell what it might have been... *once*. His wings had withered on his shoulders, and the sharp little points of his ears had turned and drooped.

"It's very nice to meet you," said Wish, giving the Once-sprite a shy wave. The Once-sprite did not look as if he had forgiven Wish for her mother's actions. He stared stiffly into the distance, as though Wish were not there.

But Wish was too happy in that moment to mind.

The truth is, if you spend most of your life with your only real friends being an Assistant Bodyguard and a spoon, it's very nice to meet up with some other people who are on the same wavelength, even if some of them *are* a little annoying sometimes, and supposed to be your deadly enemies.

All of a sudden, Bodkin screamed, "Werewolf! Get behind me, Wish! There's a werewolf!" as he saw Lonesome for the first time, prowling in the shadows behind the other wolves, his tail swaying ominously from side to side.

"Oh, no, that's fine. He's a friend," explained Xar with a careless wave of his hand. "I met him in Gormincrag."

"A *friend*? You're friends with a *werewolf*?" said Bodkin. This really was too much, even for Xar. "But werewolves used to be known as companions for Witches...and what were you doing in Gormincrag? Isn't that some kind of prison?"

"Lonesome was innocent. He should never have been in prison in the first place," said Xar. "And for a Loner Raving Fangmouth werewolf he's really quite friendly. He just needs a bit of help with his manners."

"Doesn't EVERYONE in prison say they're innocent?" said Bodkin, looking very dubiously indeed at the werewolf, who was pawing at the ground in a

manic sort of way, as if he was barely repressing the urge
to rip them all to pieces.

The werewolf bared his teeth menacingly at Bodkin.

"Oh, Bodkin, don't be so prejudiced," scolded Wish.
"This werewolf may be a very *nice* werewolf for all we
know..."

The werewolf paused for a moment, stiffening a
little in surprise. He had never met Warriors before,
having spent his whole life locked up in Gormincrag,
and this was the first time that anyone had ever
described him as "very nice." Mostly people just ran
away screaming.

"Why were you in prison, Xar?" asked Wish. "And
why do you want the Spelling Book? I'd have just *given*
it back to you; you didn't have to sneak in and steal it."

"Caliburn didn't want me to get you involved," said
Xar. "And I need a Spelling Book so I can make my
father's staff work properly. I'm going to need all the
Magic I can get in the quest I'm going on...A quest to
get rid of...*this*."

Xar took off his glove.

Wish and Bodkin let out horrified gasps.

"I *wish* you'd stop doing that," moaned Caliburn,
putting one wing over his eyes as the sprites burned
with green fire, hissing and cursing in alarm, and the
snowcats and the wolves crouched down, growling. A

trembling Squeezjoos flew into Wish's hair and made a little nest there.

"Oh...my...goodness!" whispered Wish in horror. "What happened to your hand? It's the *Witch-stain*, isn't it? But I thought the Stone-That-Takes-Away-Magic had taken the Witch-stain away? We all saw it happen, in my mother's dungeon!"

"Yes, well, it didn't take all of it," said Xar. "The great thing about it is that I can do Magic now, and that was wonderful, at first. But the bad thing about it is..."

"It's *bad* Magic," finished Caliburn. "Very, very *bad* Magic. And, as you can see, it's getting worse."

Bodkin and Wish shivered as they looked at Xar's hand.

"It looks so *awful*. You don't think...You're not worried that...it might turn YOU to the bad, Xar?" suggested Wish tentatively. She laid a gentle hand on Xar's arm.

She could feel a slight coldness as she touched him, like ghost-breath on the back of the neck. Xar wasn't looking well. His hair was damp, as if he had a temperature. The green of the Witch-stain had crept all the way beyond his wrist, there was a feverish look in his eye, and he shivered now and then, as if he was about to catch a nasty bout of the flu. Sometimes his hand stiffened, and his fingers curled and turned into claws...

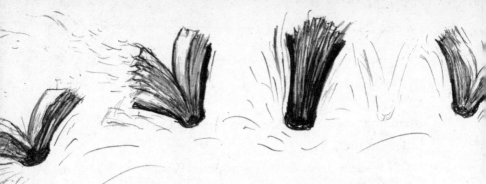

And even Xar found that a little scary.

"The Droods found out about the Witch-stain and shut me up in Gormincrag. They said they were trying to find a cure, but they were *lying*, and my father believed them," said Xar moodily. "They all just want me to stay in Gormincrag forever. My father doesn't care...Well, I'll show *them*!"

"But what are you going to do, Xar?" said Bodkin. "The Stone-That-Takes-Away-Magic is broken, you can't use that anymore!"

"The only way to get rid of a Witch-stain is to get rid of the Witches *themselves*," said Xar. "So that's what I'm going to do. I'm going to go out there and destroy them."

Bodkin looked at him with an open mouth. He had met Witches before and knew exactly how scary they were. "You're going to go out there and face a whole horde of acid-blooded nightmares *all on your own*? On *purpose*? But you're just one small boy!"

Caliburn coughed. "And it's all very well saying you're going to destroy them, Xar, but HOW, exactly? That's been my point along..."

"Well, that's why I need my Spelling Book," said Xar. "I'm sure there will be something in there that can

The Spelling Book FLEW up into the air and into Wish's hands...

help me..."

"This is the most extraordinary coincidence!" cried Wish excitedly.

"What coincidence?" moaned Caliburn, feeling the beginnings of a serious worry coming on. "I hate coincidences..."

"I've JUST TODAY found a spell in the Spelling Book to get rid of Witches!" said Wish triumphantly. "In fact, that's exactly why I broke out of the Punishment Cupboard—I wanted to get the spell to you and your father...Bodkin, show Xar!"

As soon as she said these words, the Spelling Book flew out of Bodkin's pocket, and up into the air and into Wish's hands, growing larger as it flew.

Wish tapped the letters on the contents page to take them to the right part of the book.

"It was quite strange really. I didn't *find* it so much as *write* it," admitted Wish. "I was using the feather that Caliburn gave me to write with, and it was almost as if Caliburn's feather was writing *on its own...*"

They all crowded around the Spelling Book to see the page.

The Spelling Book

A Complete Guide to the Entire Magical World

The Spelling Book
Bloody Barbeards

Bloody Barbeards are dangerous mer-people who live in the Drowned Forest. They have a grudge against all Wizards, the reasons for which have gotten lost over the centuries, but any Wizard found swimming in the Sea of Skulls will be dragged down to the bottom of the ocean by a Bloody Barbeard.

page 3,284,956

The spelling book

Three-headed
Bugbear

Bugbears are large, annoying creatures with great
tracking abilities. Once they are on your trail, they
will very rarely give up.

The third head on
this Bugbear is invisible.

page 3,284, 957

THE SPELLING BOOK

Telekinesis

Moving
things
with your
mind..

The power of moving things with your mind. Most
Wizards have to use a staff to move things through
the power of mind control, but a few can use their
hands, or in this case, a Magic eye.

It takes years of practice to
perfect this art.

The Spelling Book
The Magic Eye

Wizards with a Magic eye are extraordinarily rare and will have more than one life. The Magic eye allows the Wizard to perform Magic without a staff (normally a skill that takes decades to learn). However the Magic is so powerful it is extremely difficult to train and control.

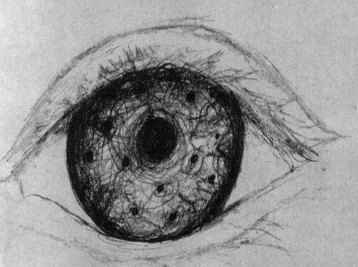

A Magic eye only appears
once in every couple of generations.

page 582,130

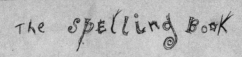

Transformation

Transformation is one of the most difficult Magic
spells, and extremely dangerous. For it is one
thing to transform into another form—it is quite
another to come back. If you stay too long, there
is a risk that you might remain as the creature you
transformed into forever.

The stronger the Wizard's magical
powers, the longer they can stay
transformed and still come back.

House Sprites

Most forts, either Wizard or Warrior, are infested
with house sprites. These mischievous little creatures
hide like mice, in the walls or under the floorboards,
and they come out at night to steal food or play
tricks on the inhabitants of the forts.

PAGE 60,486

THE SPELLING BOOK
Write Your Own Story

Noo Year's Ressohishuns

1. I well work hard at my reeding and riteing and arithmatic so I can be topp of the klass.

2. I wull mak a gud impreshun on the teacher.

3. I wull impress my muther so she dus not think I am a Dissapointment.

sined :

Wish

page 2,304,587

The Spelling Book
Write Your Own Story

A Spell to Get Rid of Witches

Gather all ingredients and STIR into a living spoon.

Ingredients:
One: Giant's Last Breath from Castle Death
Two: Feathers from a Witch
Three: Tears from a Frozen Queen

page 2,304,588

The Spelling Book Thanks You For Reading,

and Would Gently Remind You That Things

Generally Turn Out All Right

IN THE END.

(Hopefully)

DIE!

SnoCats FoREVER

Niteye eating Looter

When my MAGIC comes in I will bee the MOST MAGIC ~~pursonn~~ purson in the UNIVERSE

I ♥ Spoons

This booK has ben lent to mee. Wish

"Look! It's a recipe! Maybe the Ssspelling Book wants us to EAT the Witches?" said Squeezjoos, excitedly, for Squeezjoos was always hungry.

"That's not a recipe!" said Xar. "Oh my goodness! *You're right!* It's a Spell to Get Rid of Witches!!! I knew it!"

They all gazed hopefully at the spell.

"You wrote this with MY feather, did you, Wish?" said Caliburn, so worried now that the feathers were dropping from his back like leaves in autumn. "Oh dear, oh dear, oh dear...Sometimes I forget what happened in my former lives, but the memory lives on in my feathers."

"You've lost me there, Caliburn," said Bodkin, shaking his head. "I have no idea what you're talking about. Former lives?"

"Yes, I have lived many lives as a human, but this is the first time I have been reincarnated as a bird," explained Caliburn, as if this was the most normal thing in the world. "So perhaps the feather is writing a message TO me, FROM me in one of my former lives?"

Bodkin's head was going around and around. These Wizards and Magic things were so complicated. Having just the one life as a Warrior Assistant Bodyguard was so much simpler than all this reincarnating, turning-into-birds business.

"But I've never heard of a spell so strong that it could actually get rid of Witches ENTIRELY," said Caliburn.

"Did I really know that in a former life? *What does this mean?*"

"It means," said Xar animatedly, "*that we're going spell-raiding, guys!* Oh, this is so exciting!"

Spell-raiding was a rather disreputable part of the Magic world. Spells needed ingredients, and some of those ingredients were hard to get hold of. So wild wingless young sprites called "spell-raiders" specialized in collecting and stealing spell ingredients. They flew at night, on the back of specially trained peregrine falcons, in order to make a quick getaway.

The Once-sprite cheered up no end. He had been drooping sadly on the back of the peregrine falcon, but now he sat up, so excited that he might have an important role to play in the world once more that he accidentally fell off his bird, scrambled up on its back again, and saluted Xar, saying, "I won't let you down, Xar! Youssss can rely on me!"

"Me too! Me too!" squeaked Squeezjoos. "*I's* wants to be a spell-raider too!"

"Youss too young to be a ssspell-raider..." said the Once-sprite. "It'sss very dangerousssss...You can guard some of the collecting bottles that we're going to put the ingredients in..."

The Once-sprite rustled in his spell bags and gave a few collecting bottles to Squeezjoos, who said, "Is'll guard them with my life!"

"All right, let's see, what's the first ingredient?" said Xar excitedly. "*Giant's Last Breath from Castle Death...*"

The werewolf started to growl and gesticulate urgently. What he said was: "*REOOWR, grunt, GROOWGGRGLE, grunt, weoorrrrr!*" And then a loud spitting noise, and a stamp of the hairy foot, followed by, "*Creargle Urgh.*"

"Look! Lonesome is agreeing with us! He's saying we have to go IMMEDIATELY to Castle Death," said Xar.

"You speak werewolf?" asked Wish, deeply impressed.

"Oh yes, fluently," said Xar carelessly.

"Would you say *fluently*?" said Caliburn, to no one in particular.

"Fluently," repeated Xar firmly. "We Wizards all get lessons in werewolf language."

"Xar's *brilliant*, issn't he?" said Squeezjoos proudly. "Speakss werewolf like he'ss a werewolf himself."

"Your lessons sound so much more interesting than *our* lessons," said Wish longingly.

"What's he saying now?"

The werewolf repeated rather more urgently, "*Grunt, weoorrrrr!*" Spit! Stamp!

"Don't worry, Lonesome, I understand," said Xar. "We need to go to Castle Death. Immediately."

Unfortunately that *wasn't* what the werewolf was

159

saying. Xar really should have concentrated harder in the werewolf language classes. *"Creagle Urgh"* does indeed mean Castle Death, so Xar had gotten that bit right. But "go to" in werewolf language is *"grunt, weeiiiroh,"* whereas *"grunt, weoorrrrr!"* means "stay away from."

The spit and the stamp were just for emphasis.

So what the werewolf was *actually* saying was: "For goodness' sake STAY AWAY from Castle Death!"

The werewolf got more urgent still.

"Reaaghhh cccrooogllie sfocccan Burgan!" Stamp! Spit! *"Purgan GRUNT WEOORRR, nurgan GRUNT WEEIIROH! GRUNT WEOORRR Creagle Urgh! Pi urglly discottle agly rewooooow peroooooow."*

And what *that* meant was, "That's not what I *said*, you stupid human! 'Stay away,' not 'go to'! STAY AWAY from Castle Death if you want to hang on to your pathetic little human lives!"

And then Lonesome threw his head back and started howling.

"Lonesome's just becoming a little frustrated because he thinks we should be getting a move on," said Xar. Xar patted the werewolf kindly on the paw. "Don't worry, Lonesome, we're going there. We're going there as fast as we can..."

"I think *we* should go too," said Wish decidedly.

"Whaaaaaaaat????" said Bodkin.

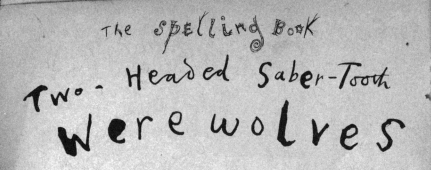

THE SPELLING BOOK

Two-Headed Saber-Tooth
Werewolves

Werewolves do not only come out at night, as the
legends suggest, and some are more friendly than others.
This Two-Headed Saber-Tooth
werewolf is remarkably speedy
and very savage, so best
avoided (unless you are a
very fast runner).

*Best avoided, unless
you are a
very fast
runner.*

8 · Following the Sweet Track

ut you promised your mother!" said Bodkin in an agonized sort of way. "You said you'd go back home straightaway! This isn't our problem!"

"It IS our problem," said Wish. "We ALL let the Kingwitch out of the stone, and Xar is our friend, so we have to help him. We can't just sit behind the Wall twiddling our thumbs while Xar goes through all this on his own."

"I have to agree with Bodkin the bodyguard," said Caliburn. "That's a REALLY, REALLY bad idea! Your type of Magic is very dangerous, Wish...and the Witches WANT that Magic. On the other side of the Wall, the Witches can't get at you, but over *here*..."

"You need our help!" argued Wish. "The spell talks about how you should 'stir the ingredients with a Living Spoon,' and *I'm* the one who has the living spoon!"

The Enchanted Spoon, delighted to be playing such an important role, gave a small, proud bow to the rest of the company.

"You should both go back to your parents!" moaned Caliburn to Xar and Wish. "I know they're a little unreasonable, but if you explain everything to them, maybe they could help you. This is a bigger problem than the two of you can deal with…MUCH bigger … MUCH more dangerous. This is a Longstepper High-Walker GIANT of a problem!"

"All right, Crusher, what do YOU think?" Wish shouted up to Xar's giant.

Crusher was picking leaves from the topmost branches of the trees and eating them.

He put his face down a little closer, and you could see that it was covered with wrinkles and laughter lines like the wandering paths on an old map, and his eyes were kind and wise.

"I was thinking," said Crusher dreamily (speaking v-e-r-y slowly, for giants operate in a different timescale from everyone else), "about LANGUAGE and how in *English* two negatives make a positive, but in *spriteish*, a double negative is still a negative. However, there is NO language in which two positives make a negative…"

"Yeah, right, like THAT'S the problem," said Xar sarcastically.

"I hadn't thought of that!" said Crusher in gentle surprise, but delighted that Xar was engaging with his mental processes. "You're correct, Xar. 'Yeah, right' IS a statement in English where two positives make a negative…"

Crusher was a wonderful giant companion, but he could sometimes be on a different planet from everyone else.

"That wasn't what I meant!" said Xar, in exasperation. "*Stop thinking Big Thoughts, Crusher!* The *real* problem is, should Wish come with us or go back to her scary mother?"

"Oh!" said Crusher, even more thoughtfully.

He paused for an impressively long time, and then said, "Well, Wish should come with us, because I like her."

Strangely enough, it was this simple statement that changed Caliburn's mind.

"All right!" he said with a sigh. "I suppose this is all such a disaster that it doesn't really matter WHAT we do, as long as we're with our friends and we do it TOGETHER.

"And as long as everyone promises that we will take breaks for lessons along the way," he went on. "I don't want any of you getting behind in your studies! You three need all the education you can get."

They looked up the way to Castle Death in the maps section of the Spelling Book, which very helpfully lit up the various routes across the wildwoods with different colors of sprite dust. Purple dust was a warning to the traveler to be careful, red dust meant

exceptional danger, and yellow dust marked the safer passages.

Castle Death, on the edge of the Witch Mountains, was across a land to the west called the Slodger Territories, a vast, boglike desert that stretched for miles in every direction.

And the Slodger Territories were dangerous, for Grindylows and Greenteeth lived in those marshes, strange, part see-through creatures, with huge sad eyes, who reached out skinny arms and dragged you down under the muddy water, with little satisfying belches of the bog.

The only safe way, marked in yellow, across the Slodger Territories was the Sweet Track, an ancient road like a long, winding bridge, built and blessed by Wizards long ago. You can't be attacked on the Sweet Track, for it was guarded by a very ancient power and spells too old to unravel.

They didn't want to use Magic to get there, for Magic was tiring, and Wish was already so exhausted by the effort of making the door fly and keeping it in the air by her sheer will, that she could feel every muscle in her body aching. Also, the use of Magic would make it easier for Witches or other bad things to trace them.

The broken door had smashed to pieces on landing, but they might need it later, so it was the sprites who put it back together again with their wands.

A fairy making a spell is a little like someone taking a golf shot, or a baseball swing in another time, another place. It's not just a matter of pointing the wand in a careless fashion. The spell is thrown up in the air, the wand goes right behind the head and then smashes the spell toward the thing that it is wanting to enchant, preferably, for full power, with a great deal of follow-through.

ZING!!!! The spells spun through the air, singing the word "reconstruct," and scoring a direct hit on the smashed door, and the pieces instantly sorted themselves out, organizing themselves swiftly on the floor like a puzzle rearranging itself, at first forming a ridiculous pattern that didn't look like a door at all, before whizzing back together again magically in the right place, as if magnetically attracted to one another.

Crusher put the Enchanted Door in his pocket, and Xar, Wish, and Bodkin climbed aboard the snowcats' backs, and the giant slowly walked his way through the holloways to the beginning of the Slodger Territories, the wolves and the snowcats running by his side, the sprites and Caliburn flying overhead.

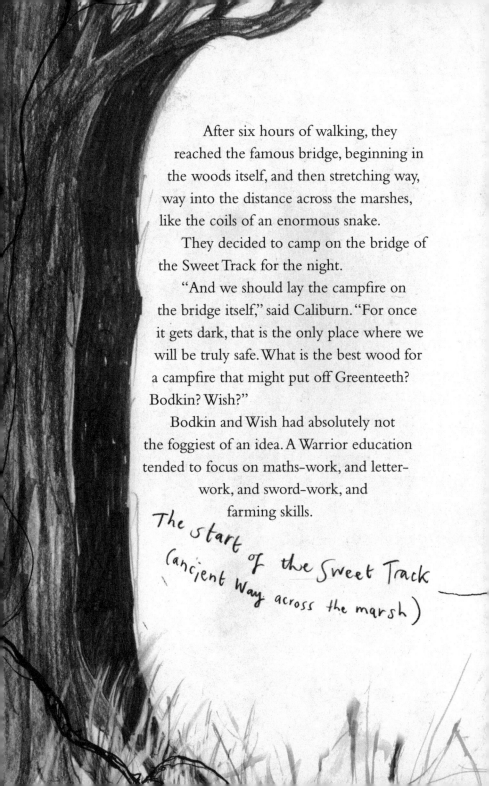

After six hours of walking, they reached the famous bridge, beginning in the woods itself, and then stretching way, way into the distance across the marshes, like the coils of an enormous snake.

They decided to camp on the bridge of the Sweet Track for the night.

"And we should lay the campfire on the bridge itself," said Caliburn. "For once it gets dark, that is the only place where we will be truly safe. What is the best wood for a campfire that might put off Greenteeth? Bodkin? Wish?"

Bodkin and Wish had absolutely not the foggiest of an idea. A Warrior education tended to focus on maths-work, and letter-work, and sword-work, and farming skills.

The start of the Sweet Track (ancient Way across the marsh)

Wood-work was not really part of anything they knew.

"Goodness gracious!" said Caliburn, very shocked. "Don't they teach you anything over there in iron Warrior fort? This is elementary stuff. How do they expect you to survive in the forest if you don't know *that*?"

"I's know! I's know!" said Squeezjoos. "Alder or rowan is for protection…and hawthorn makes a nice hot fire…"

So Xar and Wish and Bodkin gathered alder wood from the forest, and then they arranged a little ring of stones to put the wood on to make their campfire.

"Let *me*
practice lighting it
with staff-Magic!" said
Xar.

"I'm not sure that's a
good idea," said Caliburn
hastily.

"I have to practice controlling
the Magic! And you were the one who
said we should be doing lessons!" said Xar.
He looked up the spell in the Spelling Book and
then held out his arm with the Witch-stain on it, his
father's yew spelling staff grasped firmly in that hand.

"Let the Magic come out slowly," advised Caliburn,
"in a controlled and focused manner…Think gentle,
calm, happy thoughts…Be patient…"

But nothing happened. And Xar was not a patient person.

He went red in the face with exasperation. He shook the staff crossly. "Why isn't it working?"

"Oh, I've been looking up about spelling staffs. I think you might be holding the staff at the wrong end—you hold it like *this*," said Wish, helpfully putting her hand on the staff to show him the grip she had read about in the Spelling Book.

And the moment that Wish put her hand on it as well...

BOOOOOOOM!!!!!!!! The Magic came screaming out of the staff with such force that the little campfire of alder and hawthorn twigs EXPLODED, and Wish and Xar and Bodkin and the wolves and the snowcats and the werewolf were all blown off their feet by the force of the explosion, and into the bog.

"Don't get discouraged, everyone!" announced Caliburn, as they all staggered muddily to their feet, amid a strong smell of burning feathers and singed-fur-of-werewolf. "It can take quite some TIME to learn how to control Magic."

The explosion had blasted a great big
hole in the bridge of the Sweet Track,
where the ancient timbers, which had
lain there quietly and peacefully
for so many centuries, had been
smashed in two, and now smoldered
ominously with little flickering
green flames at the blackened
edges.

"Oh dear, was that me?" said Wish apologetically. "I'm so sorry. I've always been a bit clumsy..."

"No, no...it could happen to anyone!" said Caliburn, with a nervous glance at Wish, for the power that protected the Sweet Track was a very ancient power indeed, and the bridge really ought to have remained intact whatever spells were thrown at it. He had never heard of any Magic, past, present, or future, that could have an effect on the Sweet Track.

It didn't seem the best of omens for the start of their expedition.

They regathered wood and relaid the fire a bit farther down the bridge, and Bodkin lit it by the Warrior method of using a little iron fire striker against flint, which deeply impressed the sprites. Less spectacular than Xar's way, but more effective.

The sprites then blew *out* the fire, in order to show off to Bodkin that they could relight it with their sprite-breath, in all sorts of beautiful colors—yellow, red, green, blue.

Look what I've done to my father's Spelling Staff!!

Wish tore up the note she wore around her neck saying "I am a Fule" and put it on the fire, and the note burned happily, with rainbow brightness.

And then they made a delicious nettle stew. Crusher gathered the nettles, stuffing his pockets with handfuls and handfuls of them, for they would need food for the journey ahead, and not much food was to be found in the Slodger Territories. Wish and the sprites found water and Bodkin did the cooking. The werewolf, *thoroughly* overexcited by his newfound freedom in the wildwoods, returned from his own hunting expedition with an entire mouthful of worms, which he deposited triumphantly in Wish's lap as a helpful addition to the stew. (The werewolf seemed to have taken a bit of a shine to Wish.)

"That's a LOVELY idea, Lonesome!" said Wish tactfully, not wanting to hurt his feelings. "But maybe you could have those on the side or as a starter? I think Bodkin may be allergic to worms, aren't you, Bodkin?"

"Definitely allergic to worms," said Bodkin firmly.

Xar wanted to try one, but Caliburn wouldn't let him.

The Enchanted Spoon stirred the stew with such enthusiasm that he turned it into a positive *whirlpool*, and on a couple of occasions the spoon very nearly fell in and had to be rescued by Xar or Bodkin or Wish.

175

Bodkin announced that the stew was ready, and the werewolf leaped up and thrust his entire head into the saucepan and began noisily slurping. Xar pulled him out, and Caliburn explained to the rather crestfallen werewolf about manners, while the sprites cartwheeled through the air in fits of giggles.

Xar had managed to steal a saucepan while he was on the run, but he hadn't gotten any plates, which was fine, because they just ate off large leaves.

And I don't know whether it was the cold night air and the adventure of the day or the way that the Enchanted Spoon stirred that stew, but it was the most delicious stew that anyone had ever tasted.

That was a happy, happy evening. Even Bodkin was happy. He couldn't quite think why. He had lost most of his armor, which should have left him more anxious, but somehow he felt lighter and braver. At least he could bend over.

He joined in with the songs around the campfire.

The moon came up over the marshes, a big round full one, and the werewolf howled at it, and Xar joined in. *"URR URR URRRRR!"*

"Is it just me," whispered Bodkin to Wish, "or is that werewolf not a very good influence on Xar?"

"Give the werewolf a chance," said Wish. "He just hasn't been around people very much..."

Eventually they fell asleep on the boards of the Sweet Track, and even though the air was bitterly cold, they were all snuggled around with the wolves and the snowcats and the bear, and their shaggy coats kept them warm. The smoke from the fire curled gently upward, constantly changing color—blue, red, orange, white.

Crusher stayed awake, watching out for Witches and other bad things. He sat cross-legged in the bog, humming and singing very softly to himself.

Much later, Wish woke up.

"Having trouble sleeping, little one?" said the giant, stopping singing for a moment and bending down to look at her.

"I'm worrying about

going to Castle Death…and the Witches…" Wish shivered. "How can you *not* worry, Crusher?"

The giant laughed. "What *I* generally find is that if there is some GIANT problem in the world some GIANT answer turns up just in time to solve it."

The raven, who was also awake, harrumphed a little, but he did admit, "That IS the lesson of history."

"Worrying won't help it turn up any sooner. And look!" continued the giant. "If you waste your time *worrying*, how will you have a moment to see how beautiful the world is?"

His giant fingers closed around Wish, and gently he carried her up, up, up into the air. Wish had a heart-stopping moment of excitement to find herself looking DOWN on the world rather than UP at it. Crusher put her into his pocket and she peered over its rim, the wind blowing her hair back. From here in the moonlight she could see for miles and miles across the wasteland, and way, way in the distance the misty outlines of the Witch Mountains. Somewhere out there was Castle Death…but from the safety of the giant's pocket, all she could think of was how calm it was, how still, with the moon above the marshes and the wind blowing steadily.

The giant began to sing.

"A GIANT heart
Needs a GIANT life!
GIANT arms
Can hold a world!"

Every time he sang the word "GIANT!" he threw
out his arms wide and Wish bounced around unsteadily
in his pocket, giggling.

"Let me lead a GIANT'S life!
No LITTLE steps, no holding back!
A GIANT way, a GIANT'S track!

Let my mistakes
Be GIANT ones!

For I can't live in LITTLE worlds!

I need the space to run my fill
I need to jump from hill to hill

And if you take my woods from me
I'll wander out into the sea
And try to find another world

So I can live a GIANT life!"

And down on the Sweet Track, the sound of the
giant's singing woke Xar and Bodkin, and the sprites,
and it was so joyful it really put heart into the
little party. The werewolf even joined
in with his OWN song, which I
have translated here, because
otherwise it sounds mostly
like howling.

The Moon and I
(The Werewolf's Song)

Me and the moon
The moon and me
When all the world gives up on me
When everyone thinks bad about me
I still have the moon
It's me and the moon
It's always the moon and me

My bad wolf heart wants what it wants
So I have to keep running…Keep running…
Can't stop in case I bite someone
Keep running…Keep running…
I thought I was good, and then I looked down
My shaggy coat, my wolfy paws,
I'm bad as a snake, and meaner than grit,
Don't try and stop me, 'cause you will get bit
Let me keep running…

I'm running for the moon
Up to the moon where I can be good
When all the world gives up on me
When everyone thinks bad about me
I still have the moon
It's me and the moon
Mostly it's me and the moon

Every now and then the werewolf would break off to howl: *"Ooooouw ooow OOOOOOOOWW!"*

And Wish and Bodkin joined in with the Warrior War Song: "NO FEAR! That's the Warrior's marching song! *NO FEAR!"* While Xar and the sprites sang the Magic Lament: "Once we were Wizards, wandering free, in roads of sky and paths of sea…"

"Let me lead a GIANT'S life!" sang Crusher.

"Mostly it's me and the moon!" sang Lonesome.

"Oouw ooow OOOOOW! Ooooow ooow OOOOOOOOOWWWW!"

And as the songs blended on the midnight air, they seemed to be defying and taunting the many, many people and creatures who were now chasing Wish and Xar.

Xar's father was looking for him, searching the countryside in the form of a great golden eagle. And Queen Sychorax and the Witchsmeller.

And something WORSE was following them...

For as I said earlier, when Xar escaped from Gormincrag, there might have been some things that helped, things that had soft black wings and feathers for arms and talons like swords on the ends of their clawlike hands. Things that might have been Witches...

Well, they weren't helping him NOW.

They were AFTER him.

For Xar, all unknowing, had done what the Kingwitch wanted. He had brought Wish from behind the Wall, and now she was out in the open, unprotected, and if the Witches could get their claws on her and bring her to the Kingwitch sooner than expected, why, then, so much the better...

Xar and Wish are on this Quest together now...

but they are being CHASED by dark forces. Can they get away?

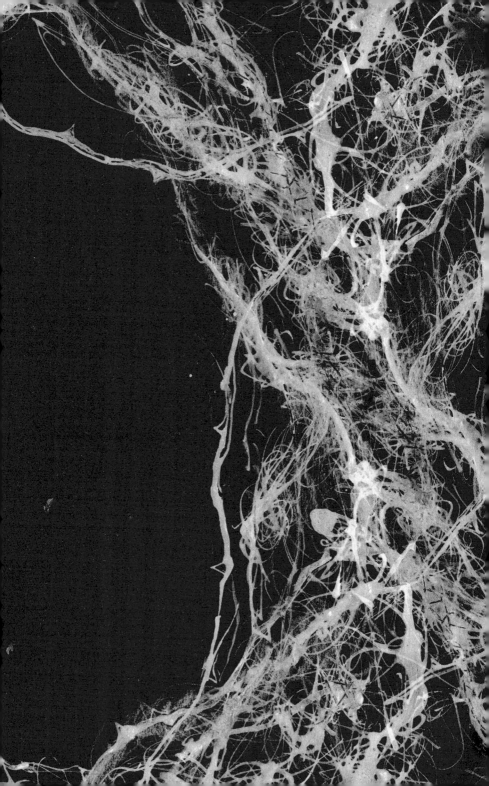

part Two

the

Witch-

Trap

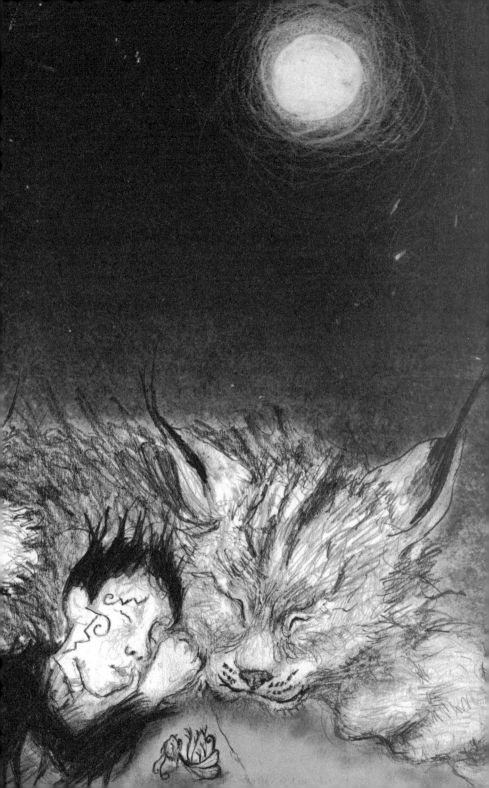

9. A Couple of Nasty Surprises on the Way to Castle Death

ar woke very early the next morning, his right arm aching and burning. He shook Wish awake, and within seconds of opening her eyes, her heart was beating as quick and panicked as that of a small forest creature who knows it is about to be attacked. There was a coldness in the air that they both remembered from before, a chill that sank into the bones and froze the blood and smudged the thoughts, and the hair on Wish's head rose up with electric, fizzing energy.

For the smell was familiar too: a stinking reek of decaying cat and corpses' breath and burning hair, with a sulfurous kick of rotten eggs...A smell that brought Xar out in a frightened sweat, for it was the smell of WITCHES.

All around them the animals were waking into instant, terrified alarm, their fur bristling around their necks in ruffs, and the sprites flew shaking up into the air, burning bright with fear, drawing their wands, sharp as thorns, reaching into their spell bags...

Wish felt for the Enchanted Sword, but to her horror she found that for some reason she couldn't take it out of the scabbard. It was stuck fast.

She could hear her own breath.

There was something under the bridge...

She had a glimpse from between the boards of something dark and feathery, moving slowly, nauseously, greasily beneath them.

"Ruuuuuuuunnnnnnnnn!!!!" yelled Wish at the top of her voice, as with a high unearthly wail...

UH-OH...

There's something under the bridge!

SLLLLLICCCCCCCCCE!

Three great talons came up from below, piercing right through the planks of the bridge a couple of yards back from where they were standing.

Wish and Bodkin and Xar ran for their lives, alongside the snowcats, the wolves, and the werewolf, along the length of the Sweet Track, with the sprites and Caliburn flying terrified above, and Crusher stumbling

to his feet and splashing noisily through the bog, following them all.

Wish looked over her shoulder as the snowcats ran farther, farther along the bridge across the marshes. There were the woods, dark in the distance. There was the broken bridge. There was the place where they had camped. There was the spot where Wish had seen the Witch's talons, but there was nothing to be seen of those talons now...Where had the Witch gone?

They ran on, on, on, along the Sweet Track, until the woods were just a distant smudge on the horizon, and the snowcats were so tired that their weary paws moved slower, slower, and...
slower...still, until they limped
and lumbered into a
panting walk.

"I think," puffed Caliburn, "that we're safe now. That Witch would only have been able to attack us because the explosion yesterday may have broken the Magic that protects the bridge at that particular point."

"Why couldn't I draw the Enchanted Sword?" said Wish, puzzled and shaken. "It wouldn't come out, however hard I pulled it, but it's coming out really easily now…"

Sure enough, now they were out of danger, she had taken the sword out of the scabbard with one light touch.

"I always said that sword was a bit wayward," said Caliburn nervously. "It has too much of a mind of its own."

They all stopped to examine the sword.

"That's odd…" said Bodkin, noticing something for the first time. "The writing on the blade looks different."

"It must have gotten scratched or worn away at some point," said Wish.

It was an unfortunate scratch. For somewhere since their last adventure a deep scrape on the blade had changed the inscription from *Once there were Witches …but I killed them* to *Once there were Wishes …but I killed them.*

It was a much gloomier message somehow, the idea of "wishes" being buried, and particularly gloomy when one of your party is actually *called* "Wish."

"It's just a scratch," said Wish, firmly putting the sword back in the scabbard. "It was an accident. It doesn't mean anything."

They kept on walking, trying not to see this as a bad omen, and to put as much distance as possible between themselves and that Witch attack.

But it was only much, much later in the day that Wish's heart began to beat a little slower again.

That little incident made the spell-raiding band somewhat uneasy, as you can imagine.

But you can't stay frightened forever.

And over the next few days, there was absolutely not a hint of a Witch, or even a Grindylow or a Greenteeth, only curlews and kingfishers, lapwings and snipe, wheeling and calling and singing over the bog.

They got back into a happier rhythm, walking across the Sweet Track, across the endless marshes, and when they stopped for a rest, Caliburn would give them Magic lessons sitting on the bridge, their legs swinging.

For Xar, the lessons were based around patience, calmness, not losing his temper when he practiced the spells. This was particularly important because Xar was working with his father's staff rather than his own one, which had been left behind in the Wizard fort when Xar was taken to Gormincrag. Encanzo's staff was not supposed to be used by beginners, particularly those who have a Witch-stain, so things often went wrong.

For instance, Xar helpfully tried to make Caliburn's feathers grow back, because the old bird had lost so many from the sheer worry of being Xar's advisor. He pointed his father's staff, as calmly as possible...and the feathers went on growing and growing and growing, until Caliburn had a tail as long as a peacock's, that trailed over the edge of the bridge and into the bog below. Squeezjoos and the hairy fairies were in fits of giggles. It took a couple of hours of concentrated spellwork for Ariel and the sprites to get the feathers to grow small again, and two days later, Caliburn still had an amusingly fluffy bottom.

Caliburn was a dignified bird, so he got very cross if he caught the hairy fairies pointing and laughing at it.

With Wish, Caliburn concentrated on things that were easiest for her first, to build up her confidence. Wish found things made out of iron the simplest to move, so Caliburn had her pushing up her eyepatch a little, and practicing with her pins, making them dance,

and moving them like little armies, and even getting them to have pin fights with each other.

"I understand things so much better when YOU'RE teaching me, Caliburn, rather than Madam Dreadlock!" said Wish triumphantly. "Madam Dreadlock is just a little too... *shouty*...and it's difficult to focus when someone is yelling at you."

The key from the Punishment Cupboard had decided it was in love with the Enchanted Spoon.

BOING

BOING

The head of the key formed a mouth, and every now and then it would shout in its enthusiastic, creaky little voice: "Sppooooon!!! Where are yooooooouuuu?" The Enchanted Spoon was a bit frightened of the key and had taken to hiding, because the key kept on wanting to kiss the spoon.

Wish was so delighted with her success in bringing the spoon and the key and the pins to life that she

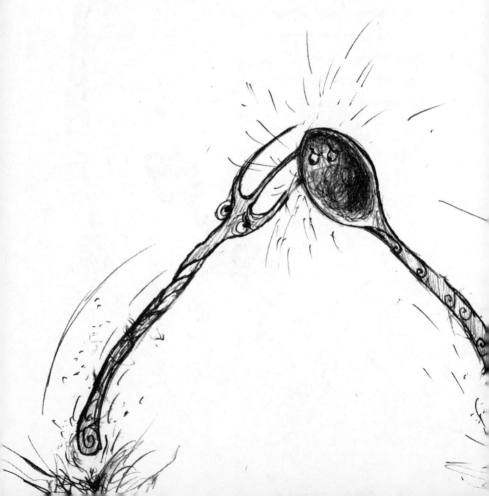

accidentally did the same with Bodkin's fork, and regrettably that created a love triangle. The fork decided that *it* was in love with the key, and that the unfortunate spoon was its main rival. So Bodkin would be trying to eat his supper, and the fork would leap heroically out of Bodkin's hand to pin the Enchanted Spoon to the ground.

Or the spoon would find himself being stalked…and the fork would challenge him to a fight…and the spoon would stick out his chest like a proud swordsman, and the two of them would conduct a complicated spoon-and-fork fight, lunging and parrying and dueling and ambushing each other across the Sweet Track.

Oh, be careful, my love!

Caliburn progressed from lessons on "moving things" into lessons on "magnetism." The Enchanted Spoon was very patient when Wish gave him many variations of hairstyles made out of pins that she made magnetically attach to his head.

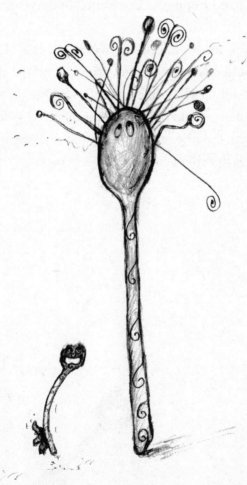

Nice hairstyle, handsome!

One day, Wish's hand slipped on her eyepatch and the spell from her Magic eye was a little too strong. It sent the Enchanted Spoon cartwheeling through the air like a spinning spelling staff, pins scattering in all directions, before he landed upside down, stuck fast to the top of Bodkin's forehead.

And there the spoon stayed, doing a headstand, his handle moving up and down like a kicking leg, as the key cuddled up to him, cooing, "Poooor sppooooon...poooor spooooon..."

This all passed the time very merrily, until after a week or so, they reached the edge of the Witch Mountains, which rose eerily out of the edge of the marshes.

Castle Death was somewhere on the edge of those mountains, but all the paths on the map had petered out, so there was absolutely no sign of how to get to it.

"Whoever lived in Castle Death long ago didn't want to be found," explained Caliburn.

"How are *we* going to find it then?" asked Bodkin, very reasonably. "This mountain range is huge! We could be searching for this castle for the next twelve months!"

They had to leave the Sweet Track to get to the Witch Mountains.

This led to the SECOND bad thing that happened on the way to Castle Death. And it was far worse than the first, even though in a way it solved their problem of how to find the castle.

Camping on the edge of the marshes, Wish was woken early one morning by a cold presence.

She tried to draw the Enchanted Sword...and for some wayward reason of its own, once again it would not budge, however hard she pulled it.

Crusher reached out his giant hand to protect Wish, the snowcats pounced...*too late.*

"My spoon!" cried Wish in horror. "He's GONE!!!! Something's taken my spoon!"

No SPOON,

"What do you think it was?" asked Bodkin. "Was it a Witch? Was it a ghost? Was it a Grindylow?"

But neither Wish nor Crusher had seen what it was, and there were all sorts of nasty creatures who lived in the Witch Mountains.

"It can't have been anything magical," argued Xar. "Magic things are afraid of iron...maybe it was a bear or something?"

They searched and searched, but they could not find the spoon anywhere.

Poor Wish was inconsolable. "I should never have led my spoon into all this danger!" she wept. "He's going to be so frightened..."

And then, a while later, and a hundred feet or so away from the edge of the campsite, the Enchanted Key gave an excited squeak, and it and the fork and the pins came hopping back to Wish, the key crying in its little creaky voice, "We've picked up his trail!"

Wish's heart leaped, and the little party followed the enchanted things, who hopped purposefully ahead, pausing every now and then to smell some scent that only other enchanted things could detect, that was telling them which way the spoon had gone.

Sad Key

At first, Wish was hopeful that they

might find him quite quickly, but minutes turned into hours, and darkness fell, and they still had not found the spoon, and eventually they had to decide to camp for the night and carry on looking for him the next day.

And a brokenhearted Wish had to go to sleep without her spoon.

They didn't find him the next day either.

Or the next.

"Don't worry, Wish!" said Xar on the fourth day. "We WILL find him, I promise! Don't give up hope…I know what it can be like, losing a great companion…We're constantly losing *you*, aren't we Squeezjoos? But we always find you again in the end!"

But each night they had to camp without finding him, it got harder and harder, and Bodkin lay awake by the campfire, looking up at the stars, realizing bleakly that adventures were wonderful and exciting, but the stakes were high and the peril was real.

Even Xar understood that they had to find the spoon before they could start looking for Castle Death.

And though the snowcats' paws were weary, and Wish cried herself to sleep every night for love of the Enchanted Spoon, they followed the Enchanted Key and Fork deeper and deeper into the Witch Mountains.

When, long ago, the iron Warriors were on the warpath, the Witches retreated farther and farther west, driving the giants out of their homeland of peaceful Gigantica, forcing many of them to wade out to sea along the way of the Giants' Footsteps, never to be seen again. It was the Droods who struck the final blow against the Witches, ambushing them in their stronghold between the woods and the sea, and getting rid of them entirely. That was when the Kingwitch was defeated and put inside the stone...

After that, the country was ruled by a great Wizard called Pentaglion, but something terrible happened to him, no one quite knew what. It was rumored that if anyone dared enter the ruins of Pentaglion's castle, Castle Death, a giant of unsurpassable size would take revenge with his very last breath.

The Witch Mountains were built on a scale that was unimaginably huge. Up there, the clouds formed and re-formed and fogs descended with such suddenness that it was hard to tell what was land and what was sky. Wish

Oh, Spooon!

had a horrible feeling they were being followed, but every time she whirled around there was nothing there. Higher and higher they climbed, and the deer paths teetered over impossible crevasses, and at times turned into rope bridges half smashed out, so that they had to clamber across them on the backs of the snowcats in driving rain.

And then they climbed a peak that looked like it might be any other peak, exhausted, having almost given up hope that they would ever see the spoon again.

And it was there.

Not the spoon.

But *Castle Death.*

The Enchanted Key and the fork jumped in excitement, the fork pointing all its prongs at the castle, and the key squeaking, *"The spoon's in there! The spoon's in there!"*

"We weren't looking for the castle but we found it anyway!" said Wish in delight. "Oh, Xar, this is marvelous! We can get back my spoon AND the Giant's Last Breath all at the same time!"

"Oh dear, oh dear, oh dear," moaned Caliburn. "That's

quite a coincidence. I HATE coincidences...because, are they really coincidences, or did someone or *something*, really intend them all along?"

But Wish was too thrilled thinking that she might find her spoon again, and Xar was too pleased thinking that they were going to get the first ingredient in his spell, to be anxious that this coincidence was a little suspicious.

They pressed forward, even though the castle was not exactly inviting.

Castle Death was half buried in vegetation, a sad corpse of a building, surrounded by a mass of thorns and briars and treacherous fogs, and with such an ominous feeling of decay about it, that hopeful and determined as they were, it was still hard to resist the urge to run away as fast as possible in the opposite direction.

Crusher's eyes filled with tears. "The halls of my ancestors..." he whispered. "Ah...I never thought to see such a place..."

This had been the ground of many a battle.

In front of the castle was an extraordinary clatter of rock formations, covered in vegetation. But these weren't exactly what they at first seemed. As Nighteye slipped on a slimy boulder, Xar looked down, and realized it wasn't a stone at all, but the hilt of an enormous sword, a sword so huge that it could only have been wielded by a giant, wound around and around with layers of brambles and thick with a cushion of a century of moss.

And none of the rocks they were scrambling over were stones after all, but a carpet of these impossibly huge weapons—broken spears, the tip of a smashed, enormous shield, half-buried arrows—that the trees had grown through and up and around.

The sign of Pentaglion was a raven. So there were carved ravens on the shields of the giants, ravens scratched into the cracked stones, ravens decorating the broken ramparts of the castle.

"We shouldn't go in there," groaned Caliburn. "This is a really bad idea. I just know it's a really, really bad idea…It's CURSED! I mean, who thinks this is a good idea? Because *I* don't…"

The werewolf enthusiastically agreed with him, making loud gargling noises and pointing down the mountain to indicate the direction he thought they should be going. DOWN.

"The werewolf wants us to go in anyway!" said Xar. "He says, 'Look at how far we've come…We can't turn back now!'"

Xar was going in even if the castle WAS cursed.

CASTLE DEATH →

This could be his chance not only to get rid of his aching, worrying, burning Witch-stain, but also to get rid of the Witches themselves.

"We HAVE to go in," said Wish excitedly. "For the sake of Xar's spell, and to find the spoon. He's here, somewhere, I know he is! Spoo-oon! Where are you???"

And the Enchanted Key repeated after her, "Spoo-oon? Yoooo-hooo!! Where are you?" And their two voices bounced together and mingled as their echoes came back spookily from the gigantic ruined rooms.

"Shhhhhh!" whispered Bodkin, who had drawn his sword. "We don't know what's in here. And if there IS something, we don't want to wake it up!"

They tiptoed forward. Everything was built on such an enormous scale that it created the extraordinary impression that someone had waved their staff and had turned the spell-raiding party into mice. And yet people their own size had obviously lived here too—giants and humans together.

When sprites are concerned, their hearts glow green, and they give off a sulfurous smell to warn the other sprites not to go farther, and all around, those sprites were burning a hot chartreuse, green as emerald, smoky with fear, queasily circling and buzzing and hissing out protection spells with so many consonants in them that the words whistled and spat like hot fat in a pan. "Bklftttllkprt! Kkllfrkkkfllff! Rkrbptt!!"

For the dead castle seemed to be coming alive again as they entered it and the ears of the sprites could hear the music it was singing and it was a terrible song indeed. "A song without music, a sword in the senses, a storm in the heart, and a fire in the brain..."

The pointed ears of Ariel swiveled to catch the sound. He opened his little forked-teeth mouth and cautiously drank a bit of the air, and his face crinkled in disgust and alarm at the searingly bitter taste of it.

211

"Lissten…" whispered Ariel. "Taste…"

"I can't hear anything," said Bodkin, swallowing hard and holding very tight to his sword.

"Ssstupid humansss…" hissed Tiffinstorm in exasperation, holding equally firmly to her wand, sharp as any thorn. "Your dull earsss can never catch the important sstuff…I don't know how you have ever sssurvived…"

"Let's leave now, Xar!" said Ariel. "We must go no farther! Trusst us, trust us, trussst us!"

"This castle wants revenge," explained Tiffinstorm softly, blinking into visibility beside them. "Every stone is singing of it…every creeper…every broken glass…The hum of revenge is all around us. Can you not taste the bitterness of it? Can you not hear the anger of it?"

Wish peered around. She could hear

nothing, but even *her* dull human senses could feel the
savage melancholy of the atmosphere. And then, was
it her imagination, or were the creepers, the ivy, the
bracken that had with infinite and minute slowness
pushed their green vegetative tentacles up through
the broken flagstones, were they now…*moving*?
At a rate that was visible to the human eye?
Yes…there it was, the ivy was moving like
snakes, rustling like serpents, reaching out either
pleadingly or menacingly toward them…
"Are any of US doing that?" cried Wish
in alarm, already knowing the answer, but
the werewolf and Xar and all of the
sprites had gotten out their staffs and
were performing encircling spells of
protection to stop the encroaching
plants reaching out
toward them.
"Somebody
knows we're here!"
whispered Wish.
"We should go
back!" cried Bodkin.
And even as he
said the words the great
broken door slammed

213

behind them, and the vegetation choked up behind, closing the way, great roots and thorns spearing upward like crossing swords.

Xar swallowed hard. "Of course it's going to be frightening," said Xar stoutly. "We're looking for the ingredients of a spell to get rid of Witches, and Witches are not going to be vanquished by a smell of roses. Revenge is going to be a wonderful ingredient for our spell."

"But we don't know who the castle wants revenge *on*," Caliburn pointed out nervously.

He had a horrible, horrible feeling that he was returning to a forgotten past. It's a dreadful problem for a raven who has lived many lifetimes. He had some dim memory of the familiarity of the place, but he couldn't for the life of him recall any of the important details.

"Well, it stands to reason that this castle will want revenge on the WITCHES, won't it?" said Xar. "The Witches took this territory from the giants, so

of course the giants' castle is going to be angry
with the Witches…"

"But Xar, you don't know that…" groaned Caliburn.
"Stories and histories are often more complicated than
they look."

And then they came across the shoe.

It was lying in front of them, on the steps, on one
side, as if someone had been in a hurry and lost it. At
first they thought it must be some sort of leather tent
or house, before they realized it was in fact a gigantic
BOOT, a shoe so large it dwarfed even Crusher, the top
of the rim of it coming up to the Longstepper High-
Walker's waist. Crusher peered over into the cavelike
depths, an expression of mild worry on his face, which
was a cause for concern in itself because Crusher did not
normally worry about much.

"Impossible," marveled Xar. "This can't be true!
Giants don't grow that big…Something that huge just
could not exist!"

"The ancient giants were supposed to be much
larger than our present giants and ogres," said Caliburn.
"Gog and Magog and their descendants…We are
trespassing in lands we do not understand…with
mysteries and forces much bigger than we know…"

But Xar was now thoroughly overexcited. "There IS
a giant in this castle after all!" he said, drawing both his

father's staff and his sword at once. "So that means we can get the Giant's Last Breath! And that breath will be the breath of REVENGE!"

"But the giant is HUMONGOUS!" exclaimed Bodkin. "If he's alive, we'd have to kill him if we want his last breath, and we couldn't possibly do that because I like giants and so does Wish and so do you! And if he's dead we can't get his last breath anyway!"

Xar wasn't listening.

"We'll just sneak up on him and check the whole situation out," said Xar.

"But whatever-he-is already knows we're *here*!" wailed Bodkin.

Now Wish knew what it must feel like to be the size of a sprite, for that is how small they were in comparison with this boot.

With shaking steps they inched forward, and the Enchanted Pins, Key, and Fork led them to an enormous door, hidden in cobwebs and darkness. Behind the door was a staircase that led down, down, down underground. Crusher had to lift them all down the steps, and when they got to the bottom of this staircase they came to a hall that was way, way bigger than the last. It was impossible that a room could be that huge. A table so high that each one of its legs was as tall as one of those tree trunks from the High Forests outside. A chair so enormous its existence was beyond imagining. And underneath the table was a boot to match the boot outside, and a gigantic foot, with huge toes that were turning a rather unnatural green color. And above the foot, way, way above, stretched the leg, and out of their sight, must be the body of the giant.

A giant larger than anyone had ever seen before, or dreamed of.

10. The Giant's Last Breath

I t took every single ounce of nerve in their bodies to make them move forward. Bodkin could feel his heart beating so fast it felt like it might leap out of his chest and make a run for it. *He* wanted to do that anyway...

But then he thought of poor Xar, shivering in the night as the Witch-stain crept up his arm. Xar would have to stay forever locked up in Gormincrag if they could not find the ingredients for this spell. The Witches were not going to go away if they closed their eyes and hoped for it...So Bodkin walked on.

Each one of the toes of the giant came up to Wish's waist. The toes were absolutely still, unmoving. They appeared to be green, now they got closer, not because of gangrene, but because they had been there so long that moss was growing over them, so they must not have moved for a very long time.

"Is he alive, this giant?" whispered Wish. "Or is he dead?"

"Find out, sprites!" ordered Xar fiercely.

Bravely, Tiffinstorm and Ariel and the Once-sprite flew up to the head of the giant.

Tiffinstorm flew back down first. "Dead," said Tiffinstorm.

"But he can't have been dead for very long," argued

Wish. "Because after a while, don't dead bodies...sort of
decay?"

"Yucky!" said Squeezjoos, inspecting the giant
for signs of decay with delight. "They's do! Letsss me
look...letsss me look!" The hairy fairy buzzed around
excitedly, but returned extremely disappointed. "He'ss
just the sssame asss when he wasss alive...No yucky bits...no
squidgy bits...The green is just moss..."

"It's some kind of enchantment," said Caliburn,
shivering. "An enchantment so strong I'm not sure I
want to know what it is..."

"Which may mean," said Xar triumphantly, "that we
CAN get his last breath! The spell to get rid of a Witch-
stain must be true! And this giant here must have been
waiting for us to come so that he can die..."

"You're making a whole load of assumptions there,"
said Bodkin, terrified. "Maybe he's waiting so that he can
eat us."

"We keep telling you! Giants are vegetarian!" said Xar.

"Yes but, Xar, we don't know much about the really,
really big ones..." said Bodkin. "Most of them waded
out to sea hundreds and hundreds of years ago."

But Xar wasn't listening. "Follow me!" he ordered.

The snowcats and the werewolf climbed each table
leg as if they were tree trunks, claws gripping either
side, with Wish and Xar and Bodkin on their backs.

Xar had never been on a giant's table before. The
plates were larger than any he had ever seen, more
like enormous silver lakes. The three young heroes
steered their way around the massive cups and knives.

  The Enchanted Fork perched on the rim
of one of the spoons, gazing down
with admiration at its unfeasibly
enormous cousin, a monster in
spoon form.

The fork shook its head, as if to say, "Will I ever grow that big? Could I?"

Squeezjoos and Bumbleboozle and the baby, always easily distracted, had a great time slipping down the center of the giant's spoon as if it were some sort of gargantuan slide, until Xar snapped his fingers to get them to concentrate.

"We're on a mission here," whispered Xar. "There's no time to mess about! Once-sprite, you're the Chief Spell-Raider. How do we get the last breath out of the giant, if there's still one in there?"

Up above them was the giant's head, tipped to one side. He certainly LOOKED dead. His eyes were closed. His great wrinkled map of a face was covered in bracken and ivy, and if they had not known that it was a giant and seen that foot down below, they might have thought it was a rock face, or some other broken landscape, covered in a rich tangled mess of briars and thorns as if it wore a mask.

A sad face.

A broken face.

A lost face.

The Once-sprite flew the falcon upward, and leaped from the bird's back. He swung for a second from one of the giant's nose hairs, peering up into the dark depths above as if it were some sort of enormous snot-filled cave.

He poked his spear into one edge of giant nostril.

The giant did not move.

"He's dead," announced the Once-sprite, dropping back onto the falcon.

"Yes, I know he's probably *dead*!" said Xar impatiently. "The point is, how do we get a last breath out of him?"

And then, as if in response to Xar's question, and making them all jump, there was a reverberating sound like the noise of a muffled distant drum, and a slight wheezing wind poured faintly out of the nostrils above like the breeze in coral caves.

Oh, by green things and white things and mistletoe and ivy...

The giant wasn't dead after all!

"The beassst isss alive..." whispered Ariel, burning so bright green with alarm that he shone like a torch.

The giant twitched.

"Ohhhhhhhhhhh my! Ohhhhhhhh my! He's moving!" said Squeezjoos.

Slowly, slowly the great eye above cracked open the mess of thorns above it, and one enormous eye focused grimly on the children—an eye you could lose yourself in, a mighty desolation like the desert of the ocean. And then the great mountain above them jerked upward with such startling suddenness that the plates bowled over, and the young heroes lost their balance on the table, set a-shaking by his sudden coming-to-life. They all forgot that giants are not ogres and that they're supposed to be vegetarian, even the really, really big ones, and they scattered like scurrying ants across the table, for safety under the plate rims and to hide under the forks.

Their hearts beating like rabbits', they cowered, Bodkin under a plate rim, Xar flattened behind a salt cellar, Wish under the spoon.

"Don't move…" whispered Xar.

Was the giant friendly? Or was he *unfriendly*? Did he know they were there? Had he seen them?

They could hear the giant breathing now, the wheeze in and out of his lungs like some great wind, and suddenly it seemed that their quest might have been a little, well, *foolish*.

Bodkin held his breath.

Maybe the giant *didn't* know they were there…

Minutes passed.

There was silence again.

Bodkin began to breathe a little easier.

And then a very beautiful voice, one that definitely could not have belonged to a giant, said sweetly and out of nowhere: "There's one hiding under the plate…"

And…

BLAM! The sheltering plate above Bodkin went spinning from above his head and sailing across the room, where it smashed with ear-shattering violence.

That was a little too, well, ROUGH for the giant to be entirely friendly, and when Bodkin looked up at the face looming above him like a great green god, the glowering fury of his expression was unmistakable.

It's all very well, people telling you not to *move* when you're being charged by a forest animal, or if a great desolation of a giant is poised over you, but in those sorts of situations instinct tends to kick in, and Bodkin ran across the table with some considerable speed.

SLAM!!!! A fleeing Bodkin was caught by a mighty force from above that sent him sprawling—OOF!—onto his stomach, and when he scrambled, petrified, back to his feet, an immense hand imprisoned him like a great green cave.

Peering out from behind the spoon, Wish shouted, "Bodkin's been trapped!" Forgetting all about how much she liked giants, she ran forward and jabbed one of the massive fingers with her sword, and it couldn't have been much more than a pinprick, but the fingers startled upward, and then all three humans were scurrying and running, and weaving and dodging across the table with the giant and frankly not-very-friendly hand slamming down around them, trying to catch them.

Which it did, eventually...

Xar and Bodkin hid in the salt cellar, but the giant shook them out and pinned them to the table between the prongs of a fork.

And then the giant took a cup and slammed it over Wish. For one horrible moment she thought she would be trapped there forever, but the giant flipped the cup over, picked her up, and dropped her in it. And there she hung, peering with one terrified eye over the rim, into the grim eyes of the enormous and, let's face it, extremely annoyed giant.

An unintelligible noise came out of the giant's mouth. It was opening and shutting as if it were making words, but the wheeze of his voice meant it was impossible to hear what he was saying. He paused.

The three children looked at one another, terrified. None of them could make head nor tail of what he was talking about.

The giant spoke again, equally unintelligibly, soft anger in the wheezing.

Caliburn bravely flew up to the giant's mouth, so that he could hear more clearly.

The giant seemed to be choking,

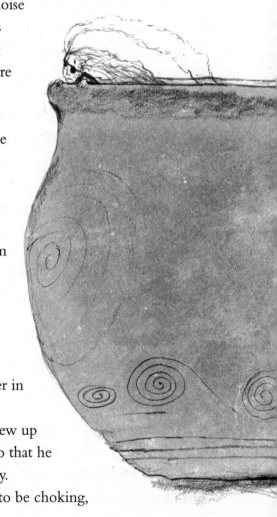

fighting for breath, until from out of nowhere an ethereal little *something* appeared in a trail of light, something so bright it made you blink to look at it, and the something poured a little potion into the choking giant's mouth, and the dusty desolation drank it down greedily.

"What is *that*?" asked Wish, with an open mouth, trying to look at the brilliant little something as it dashed past. It didn't look quite like any other sprite, or elf, she had ever seen before.

"I am a Frost-sprite who once belonged to the great Wizard Pentaglion," said the little *something*, moving so quickly they still couldn't see what it was, "but you can call me Eleanor Rose...That is not my name, but it's a very pretty one, don't you think?"

Eleanor Rose, for that was *not* her name, had a very beautiful voice that reminded you of running water, or bells. It must have been she who had told the giant where they were. "And this big decaying chap here is Proponderus," said Eleanor Rose, as if they'd all dropped in for a cozy chat, rather than broken into a ruined castle whose name was Death. "So, since we're all here, perhaps you might introduce *your*selves? Proponderus and I have not had company for many a long year. And even when we do, uninvited guests tend not to stay very long...particularly if they are burglars..."

There was something a little sinister in the last

Eleanor Rose

228

statement, even though she said it perfectly good-
naturedly, even somewhat sadly. They didn't need
Caliburn to whisper, "Don't trust her..."

Eleanor Rose didn't appear offended. She even
agreed and might have been nodding her head if she had
been still enough for them to see her. "Yes, it's probably
wiser for human beings not to trust me...Frost-sprites
have no hearts, you see..."

The giant spoke in a wheezy whisper, which was
nonetheless very loud to human ears, for he was so very
large a giant.

"Who," said the giant, "are YOU, little ants,
little nothingnesses, and how dare you
disturb the peace of a giant of the ancient
lines who is on the verge of dying? Is
nothing sacred?"

"Oh, you're on the verge of dying are you?" said
Xar, without thinking, and heartily pleased to hear it.
"Excellent!"

The giant blinked down at them.

Bodkin prodded Xar frantically.

Xar started, suddenly realizing that it wasn't very
polite to be seeming to welcome the imminent death of
your host.

"I mean, we're *very* sad to hear that," said Xar
hurriedly.

Eleanor Rose laughed again. "Oh, don't worry!" she said kindly. "*You're* on the verge of dying too!"

"A-are we?" stammered Bodkin anxiously.

"Of course you are!" said Eleanor Rose with great humor. "What did you expect? You are entering, uninvited, a castle whose name is Death, with the burglarious intention to steal something infinitely precious from one of the inhabitants within who also happens to be your unwilling host...Don't bother to deny it!"

For Xar had opened up his mouth in instinctive denial.

"Unless..." said Eleanor Rose.

"Unless?" prompted Wish, ever-hopeful.

"Unless...you are the people we have been waiting for, which is terribly unlikely, considering the amount of people there are in the wildwoods, and how surprising it would be if they were to accidentally make their way here," said Eleanor Rose. "Which is the reason we have been waiting such a very, very long time. So, who are you?"

Oh dear, oh dear, oh dear.

They had to hope the Spelling Book had not tricked them. They had to hope that their names would be good enough.

"Tell the truth," Eleanor Rose advised them.

"I am Xar, son of Encanzo, boy of destiny," said Xar. "And this is Wish, daughter of Sychorax...and this is Bodkin, Assistant Bodyguard."

There was a long, long silence, and Eleanor Rose was still enough for Squeezjoos to see her clearly for one, tantalizing second, and for Squeezjoos to say with a sigh, "Oh! How pretty you are!"

"Beauty is not everything," said Eleanor Rose, on the move again, "but the universe has found that, sometimes, it helps. And impossibility isn't everything either, but it is surprising, particularly considering the nature of impossibility, how often the universe is depending on *one...*

unlikely...

chance..."

Bodkin and Xar and Wish had been holding their breaths, but now they let them out again with relief.

"Of all the numberless names of people in these wildwoods, you ARE the right ones," said Eleanor Rose.

"Thank goodness for that," breathed Bodkin.

"At last!" said the giant. "Are they worthy?"

Eleanor Rose hovered in front of all of them, and touched them one by one—Xar, Bodkin, Wish, and finally Caliburn—testing them for worthiness. Each of them cried out at the moment of contact, as if they had been hit by a sharp electric shock.

Eleanor Rose circled the room twice before she gave her pronouncement.

"There is room for improvement," said Eleanor Rose. "Particularly in the one who calls himself the boy of destiny...but what can you expect from the humans? However, when it comes to the worthiness of the bird, why the bird..."

Caliburn ruffled his feathers, preparing to make modest protestations. This was his moment.

"The talking bird is the *least* worthy of all," said Eleanor Rose.

"Oh!" cried Caliburn, very offended. "I think you must have mistook me! I am Caliburn, the raven-who-has-lived-many-lifetimes, and I have been put in charge of Xar, precisely *because* of my wisdom and my worthiness!"

"Yes," said Eleanor Rose, with an audible, dismissive sniff that still managed to sound affectionate, "and perhaps you might like to think, *why*, after all those lifetimes, you have ended up as a bird? I know perfectly well who you are, raven, and age is no proof of worthiness, or indeed of wisdom. We'll just have to make do, Proponderus, and hope for the best, as is often the case with the humans. We can't wait any longer. I am finding it harder and harder to slow down the dying process, and those are, after all, the right names."

The giant snorted with relief.

"So," said Eleanor Rose, "you have come here to steal something? Don't bother lying, just tell me what it is."

"We have come to take the Giant's Last Breath," said Xar defiantly. "We need it as part of our spell to get rid of the Witches."

"Ahhhh..." breathed the giant with desperate satisfaction in a great wind above them. "They *are* the right ones."

"That is precious, very precious," said Eleanor Rose solemnly. "It is not something the likes of you could *steal* from a giant of the ancient lines, but luckily for you he will give it to you willingly. I presume you have come prepared?"

"We have," said Xar promptly. "The Once-sprite here is a great spell-raider. He will catch the breath, and Tiffinstorm will shrink it, and between them they will put the breath in this collecting bottle here..."

Eleanor Rose laughed again. "Oh, you humans! You're so funny! Your plans are so inadequate and yet you keep making them! You hadn't a hope of doing that on your own, but I will help you.

"You shall have your wish," said Eleanor Rose, "and maybe, as is the way of things...a little *more* than you wished for, as well. Settle down, everyone, make yourselves comfortable."

Eleanor Rose did not bring out a wand or a staff or make any sort of movement that could be interpreted as spelling, but the fork lifted itself off Xar and Bodkin, and the cup tipped over gently, depositing Wish on the table.

"The giant is going to tell you a story, and I am going to help…"

Way above them, the not-quite-dead giant's words came booming out with such loudness, they had to put their hands over their ears.

"LET ME TELL YOU A STORY!" said the giant.

"A story???" said Xar, between clenched teeth, for the words really were very, very loud.

"You don't like stories?" said Eleanor Rose in surprise.

"I love stories!" said Xar. "But what is the giant doing, telling us a story? This is supposed to be his last breath! Surely you can't tell a whole story with one last breath? And we're in a bit of a hurry here…It's complicated, but the Droods and the Wizards and the Warriors and the Witchsmeller and the Witches themselves are all chasing after us, and they could be here any moment…And my companion, Wish here, has lost her Enchanted Spoon, and we have to find him…"

"Have you seen him?" said Wish anxiously. "My fork and key are convinced he's in here somewhere. He's about so high, made of iron, and—"

234

"What did I say?" interrupted Eleanor Rose. "Plenty of room for improvement. You need to learn patience, boy and girl. There is *always* time for a story. The giant will give you his last breath and in return you will listen to his story, patiently, quietly, and humbly, for those are all things you need to learn. That is your payment, if you will."

So in the heart of Castle Death, Wish and Caliburn and Xar and Bodkin and the snowcats and the sprites and Crusher the giant sat down cross-legged or put their shaggy heads on their paws or folded their wings or lay on their backs with their eight legs in the air depending on what or who they were. All of them listened quietly, obediently, and even *Xar* tried to be as patient and respectful as he could as they listened to the story.

Now, the last words of *anyone* who is dying have a magical power.

But the last words of a giant of such extraordinary immenseness…why, those have more power than most.

In real life this story was being told by a great giant the size of a small hillside, in the last stages of dying, crumbling at the edges and a trifle fly-infested, in a voice that was sometimes louder than the loudest thunder and at other times breaking and wheezing and

barely there, and when his voice broke at the edges,
like the crumbling of his fingers, and became so faint
that you could hardly hear it, the story was taken up by
the Frost-sprite, who was the absolute opposite, tiny and
ever-moving, with a voice like the never-heard music
of the universe and turning stars and the tiny bell-like
chime of time...

But if I tell it like *that* it will make it hard to concentrate
on the story, and the story is important. So I will speak it in
my own voice, the voice of the unknown narrator.

This was the story the giant told.

It was "The Story of the Giant's Last Breath."

*The story was
dying to be told...*

The Story of
the Giant's
Last Breath

Once upon a time, there was a ferocious young Warrior princess, as wild as any werewolf. She was afraid of nothing, this Warrior princess, and her hunting skills were the talk of the Empire. All alone, she fought the Frost Giants of the frozen north, all alone she captured the dreadful Grim Annis of the west, all alone she scared off the Rogrebreaths that were raiding the Warrior villages in the south.

The Warrior princess did not believe in love.

"Love is weakness," said the princess.

"I'm really, really hoping this isn't going to be a LOVE story!" said Xar in disgust, before remembering he was supposed to be quiet and respectful and hurriedly shutting his mouth again.

One day, the princess was riding alone and free through the wildwoods, in the depths of midwinter, when she realized that she was being chased by a couple of snowcats. She shot arrows at the snowcats, and two of them hit their targets, but still the snowcats pursued her. Eventually she realized they wanted her to follow them, and she was so impressed by their bravery, that this she did.

I'm really hoping this isn't a LOVE story...

238

The snowcats led her to a clearing where there was a circle
of gigantic wolves waiting patiently at the bottom of a tree.
There was a young man up in the tree, and the wolves were
waiting for him to grow so tired he would fall out, like a large
ripe apple. Two days he had been up there, and he was dropping
with hunger and thirst and fear.

At the bottom of the tree lay the young man's Wizard
staffs, for he had climbed the tree to rescue one of his
sprites.

The young man (whose name was Algorquprqin, but
that sounds like someone choking on a walnut, so everyone
called him Tor) was singing a very stupid song in the princess's
opinion, which went something like this:

"I am young, I am poor, I can offer you nothing,
All that I have is this bright pair of wings,
This air that I eat, these winds that I sleep on,
This star path I dance in, where the moon sings..."

Now, the princess knew that she should have ridden on at
that point. This young man was clearly a Wizard, and Wizards
were the Warriors' deadly enemies.

And he was also clearly a very silly young man.

But there was something so human about the silliness of
this song that it made her pause.

The princess loaded her bow and shot an arrow

toward the Wizard, not to hit him, exactly, but just to see if he would flinch.

He didn't…even though it passed so bitingly close that it grazed his left arm. The princess was impressed, for she admired bravery, even in Wizards.

The wolves got to their feet and snarled warningly at her, padding restlessly around the tree. The princess loaded her bow again, pointed it at the wolves, and called out sneeringly: "What are you doing, talking to trees, you stupid Wizard?"

"I'm not talking to trees," said the Wizard. "I'm talking to YOU."

He carried on with the song:
"See the swifts soar, they live well on nothing,
You are young, you are strong, if you'll give me your hand,
We'll leave earth entirely and never go back there,
We'll sleep on the breezes and never touch land…

"I promise you gales and a merry adventure,
We'll fly on forever and never will part…
I am young, I am poor, I can offer you nothing,
Nothing but love and the beat of my heart."

And then he just said, "Help me…"

"What will you give me if I rescue you, Wizard?" called the princess.

There was silence from the treetops, and then the Wizard replied, *"What do you want most in the world?"*

The princess replied, swift as one of her own arrows: *"I want to be the Warrior queen of this whole forest."*

The princess, you see, was always MEANT to be the queen of the whole forest, but her throne had been stolen when she was a baby by one of her evil cousins, so she was wishing for something she had wanted her very whole life.

The Wizard called Tor looked down at her.

"All right, I can't make you a Warrior queen," admitted Tor, "but I CAN give you a horse. A queen needs a good horse."

"I already HAVE a horse, stupid!" said the princess, laughing. *"I'm riding it!"*

"Back at home in my Wizard camp, I have a horse far better than that horse you are riding, a horse as black as night and as swift as spell-raiders…I will give it to you if you rescue me," said Tor. *"It isn't Magic,"* he added hastily. *"It's just an ordinary horse. You'll like it…"*

So the princess, who was really just looking for an excuse to save this silly young man, shot her arrows at the wolves, and the wolves began to chase her.

They hunted her through the forest, the princess shooting back at them over her shoulder. And Tor climbed down from the tree, picked up his Wizard staffs, and followed after her on his injured snowcat. He caught up with her at just the moment when the wolf pack took down her horse.

The princess drew her sword and he used his spelling staffs, and together they fought the wolves, but there were so very many of them that they had to climb aboard the snowcat to run away, and leave the wolves with the horse.

"You've made me lose my horse!" protested the princess as they rode together through the forest on the back of the snowcat.

"It was the horse, or us . . ." said Tor, "that's why I offered you one of my own horses if you rescued me."

And that was the moment that the princess realized that Wizards were tricky.

The princess didn't mind that.

LOVE...

Y-Y-UCKY

She was tricky herself.

The Wizard, now that she could see his face up close in the moonlight, was a very silly, tricky young man, but undeniably a little bit handsome ... and he hadn't flinched when she shot him ...

And that was how the princess lost her heart in the forest.

"It IS about love!" said Xar in disgust.

"Shhh!" hissed everyone else, because they wanted to hear the end of the story.

The Warrior princess agreed to meet the Wizard in the same clearing a week later so he could bring her the horse.

"This will be the last time I meet him," said the princess to herself.

Tor gave her a horse called Thunderbird, which certainly wasn't swifter than spell-raiders or darker than midnight. It was a perfectly normal horse ... except in one respect.

Every second Thursday, if she happened to be riding it, it would carry her off, and however hard she pulled on the reins it would take her through the forest, back to the clearing where she first met Tor.

"It IS = about love!" said Xar in disgust.

243

Tor would be waiting for her, and they would spend the afternoon being silly together.

The young Warrior princess swore that she would marry Tor. She promised on her heart that they would run away together and find themselves a world where it did not matter where they came from, where Wizards and Warriors could love and live in peace.

And then...And then...And then...

TRAGEDY.

The princess's wicked cousin died, and that meant that SHE was now queen of the Warriors.

She had all that she had ever been wanting, for her very whole life...

And now that she had it, she found that she did not want it after all.

Oh, you must be careful what you wish for, guys...

IT MAY COME TRUE.

For here is the thing about becoming a queen. It brought with it responsibilities, duties. The new queen's people needed her, for if she were NOT the queen, it would be one or other of the wicked cousins, with their taxes, and their wars-of-vengeance, and their endless thirst for such delicacies as blood-of-werecats as an aperitif, which may have been delicious, but was costly in human lives.

So the young princess felt she HAD to be the queen, and a queen of Warriors cannot marry a Wizard.

But how should she get rid of her love?

A true love's kiss is the strongest thing in the world. It cannot be gotten rid of by sneezing.

So the young princess did a terrible thing.

She had heard of an extremely powerful Wizard called Pentaglion, who was living all alone, and was doing experiments into looking into the future…dabbling in that dangerous practice. She traveled to see him. They looked into the future together, and what they saw there was that if she were to marry the young boy called Tor, the Witches would return to the forest…

SO THE PRINCESS HAD TO GET RID OF HER LOVE FOREVER.

And there was only one way.

PENTAGLION GAVE HER THE SPELL OF LOVE DENIED, WHICH IS A VERY, VERY DANGEROUS SPELL INDEED.

The sprites all gasped at the sound of the Spell of Love Denied. Squeezjoos curled himself up so tightly in Wish's hair that she let out a small squeal. Only Squeezjoos's eyes were peeping out, wide with alarm.

The Warrior princess drank the spell and the love died in her heart.

She wrote a letter to the Wizard boy called Tor,

written in poison ink and bitterage, saying she did not love him, and never had.

Meanwhile, Tor waited many long weeks in the appointed waiting place and the Warrior princess never came. He got the letter. He read it, refused to believe it. Two years he waited. A hut grew around him, and the sprites in the forest felt so sorry for him, they brought him food and water. They called him "the Wizard-who-waits."

Tor knew in his heart of hearts that the princess had betrayed him, and eventually he came to believe the letter. He got word that the Warrior princess had married someone else and was now calling herself the queen of the Warriors. The Wizard went so mad with unhappiness, he went to fight in the hinterlands and became a Shadow Man ...

"Oh, how cool ..." breathed Xar, for the Shadow Men were legendary.

"And now we reach MY part of the story ..." said the giant. "You see, the castle you are standing in was once the castle of Pentaglion ..."

Xar and Wish and Bodkin held their breaths. They had gotten so caught up in the story they had forgotten that it might be true. They looked at the smashed remains of the castle all around them.

What had happened here?

The Spell of
LOVE DENIED

A tERRIBLE Spell indeed,
with TERRIBLE consequences

"*And the giant you are listening to is Pentaglion's giant, and this is where I come into the story.*" The giant's voice was drenched in bitterness at this point. "*Unfortunately one of the essential ingredients of the Spell of Love Denied was the tears of a Drood, and Droods don't like having their tears taken. The Droods set about tracking the man who had taken their tears, and when they found him, they killed not only the extremely powerful Wizard Pentaglion, but they tried to kill his giant and took his little baby werewolf into captivity...*

"*And that giant,*" finished the giant, "*was ME. So many years, I have been angry, so angry at the injustice of it, that I have not been able to die.*

"*I have BURNED with anger!*" roared the giant. "*The boiling impossible heat of my fury has kept me here...*

"*SO ANGRY!*" thundered the giant, and the sound of the giant's anger, even though he was dying, rumbled out of his great giant chest like a thousand bears a-roaring, echoing its way around the room, sending the table shaking.

"*I am not afraid to die, but I have had unfinished business...*" said the giant. "*And with my last breath I urge you...*"

Oh..h..h...
REVENGE!

The Giant
Wants revenge!

There was a great pause.
For the last breath of giants is a terrible thing.

"Revenge!" whispered Xar, highly excited. "He wants REVENGE! Don't worry, giant, I'm pretty angry with those Droods myself...You can pass that quest right on to me. Xar's your man!"

Xar was delighted because the last breath of a giant was one thing. But the dying VENGEANCE wish of a giant...that was a very powerful ingredient indeed. THAT would be extremely helpful if you wanted to get rid of the Witches.

"Get ready, everyone!" shouted Xar. "The giant's about to go!"

"Oh, poor giant!" said Wish. "Have a little respect, Xar! These are his dying moments!"

"He's been dying for YEARS!" said Xar. "We're doing him a favor! You're ANGRY aren't you, giant? So angry you haven't been able to die...Give us your fury! We need all of it!"

"With my last breath I urge you..." said the giant. He *clutched his throat...He was about to go, fighting for breath.*

"I urge you...

"I urge you...

"FORGIVE THEM."

11. The Story Takes a Surprising Turn, as Is the Way of Stories

"Whaaaaaat?????" said Xar, so absolutely flabbergasted, he momentarily forgot the quest.

"*GET THE BREATH!!!!!!!!*"

yelled Bodkin.

It was a beautifully synchronized operation.

You'd have thought they'd done it a thousand times before.

The giant fell backward, with a CRASSSHHHHHHHHHHHH that shook the hall to its remaining foundations, and the last breath was up and out of his mouth in a great cloud. Tiffinstorm zapped an appearance spell to make it visible, and there it was, in a great shaggy cloud, for one tantalizing moment before—*reoow!* Hinkypunk's shrinking spell failed to shrink it more than an inch or so—but that was where Eleanor Rose came in. She flew right over it, holding her little arms apart, and the breath shrunk to pea-size and, with a glorious flurry of wings, the peregrine falcon swooped, and the Once-sprite caught the now-tiny little ball

Whaaaat?.??

of breath in his collecting bottle, putting in the
stopper as the falcon dived down and then up,
up again, out of the way of the rising dust.

And then he dropped the little bottle into
the waiting hands of Squeezjoos, the official
sprite assistant to the spell-raiding team.

Wish ran over to the prone body of the
giant. Eleanor Rose held up both her arms
again, and in front of their eyes the great
body of the giant simply melted away, into
the ground beneath them.

"Where has he gone?" whispered Wish
with round eyes.

"Where he should have gone a long, long
time ago," said Eleanor Rose. "Do not be sad;
he is free at last, the poor giant."

"Oh, but we *are* sad!" said Wish, and all of them

were, for the giant had been so noble and had been treated so badly.

"As am I," Eleanor Rose said briskly. "Not sad, of course, but free. And what a last breath it was…after all these years of anger, he forgives them!" she said in amazement. "How wonderful!"

"Mission accomplished!" the Once-sprite said proudly as the peregrine falcon came to rest on Xar's shoulder.

Squeezjoos held up the bottle. There, right in the middle, was a small, odd-looking round thing, curled up in on itself like a flower.

The sprites let out a great hissing cheer, and the wolves and the snowcats howled their appreciation. *"We issss spell-raiderssssssss!"*

The wolves capered up and down; the snowcats chased each other around the dinner plates; Lonesome sat down and howled.

The only one who wasn't dancing gloatingly around the giant dinner table in glee was Xar.

Which was unlike Xar, who was normally Gloater-in-Chief.

It was as if having to sit quietly for five minutes without fidgeting had been such an effort that he had to burst out now with his real feelings.

"It should be a *Revenge* Breath!" said Xar angrily.

"What use is a *Forgiveness* Breath, even a *giant* one, if you're fighting Witches, the greatest peril the world has ever known?"

It was only Xar who had failed to understand the true meaning of the story.

For most of the others in the room, the story had thrown all the pieces of what they knew up in the air, and when they came down again, everything had changed.

Stories can change lives...

And this was one of those stories.

Secrets had been told that had been kept buried and hidden away in human hearts for a very, very long time.

"Don't you understand, Xar?" said Wish. "The princess in the story was my mother! And the young Wizard was your father Encanzo..."

"What?????" Xar's jaw fell open. "Nonsense! The young Wizard was called Tor!"

"Maybe that was your father's name before he became an Enchanter," suggested Caliburn, which was possible—Wizards did tend to take a new name when they rose to that status.

"But it's impossible," said Xar. "My father would never be so sappy as to fall in love with the human iceberg that is Queen Sychorax..."

"Is this why I am Magic, Eleanor Rose?" said Wish through white lips.

"Yes. A Warrior queen could have a daughter who was Magic, if she once loved a Wizard," said Eleanor Rose. "The kiss of a Wizard, if it was a true love's kiss…that could stay in the blood. The Magic could still be in there, even after the love had died."

So there was the truth of it.

Once, long ago, Sychorax and Encanzo had been in love.

And Sychorax had taken the terrible Spell of Love Denied…

And the love had died.

She had married a Warrior, like she was supposed to…

But somewhere, somewhere behind Sychorax's iron breastplate…the lingering true love's kiss of a Wizard had made her daughter Magic, even though she was the daughter of two Warriors.

"Oh dear, oh dear, oh dear," moaned Caliburn. "*They broke the rules!* And rules are there for a reason! Wizards and Warriors aren't supposed to fall in love…And now we see why! A child has been born—Wish—who has Magic-mixed-with-iron…and that has changed the course of history. For Magic-mixed-with-iron is what the Witches have been waiting for, for so many, many years…"

Xar was still finding this hard to absorb. "My father is always lecturing ME about not breaking rules, and you're telling me HE broke the biggest rule ever?"

"Maybe this is what our quest has been all about!" said Wish excitedly. "My father died years ago in a battle against the Grimogres. What about your mother, Xar?"

"She died when I was a baby," said Xar.**

"So *your* father and *my* mother are free to fall in love all over again!" said Wish excitedly. "We can help them by undoing the Spell of Love Denied!"

Both Xar and Bodkin looked at her as if she were crazy.

"If my father made the mistake of falling in love with that dreadful polar ice cap that is your mother *once*, he's never going to do it TWICE," said Xar in disgust.

"And oh dear, oh dear, oh dear," said Caliburn, in great agitation. "Undoing the Spell of Love Denied would be IMPOSSIBLE! What was Pentaglion thinking to cast such a spell?"

Eleanor Rose sniffed disapprovingly. "Yes, sometimes it is the ones who think they are wisest who are in fact the most foolish. You're never too old to learn ... Now, good-bye, little humans and other funny creatures," she said.

"Oh, don't go!" cried Wish. "We really, really need

**The narrator would like to gently point out that life was a whole load more uncertain in the Iron Age, which is why there are so many stepparents in fairy stories.

Oh dear ... I hope this wasn't my fault ...

your help! And you never told me where the spoon was! Do you know?"

"I do know where he is," agreed Eleanor Rose.

"OH!" cried Wish in delight. "Please tell me where he is!"

"I can release him for you, but after that you should leave here *as quick as you can*," warned Eleanor Rose. "Us Frost-sprites are not really supposed to interfere with the affairs of the humans, you see, which is one of the reasons I can't kill THAT," she said, gesturing upward. "For that really would be interfering. And besides, I made THAT a promise..."

"What is THAT?" said Bodkin, looking up at the ceiling, where he thought he could see something, he wasn't sure what, but *something* lurking up there. They hadn't noticed before, but whatever it was was dripping, one small drop every minute or so, like a stalactite in a cave. *Drip..! Drip..! Drip..!*

Bodkin moved forward, peering upward, trying to see what it was...

And just as Bodkin was staring upward…

Something rather LARGER than a drop of water melted from the dark thing it was attached to and landed on the floor with a bright clear ringing noise like a bell.

CLING!!! *Cling! Cling! Cling! Cling!*

Something that bounced around brightly on the floor before lying quite still.

Something about the size of…

an Enchanted Spoon.

Wish rushed forward, with a cry of joy. "My spoon! *My spoon!*" and she caught the spoon up in her arms.

"He's *fine!*" she exclaimed, in jubilant relief. The spoon was cold as ice, but she could feel him warming and beginning to move, and the fork and the key and the pins curled around him gleefully, the key making purring noises, and even the sprites

Oh
bother.
I
hoped
we'd
lost
him
forever,
thought
the
fork.

and the hairy fairies were pleased for Wish at this
reunion. Xar and Bodkin patted her on the back,
and the snowcats and wolves capered around in
happy circles.

Wish turned to thank Eleanor Rose.

But Eleanor Rose had already left.

Off she flew, up and away, rocketing like a tiny
shooting star, pausing a moment at the rim of the
battlements, and then sending down some sprite-
writing as an afterthought, before continuing on
in the direction of the north.

The sprite-writing hovered in
front of them, for a few beautiful
flickering moments before
disappearing too, like
smoke into the sea.

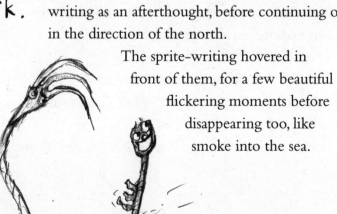

"Remember…" said the sprite-writing.

"The universe often depends on

one…

unlikely…

chance."

"Oh, I LIKED her!" said Wish, sighing and hugging the spoon very tight. "She cared far more than she thought she did! And I felt somehow better when she was here to protect us…"

For as the spoon grew warm and wriggly in her arms, she could tell by his body language that he wasn't as joyful about this reunion as he ought to have been. He seemed agitated. He was jumping, sluggishly but anxiously, on her hand. He seemed to be trying to point to something…something up above their heads…

"What is the spoon trying to say?" asked Xar as they looked around themselves, and realized that they were suddenly very alone in the castle, with the giant and Eleanor Rose gone. Some haunting spell had left it, and it felt…peaceful, and no longer sad, but also no longer alive.

But nonetheless…the silence was a little…

Ominous.

"Why do you think Eleanor Rose said we should get out of here as fast as we can?" asked Tiffinstorm uneasily.

Bodkin was slowly backing away as he looked upward,

Remember...

The universe often

depends on

one ...

unlikely ...

chance ...

at where the Frost-sprite had pointed a few minutes earlier, at the exact spot the spoon had dropped from.

There was *something else* hanging from the ceiling, like a gigantic vampire bat. A still thing, folded in on itself, quiet and malevolent and patiently waiting. It had witnessed the story. It had hung there for weeks. It had been there all along, and they had not noticed it.

A plotter.

A planner.

A thing with wings.

"What issss that?" hissed Tiffinstorm, drawing her wand, as sharp as any thorn.

Wish and Xar and the sprites and the snowcats and the wolves turned their own heads upward to follow Tiffinstorm's pointing finger. The werewolf stiffened, sniffed the air as he smelled something wicked, and raised his shaggy head reluctantly.

"Hissssssssss..." hissed the sprites, bright as fire. How could they not have smelled that smell before? That stink, that reek, that corpselike stench...

Because whatever–it–was had been frozen until that very moment.

Bodkin had been staring up at the thing for a while now, and he was so scared he could barely get the words out.

"*That*," said Bodkin, "is the Kingwitch. We need to get out of here NOW."

We need to get
out of here
NOW.

12. A Bad Moment for Your Escape to Get Held Up

As they all looked upward in horror, mouths open, at the great dark nightmare hanging above them like a sword about to drop, some more sprite-writing appeared, shooting down from above. It was a little wobblier and harder to read, for Eleanor Rose was now very far away, on the way back to the pole where she belonged.

"The giant and I promised the Kingwitch we wouldn't kill him, if he brought you all to this place together," said Eleanor Rose's sprite-writing. "I've frozen him for the moment, but the farther I get away from the castle, the harder it is for me to keep him that way, so, I repeat, you will have a bit of a head start but you need to get out of there as soon as you can…"

"Oh brother, oh brother, oh brother," moaned Xar, drawing the Enchanted Sword.

"Sorry about that," finished the sprite-writing, getting fainter every second. "But the ends justify the means…a fine outcome excuses a bad method…all in pursuit of a higher good, you know…You'll understand when you're older."

Uh-oh.

Uh-oh, uh-oh, uh-oh, uh-oh...

They scrambled to get off the giant's table and out
of that hidden hall before the Thing moved. The sprites
launched themselves into the air; the humans leaped on
the backs of the snowcats, who ran down the table legs,
scrambling to get across the hall and escape from the
castle before that THING woke up.

Up, out of the hall, and into the courtyard, the
sprites zooming overhead.

However, as the sprites and the animals emerged
shrieking and running as fast as their paws could take them
into the daylight, an unwelcome sight met their eyes.

While they had been listening to the story, their
pursuers had finally caught up with them.

Tiffinstorm gave a cry of distress, pointing her wand
to the south, where climbing up the southern ramparts
were Rogrebreaths, giants, Wizards, and the drifting
ghostly shapes of Droods.

A golden eagle and a gyrfalcon flew in through two
of the broken windows, and then swooped low over
the heads of Wish and Xar and Bodkin, as they rode the
snowcats through the ruined castle.

"Oh brother!" cried Xar, turning his head to
look up. "This is really going to hold us up!"

"What is it?" said Wish, riding Nighteye right
beside him.

"My father," said Xar. "That's my father..."

"How can that be your father? It's a bird," said Bodkin, but even as he said it, he knew it was a stupid statement.

The golden eagle and the gyrfalcon wheeled slowly around and hovered in front of the children. The long wings of the golden eagle turned into arms, and the body into the human form of Encanzo, and he landed lightly and coolly on the ground. The gyrfalcon's wings transformed into the long trailing sleeves of the Drood Commander, and he gave a grunt of satisfaction as he landed on the broken floor of the castle.

"SPLIT UP! DODGE!" yelled Xar, and the snowcats swerved—but it was already too late. They were surrounded.

The spelling staffs flew out of their pouch on Xar's back and into the hands of Encanzo and the Drood Commander.

Birds flew in from all corners of the broken castle, peregrines and crows and seagulls, and transformed into hovering hooded Droods, landing with their long ominous sleeves trailing behind them. Wolves and bears and snowcats and mountain lions appeared, each with a Wizard on its back, armed for battle, and they took out their staffs, and the castle rang with Magic spells of overcoming, so that Wish and Xar and

Bodkin could barely move, and Bodkin struggled for breath.

"Going somewhere, Xar?" said Encanzo coldly.

Xar cursed his father loud and long as the spells from Encanzo's staff carried him up into the air, legs dangling furiously.

"LET ME GO!" shouted Xar. "We need to get out of here right now! There's a Kingwitch about to unfreeze in the chamber below us!!!!"

"You will excuse me if I do not believe you, Xar," said his father in a voice of steel. "For you have lied to me so many times in the past. We are here to take you back to Gormincrag. You were put in Gormincrag to try to HELP you but it seems you are determined to prove you are beyond help!"

"Why do you never listen to what I say?" raged Xar. "That Drood there thinks I'm incurable! He just wants to keep me there forever! I am NEVER going back to Gormincrag, Father! Anyway, this is all beside the point because as I just told you, there's this Kingwitch, about to attack!"

Wish stepped forward. "Your son is right, sir…He's telling the truth…There really is this Kingwitch down there…"

Encanzo gave a start as he took in Wish and Bodkin for the first time.

"Who are you? And why are you with my son?"

There was no good answer to this question. "Oh!" said Wish. "I'm nobody...I'm nothing at all! I'm a friend of Xar's but nobody important...I'm just a...I'm a..."

What on earth could she be?

While Wish was desperately trying to think of a satisfactory answer to this question an ice-cold voice came floating out on the air from the right-hand side of the circle where all the Wizards, Droods, and giants were gathered. A voice as cold as a frost drop and as sweetly pure as the point of a freshly sharpened knife.

"She is my daughter," said Queen Sychorax, sweeping into the broken castle for all the world as if she were entering the emperor's imperial crown room far away in the Warrior capital. "And *your son* has kidnapped her. In an act of war."

13. Two Angry Parents

"Oh, great!" moaned Bodkin, in an agony of agitation. "Now EVERYBODY'S here! We're never going to get Wish away at this rate!"

It appeared that Bodkin was right.

Down in the chamber below, the dark frozen shape of the Kingwitch was twitching, rocking, twitching, rocking, as if it were going to unfreeze any second.

But the humans up above were too concerned with their own problems to worry about *him*.

The words were hardly out of Queen Sychorax's mouth than one of the Magic-hunters threw a net woven entirely out of iron wires around Encanzo. Encanzo's Magic blazed out uselessly as the net tightened around him, and the Witchsmeller stepped forward and placed iron manacles around his arms.

As soon as the iron touched Encanzo, Xar was released from the spell that held him, and he dropped heavily to the ground.

It all happened so quickly, no one had time to blink.

"Do not move! We have captured your leader, and one move, one attempt at a spell, and we will kill him!" cried the Witchsmeller.

"Ambushed!" swore the Drood Commander, cursing under his breath. "I knew that boy would lead us all into a trap! He should be locked underground forever, and we should throw away the key!"

All around the circle the Magic things crouched low, growling, the sprites burned bright with alarm and fear, the Rogrebreaths and giants grumbled deep in their great chests, but they dared not attack when their leader was immobilized and at the Warriors' mercy.

Queen Sychorax's Warriors trooped into the broken castle. The moonlight glistened off their iron helmets, their bristling weaponry, their Magic-catching equipment. Some were riding horses, others giant gray wolves.

"Forest destroyers!" hissed the Wizards.

"Wicked Magic-users! Followers of Witches!" shouted the Warriors.

"Well-poisoners!"

"Child-stealers!"

Encanzo was incandescent with annoyance to find himself overpowered and in chains so easily, and his expression became even more furious when he clapped eyes on Queen Sychorax. *She* was looking more beautiful and splendid than ever, in the manner of a particularly spectacular polar ice cap.

But her eyes were bleaker than midwinter frost.

And great
thunderclouds
steamed off
Encanzo's head, dark
with electric fury.

So the
atmosphere
was...How
can I
describe
it?

Tense.
Imagine
the foreboding
crackle in the
air and the spine-
jingling fizz in the
ground below
you if you just
so happened to
be standing on
the edge of a
volcano about
to erupt, and
then

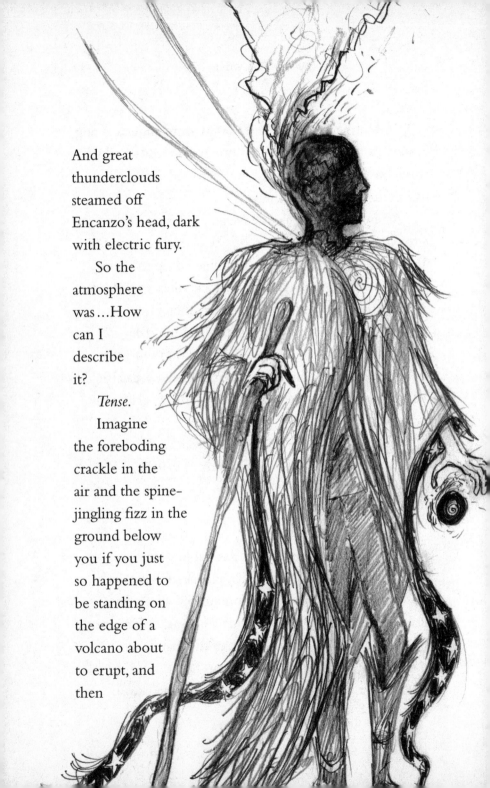

multiply that feeling by about twenty, and you will have an impression of what it might have been like on that ill-starred moonlit night when Queen Sychorax met King Encanzo on the heights of Castle Death.

tap tap tap

Not even Wish's hopeful gaze could make out
the slightest remains of past love in either of the two
monarchs' eyes. In fact, you could even say that they
were glaring at each other in what could be described as
most lively, and absolute, HATRED.

Queen Sychorax had her own reasons for being
particularly irritated at being dragged against her will
to this godforsaken blast of a doomed castle. She had
been here before, long ago when the castle had been
in considerably better condition, and she did not like
being forced to confront past deeds, and to be made to
discover the ruin that the castle had become—possibly
(who knows?) as a consequence of her own actions.

So Queen Sychorax was not in a good mood as
she stepped disdainfully across the broken rubble in her
golden slippers.

"Good evening, Queen Sychorax," said Encanzo
with bitter, icy politeness. "Ambushing a fellow royal
in neutral territory rather than meeting them in open
battle is treacherous and against your own Warrior rules,
but I gather your excuse this time is that in some way
unknown to ourselves *we* have declared war on *you*?"

(This seems like an unwise way to address a Warrior
queen who has you in handcuffs, but Encanzo was a
little too angry to be wise in that moment.)

Queen Sychorax might have been in a bad mood,

but it took quite a lot to get her properly angry. (People were so terrified of her, anger was rarely necessary.)

However, it turned out that *this* would do it.

"There is no question of excuses!" said Queen Sychorax, in a voice spitting like a nestful of infuriated hornets. "*YOUR repellently out-of-control and rude little son* has declared war on our nation by kidnapping *my* daughter, presumably on your orders!"

"I am NOT repellently out of control and rude!" snorted Xar, furious to see his father and his people overcome so humiliatingly easily by this dreadful queen. "And if we're trading insults, *you* have the largest nose on a queen that I have ever seen!"

Queen Sychorax flinched.

The entire courtyard took in a breath.

For Queen Sychorax did have, as it happened, a rather large nose. It was a splendidly, royally, *beautifully* large nose, but a trifle on the enormous side of medium nonetheless and she was a little sensitive about that.

Queen Sychorax's eyes sharpened to splinters.

"*What* did you say?"

"BIG NOSE!" shouted Xar. "Cowardly, flat-footed, no-hearted, EVIL destroyer of forests! Skulking behind your Wall while we Wizards get destroyed by the Witches! You have a nose the size of a METEORITE! You have a nose the size of a TOWER! You're the wickedest woman in the whole forest, but you also have a nose the size of a PLANET!"

"Be *polite*, Xar!" said Caliburn, in an agonized fashion. "You're talking to the person who has the power to kill your father!"

"It is entirely unsurprising that the boy should be so rude!" raged Queen Sychorax. "Like father, like son!"

"But in this case I disagree with Xar entirely," said Encanzo. "You, Queen Sychorax, have always had the most beautiful nose in the wildwoods. It is your *heart* that is the problem. The owner of the most beautiful nose in the wildwoods is also a queen who has no conscience."

The most beautiful nose in the wildwoods flared in and out with temper.

"The cheek of it! You and your entire Magic people have only been allowed to exist because of MY mercy!" said Queen Sychorax. "And I HAVEN'T left you to be destroyed by the Witches! I have personally hired this man here to get rid of them for me!"

She pointed to the Witchsmeller.

Encanzo sniffed. "One look at this man tells me he is not the right person for the job."

Sychorax's temper was not improved by the fact that she secretly agreed with Encanzo on that point.

"Enough of all this!" she snapped. "I have been

patient with you for way too long. Encanzo, you must give me your solemn word as a king that you will stop using your Magic, right here, right now, and order your followers to do the same."

The gathered Magic people gave furious murmurs.

"No, Mother, no!" cried Wish. "For goodness' sake, everyone, please listen to me! This isn't the time for doing this! We're going to need all the Magic we can get because there's this Kingwitch about to attack, just in the chamber below us…"

But Sychorax was too concerned with her fight with Encanzo to listen to Wish.

"You must stop using your Magic, Encanzo," said Sychorax, "or I will give the word for my Warriors to attack."

Caliburn flew between them both. "Sychorax, you know you do not mean that! The Wizards and the Droods do not have a hope of fighting your soldiers, for you are armed with iron!"

"Oh, but I do mean it," said Queen Sychorax, with a glittering smile.

"How strange," mused Encanzo, "for you to ask me to stop using Magic, when I have heard rumors that you are not above dabbling in Magic yourself…"

Queen Sychorax blushed. "Sometimes a queen can break the rules, in pursuit of a higher good. The ends justify the means…a fine outcome excuses a bad method…"

"Oh, is *that* what you believe?" said Encanzo, raising an eyebrow. "How extremely convenient."

"Fight them, Father!" shouted Xar.

"Your father is not the invincible person that you think he is, boy," said Queen Sychorax contemptuously, quivering with temper. "*You* see him as a terrible, powerful Magician. But a little touch of my iron, and see how weak he is!"

"My father is not weak!" said Xar fiercely. "He is the strongest person in the world!"

"No, Xar, the queen is right. Here, with my hands in iron manacles," said the Enchanter with a smile, "my Magic is useless. But however clever Sychorax may be, she still has much to learn. She can kill me, but I will still be here. And Magic cannot be destroyed; it can only be hidden."

"I hate Magic!" cried the queen passionately. "Magic is disorder! Magic is shortcuts! Magic is chaos and anarchy!

"*Choose,*" she said.

"I choose that you should attack us," said the Enchanter.

The queen looked at him in astonishment.

She stamped her foot. "Choose *wisely!*" she cried.

"I *have* chosen wisely," said the Enchanter. He laughed, and that infuriated Sychorax even more. "Was it not the choice that you wanted?"

"I am trying to find a civilized way out of this mess!" said the queen in exasperation. "I do not want violence, any more than you do. Giving up your Magic will still leave your people with a contented, happy way of life. Look at us Warriors..."

"It is very hard to be a leader, is it not?" said Encanzo sympathetically. "Sometimes hard decisions have to be made. You gave me a choice, and I took it. Now you have to let your Warriors attack."

The queen looked at him in baffled fury.

Queen Sychorax was a very, very tricky person. But...

It is possible that the queen had been out-tricked.

"No!" she said sharply.

"Too late," whispered the Witchsmeller, moving forward, purring. "He chose death."

The Witchsmeller stepped forward, sword drawn.

Encanzo braced himself for the final blow.

And Queen Sychorax leaned forward and knocked the sword out of the Witchsmeller's hand.

"What are you doing?" said the Witchsmeller in astonishment.

"Oh for goodness' sake, you stupid so-called

Witchsmeller!" snapped the queen. "Don't you know anything? I can't possibly murder an unarmed enemy king in cold blood, however much he may thoroughly deserve it..."

Encanzo's expression was unreadable.

Surprise, satisfaction, relief, anger, despair warred for supremacy in his face.

But eventually despair won out.

"You may stop short of allowing your Warrior here to slay me, Sychorax," said Encanzo, "but you do not seem to understand that in taking away our Magic and destroying our habitats, you are killing us nonetheless... You leave me no choice. Xar, you are about to have your way. You wanted war, and you shall have it..."

"At last!" said Xar, his eyes brightening. In his Xar-like way, his excitement at finally being allowed to fight the Warriors in open battle made him momentarily forget the impending doom of the Kingwitch.

At last they were going to stand up to these stupid Warriors and show them that Wizards could really *fight*!

"War it shall be," said Encanzo sadly, "and maybe, Xar, you will now see why I have gone to such trouble to avoid it.

"Magic people ... *ATTACK*!!"

14. They Really Shouldn't Be Fighting Each Other

N o! No! No!" cried Wish in distress. "Why won't you *listen*? Both of you, this is all a waste of time! We shouldn't be fighting each OTHER! I keep telling you, there's this Kingwitch, just below us, and he's about to unfreeze, and he's the commander of a whole horde of Witches, so this really isn't the moment to do this…"

"WARRRIORS, *ATTACK*!" replied Sychorax, completely ignoring her. "Be merciful, if you can be! If the Wizards surrender, take them prisoner!"

Wizard faced Warrior and they began to fight.

The Magic people were at a great disadvantage, for as you know Magic does not work on iron. But snowcats have teeth and talons, as do bears and wolves. Even sprites have fangs that sting like bees if they bite you. And Wizards and Droods carry bronze weapons with them as well as their Magic staffs if they are venturing into difficult or unknown territories.

So the sound of bronze sword on iron breastplate rang out with a bright terrible ring, and such was the volume of the roars of the wolves and the hissing of the sprites, the cursing of the Droods, and the bellows of the

giants that you could barely hear yourself think in the
cacophony of the battle.

Wish looked on in horror.

"Why do they *do* this, Caliburn?" she asked
despairingly. "They're so stupid. I told them about the
Kingwitch, but they're just not listening...I thought
maybe, after the story, that we could make my mother
and Xar's father see sense, but look at them now!"

Sychorax had made her guards remove Encanzo's
manacles.

Both monarchs drew their swords, bowed to each
other with exaggerated royal courtesy, and then lunged
simultaneously, their sword points meeting in
dreadful song, as they began their battle.

"You might as well give up now,"
spat Queen Sychorax, as she fenced

Squeezjoos
biting a
Warrior on the
bottom (it's a classic)

superbly, "for it is inevitable that you will lose. Your bronze sword is no match for my iron."

"I cannot lose more than I have lost already," said Encanzo.

Caliburn, on Wish's shoulder, sighed and shook his head. "I don't know..." he said sadly. "So many lifetimes I have lived and this is the way it always ends."

"And look at Xar!" said Wish. "Is *he* going to grow up to be as bad as the others?"

But even Xar found that *real* war was not the same as the *idea* of it.

What was he supposed to do now?

Fight Bodkin, who was running toward him? But he *liked* Bodkin.

The red mist of excitement faded from Xar's head and he paused, uncertain.

"Xar!" shouted Bodkin. "We need to help Wish get out of here! In the confusion, we can get away..."

"Oh yes!" said Xar, with a start. "Of course we can..."

Too late.

As the Wizards and Warriors fought each other, some of the combatants lost their balance when the ground beneath them began to shake.

For in the chamber below, the sinister shape of the Kingwitch had finally unfrozen.

And with a noise louder than a thousand thunderclaps

it burst up through the broken flagstones of the courtyard, creating such an outstanding noise that the people halted their fighting in their astonishment.

Up, up, it soared...

And then it dropped.

As it fell, it picked up speed, making a horrific explosive noise as the green sparks flew off it.

Someone pointed upward in alarm, at what now seemed transformed into a huge boulder plummeting down toward them, and the small party running across the hall scattered as...

BOOOOOOMMMMM!!!!!!!!!!!

What-looked-like-a-boulder landed with an almighty explosion right bang-splat in the center of the courtyard, shattering into a mass of tiny black shards and dust, and at the moment of impact, it burst into bright green flames.

"Look!" said Bodkin, pointing at the sky above them.

Above the castle, there was the sound of wings. Many, many wings. The crowd looked up. There they were, slowly turning visible in front of their eyes...the sky was thick with Witches.

"There are such a lot of them," gasped Sychorax. "How could there be so many Witches in the world and we not know about them for so long? Where have they all been?"

Five of the Witches swooped down on the gigantic, leaping fire, and flew around and around it, turning the flames as they flew counterclockwise, as if they were winding some invisible clock, making a horrible keening sound.

With trembling fingers, Xar got a good hold of the Enchanted Sword.

The Witches whirled faster, faster, shrieking in delight, as the fire burned and screamed and crackled.

And then great wings opened in the heart of the fire, wings that spread wide, slowly, unbearably.

Wings on fire…

Eyes like melting holes of hate…

A beak that screeched its loathing of the world and all the sweet good things that are in it…

The Kingwitch.

EEK!

15. The King-witch

The queen shook the boulder dust off her white skirt, sniffing.

"We seem to have a slight problem," said the Enchanter, betraying his agitation by a slightly raised eyebrow. If Queen Sychorax could play it cool, then, by mistletoe, so could the Enchanter.

The crowd stared in horror at the large crater in the center of the courtyard, which now looked as if it had been blasted by the landing of a stray asteroid.

Power reeked from that feathered thing, as slowly, slowly it unfurled its wet black wings to their full extent. They dripped on the floor, black smoking drips, as it lifted its beak and looked around at the crowd until it could pick out Xar and Wish.

Sychorax was pale, very pale.

For she knew that this was all partly her fault. She had tried to be too clever. *This* was the horror that had been hiding in her Stone-That-Takes-Away-Magic all along. Wish had told her…but there is nothing like being confronted with the actual reality to make you realize the extent to which you might have miscalculated.

White as ice, she turned to Encanzo. "Algorquprqin,"

said Queen Sychorax uncertainly. "I *think*...I may have made a mistake."

Miracle of miracles! Stiff Queen Sychorax, proud Queen Sychorax, unbending Queen Sychorax who always thought she was right about absolutely everything, admitting that even *she* might not be perfect!

"We all make mistakes," said Encanzo grimly. "Even you and I, Queen Sychorax."

"Oh, by hemlock and nightshade and all things mean and bad," whispered the Witchsmeller. "What is that?"

"*That* is a Witch," said Sychorax. "You see the difference, pest controller? Giants and fairies and Magic people, they're not really Witches at all, are they? A Witch is kind of unmistakable."

"And that isn't just a normal Witch either," said Encanzo grimly. "*That* is a Kingwitch.

"What do you want, Witch?"

Now the Kingwitch began to speak, and it was a dreadful sound indeed, a harsh, grating, guttural noise that seemed to pain him to make, and every now and again, a word was reversed, as was the fashion with Witches.

"I want the children," crooned the Kingwitch. "Give me the children."

There was a horrible silence.

"What children?" said Encanzo.

The Kingwitch pointed at Xar and at Wish.

"The boy iss mine already," said the Kingwitch. "And the girl is special..."

"There's absolutely nothing special about Wish— look at her!" said Sychorax briskly, but there may have been a little anxiety in her voice. "She's totally ordinary, and if anything, for a Warrior, just a little substandard..."

They all looked at Wish, standing uncomfortably on one leg. She didn't look remotely special, a small, skinny little child with an eyepatch and hair sticking out in all directions.

"She has something I need," continued the Kingwitch. "I already have some of it, but only as much as was in the very tip of her very little finger...Now I want ALL of it...to share with my fellow Witches...Give her to me now."

"And what," said the queen with considerable asperity, "are you intending to do with her?"

"I will eat her," said the Kingwitch.

Which was not very nice, but what did you *expect* a Witch to be like?

There was another horrified silence.

"That is ridiculous!" snapped Queen Sychorax, magnificently scornful and every inch a monarch. "Of course you can't EAT my child, you disgusting creature. I never heard of anything more barbaric!"

"Give me the child," repeated the Kingwitch. "I will swallow her whole…Give me the child…"

"I am the queen of these territories," said Sychorax imperiously. "We have a Warrior army, fully armed with iron. Take your Witches out of here, before we kill you all. Go!"

The Kingwitch gave a ghastly shriek and spread wide his great dark wings and leaped into the air, and as he flew up, up, up into the airy heights, it looked for one moment as if he was flying away, trying to escape.

Spare a thought for the poor Witchsmeller.

This was meant to be his moment.

He had been enjoying the battle with the Wizards, but this was even better!

As the Kingwitch soared upward, the Witchsmeller was rubbing his hands together.

OH, THIS WAS TOO GOOD.

All his wishes had come true at once.

A WITCH! At last he had found a real live Witch, after a lifetime of looking! And not just one Witch, a whole host of the creatures…

They weren't extinct after all!

"Get out the Witch-destroying weapon!" yelled the Witchsmeller joyfully. "Prepare to face the full force of IRON, Thing of Evil!!!"

He put down his iron visor, almost chuckling to himself.

The Witchsmeller imagined, encased in iron as he was—iron breastplates, iron helmet—that he would be quite safe against the Witch. It might look scary, this creature, but no Magic could work against iron. He would first get rid of the big one and then turn the might of the weapon on all of the others. And then he would go back to the capital in triumph and in glory, with lots of Witch beaks to show the emperor.

The Witchsmeller was just enjoying this happy little thought...

When the Kingwitch turned on him.

High up in the air the Kingwitch turned in a great beautiful glorious swoop, if you had been in the mood to admire the swooping of Witches, which the Witchsmeller most certainly wasn't, and with a grand gesture of his feathered wing the Kingwitch pointed all five of his taloned fingers at the Witchsmeller and his two imperial giant-killers, who were struggling to launch the Witch-destroying weapon.

And the Magic came blinding out of the five fingers, with the fierceness with which it might blast out of five Wizards' staffs.

Fifty years the Witchsmeller had studied Witch-hunting and the Pursuit of Magic, and now he was

looking up through his little iron visor
at the thunderous sky and realizing, oh my
goodness, that the Kingwitch was spelling at him, and
that was exactly the same moment that he had a tiny
flicker of concern as he realized, horror of horrors, how
small he was, how insignificant, how unprepared for the
spells coming down at him in brilliant stars of light.

The Witchsmeller didn't even have time to get the
imperial giant-killers to launch his Witch-destroying
weapon. It had taken years for the Witchsmeller's father
and for the Witchsmeller's father's father to design that
weapon, and they reckoned they had gotten it pretty
much perfect, but this is an excellent example of how
things that work magnificently in *theory* don't necessarily
work in practice.

The Witchsmeller got as far as shouting, "LAUNCH
THE WEAP—!" before the spells hit him.

The stars of light hit the Witchsmeller full on the
chest and bounced neatly off onto the other Magic-
hunters standing around him, one after the other.

One second the Witchsmeller was standing, in full
body armor, erect and splendid, if a little uneasy, with
his axe raised high above his head, shouting impressive
instructions.

"LAUNCH THE WEAP

— UH-OH!

The next second, the armor had stiffened around him and solidified, and he was caught within it, as if it were the trunk of a tree.

CLANG!

His visor came down.

"Hello?" said the Witchsmeller in a bewildered sort of way, and the echo of his own voice came back to him from within his metal prison. "Hello?"

And all around him, his fellow Magic-hunters were similarly caught, stuck in their armor, frozen in various poses of attack, one of them bending down to light the fuse that might set off the Witch-destroying weapon (also frozen), another with an arm above the head about to launch a spear, others in the act of taking their swords from their scabbards.

IRON. Their armor was made of IRON. How could the Witch's Magic be working on iron? With a terrible sinking of the heart, Xar realized how...

Back in their last adventure, when they first met the Kingwitch in Queen Sychorax's dungeon, the Kingwitch had drunk up some of Wish's Magic, and NOW...

For the very first time...

He had a little Magic that could work on IRON.

The Kingwitch had not taken enough of Wish's Magic to do more than make the armor freeze. He couldn't make it move or dance. But freezing was quite enough to paralyze the Witchsmeller and his band of Magic-hunters.

"Are you all right in there, pest controller?" snapped Queen Sychorax, peering through the Witchsmeller's visor. "Enjoying your first encounter with a real *Witch*?"

"Help!" said the Witchsmeller in reply. And the soldiers all around him echoed, "Help!" "Help!" "Help!" as they tried and failed to move the armor that had solidified all around them.

Queen Sychorax sniffed. "So much for your famous Witch-destroying weapon."

"The Kingwitch shouldn't have been able to do that," said Encanzo grimly.

But they didn't have time to absorb any of the implications of this.

For the Kingwitch whirled around and screamed, "Let me show you why you should do as I say.

"WITCHES! ATTACK!"

UH - OH...

295

16. The Witches Attack

ith a terrible smell of burning feathers, the Witches swooped.

When Witches attack, they assault all your senses at the same time. Their stink is unbearable, the worst smell you can possibly imagine. Their scream is like the shriek of five hundred angry foxes, and it buries itself in your brain and reverberates around your head till you feel like you might go crazy.

"WARRIORS! WIZARDS! GIANTS! LYNXES!" cried Sychorax. "Stop fighting each other! Fight THE WITCHES!"

And Encanzo held up his staff and yelled out the same orders.

Sychorax and Encanzo didn't really need to shout those instructions.

The noise and the smell were so horrid that the Wizards and the Warriors were instinctively banding together to fight these new, terrifying assailants.

Warriors and Wizards and giants were in one instant fighting back to back, on the same side. But there was an astonishing number of the Witches, a cloud of them, like a swarm of gigantic malevolent crows.

The Witches were happy to attack the Magic things. But they were still afraid of the Warriors, and they couldn't attack them like the Kingwitch could.

"HOLD FAST! DEFEND YOUR POSITIONS!" cried Sychorax, that great war leader. "FIGHT THE WITCHES TOGETHER!"

The Kingwitch sharpened his talons against each other like a blacksmith sharpening a gigantic sword.

And then, quick as a weasel he stretched up his claw and screamed an unintelligible gargle of command.

"We need to defend the children," said Encanzo, jumping up aboard his lynx, and Sychorax glided up behind him, sidesaddle, arms crossed, for she would have rather DIED than put her arms around Encanzo's waist. It was remarkable, the way that she did not lose her balance as the lynx leaped forward, but then Queen Sychorax was really rather a remarkable woman.

"Go away!" shouted Xar as Encanzo pulled the lynx to a halt beside him. "I don't need your help!"

"You have to let us defend you, Xar!" said Encanzo. "I had no idea that creature was after you..."

In the heat of the moment, and in his anxiety, Xar admitted something that he had not yet really wanted to admit, even to himself.

"The Kingwitch isn't after me; he's after *Wish*," said Xar. "*Wish* is the girl of destiny...We need to help Wish."

Above Xar's head, the whirr of soft wings. Five Witches soared, and they did not pause for Xar.

Xar was right: They were after Wish, while her Magic was still untrained, and uncontrolled.

Wish was in the center of the courtyard.

She had been about to take off her eyepatch, but the Witches had attacked with such suddenness that she had only just nudged it up a smidgeon.

And as they attacked, Encanzo leaped from the back of his snowcat and pointed his fingers toward Wish, making a defensive Magic force field the size of a very large, round, invisible boulder spring up around Wish to protect her.

The force field burned bright, as the Witches struck again and again, like great black ravens attacking a tasty morsel. Such was the force of their onslaughts that Wish was rolled drunkenly around the courtyard, thrown about inside the force field with such violence that she was unable to take off her eyepatch. Every time she put up her arms to do it, she was thrown off her balance once more.

The Kingwitch landed in a blur of wings and crouched down, long black drips of saliva pouring from both sides of his jaws.

"It's weakening!" screeched the Kingwitch, three eyes glowing red as the great slugging force of the Witches' spell-attacks began to crush the force field protecting Wish, punching great dents in it as it rolled pathetically this way and that.

Xar ran toward them, the Enchanted Sword slippy in his trembling hand.

"GET OFF HER!" cried Xar, waving the sword at the Kingwitch.

The Kingwitch crouched lower.

"You fool," he whispered. "Do you not know, boy, that you are mine?"

"I am not yours!" screamed Xar.

"You have to be careful what you wish for," crooned the Kingwitch, "and *you* wished for Witchblood...willingly took it...put out your hand and made the cut yourself. X marks the spot..."

How could Xar deny it? His whole hand beneath the glove was burning a bright, terrible green of such vividness that it turned the glove itself transparent.

"And now I control you," said the Kingwitch. "It was I who urged you to escape from the prison of Gormincrag, and I who helped you to do it. You brought her to me."

"No..." said Xar, very white, "it's not true..."

But it is only sometimes when you reach the *end* of the quest that you realize what it has been about all along.

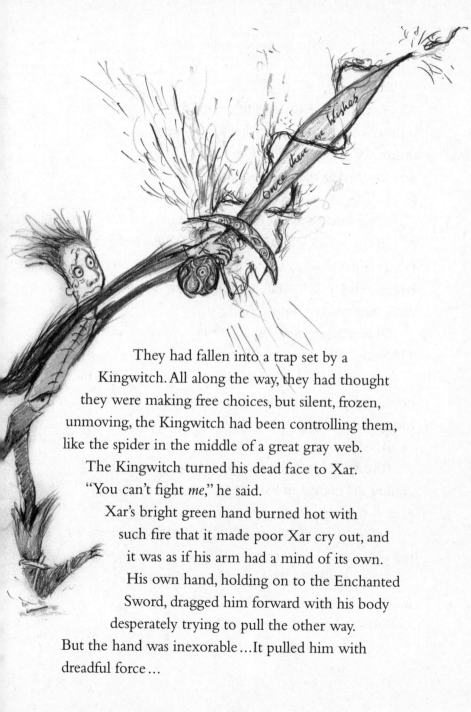

They had fallen into a trap set by a
Kingwitch. All along the way, they had thought
they were making free choices, but silent, frozen,
unmoving, the Kingwitch had been controlling them,
like the spider in the middle of a great gray web.

The Kingwitch turned his dead face to Xar.
"You can't fight *me*," he said.

Xar's bright green hand burned hot with
such fire that it made poor Xar cry out, and
it was as if his arm had a mind of its own.

His own hand, holding on to the Enchanted
Sword, dragged him forward with his body
desperately trying to pull the other way.

But the hand was inexorable...It pulled him with
dreadful force...

He tried to resist, holding on to his
right elbow with his other hand, but like it
or not, for good or for evil, the rest of his body
was attached to that hand so what could he do?
Heels dragging, he was hauled toward Wish, who was
still being thrown about in Encanzo's force field.

"If the sword kills Witches, it can kill *her* too...And
I can eat her dead just as well as alive," whispered the
Kingwitch. "You can kill her for me, boy. Humans are
weak. She won't want to hurt *you*...

"Remember who you are. You're a Wizard, and she's
a Warrior...Wizards hate Warriors..."

"I'm sorry, Wish! I can't stop it!" shouted Xar as his
bright green hand brought the sword down on the red
force field and broke through it,

BAM!

It shattered into thousands of pieces that exploded
around the courtyard like tiny splinters of bright red
glass, before melting into the air.

"Good, good," crooned the Kingwitch. "Now go for
the girl..."

Wish stood there, her fingers crooked now
underneath the eyepatch.

She couldn't lift it to fight *Xar*...

Poor Xar was still trying to control his own hand.

But the combination of his arm with the Witch-stain
and the Enchanted Sword was too strong for him, and
he was being dragged nearer and nearer to Wish, with the
sword raised above his head to attack her, even though
he was pulling in the other direction with all his might.

*I can't fight this...It's too strong for me...*thought Xar wretchedly.

"Don't think about your weaknesses, think about your strengths," shouted Caliburn. "Work with what you DO have, not with what you DON'T!"

"Use your disobedience, Xar!" ordered Queen Sychorax, shouting from behind him. "You have PLENTY OF *THAT*!"

Xar turned, and raised the sword toward the Kingwitch. He couldn't fight the Kingwitch completely, he wasn't strong enough for that, but he could work with the Kingwitch's own desires.

(Xar had learned that lesson from the Kingwitch, because that was exactly what the Kingwitch had been doing to *him*.)

"You want the sword, Witch?" shouted Xar. "You can have it!"

With every single ounce of disobedience in his disobedient body, Xar shouted, "NO! *Take that*, you stinking great feather-armed FREAK of a nightmare Witch!"

And he threw the sword with all of his might toward the Kingwitch.

There was a moment when it seemed as if the sword wasn't going to leave the green grip of Xar's hand.

But Xar had guessed right.

The Kingwitch DID want that sword, for it was a very powerful Magic object.

The Kingwitch's own wanting loosened Xar's grip… the sword sailed through the air and landed a couple of feet in front of him with a loud clatter.

"I WILL NOT do it," said Xar, chest heaving with the struggle of it. "Because I LIKE Wish."

The Kingwitch was astonished at this defiance. The boy should be his entirely! How was it possible that Xar would not do his bidding?

But it did not change the ending…

The Kingwitch would finish this himself.

He reached out his taloned hand and grasped the Enchanted Sword.

He said some very powerful words of a spell to bind the sword to his hand, so that the girl could not take it from him.

With one, two beats of his great wings he leaped in the air, wings spread wide, up up up.

And then he swooped, terrible mouth agape, to swallow the child whole.

17. Taking off the Eyepatch

And Wish took off her eyepatch. Taking off the eyepatch was like opening the door into another world.

Looking through her left eye, it was as if she was standing on the top of a snowy mountain, where the snow was so glitteringly bluey-white that it dazed you. The colors were so forceful, the reds so red, the greens so purely green that it overwhelmed her, and she cried out now, as they hit her almost like a physical blow.

She'd forgotten just how sickening this feeling was, how terrifying.

Very few Wizards before or since have ever had the rare power of a Magic eye.

A power that misted up Wish's brain with such furious energy that her hair leaped up around her like an electrical ruff and the ground beneath her swayed like a sea, and the broken walls shook further, and all around lost their balance as the Magic came screaming out of her eye and met the blast of the swooping Kingwitch's Magic.

Closer…closer the Kingwitch dived, so close that Wish could see right down the ghastly maw of his open throat, the Enchanted Sword pointed right toward her.

Oh, by the gods of water…what can I do? I have all this Magic but I don't know how to control it…

She tried to imagine removing the Enchanted Sword from the Kingwitch's hand. But it was stuck fast by the spell he had used.

What else can I do?

"Focus on what you DO know, not what you DON'T…"

Iron…thought Wish. *I know how to move iron…*

All that practicing she had done in the Punishment Cupboard, and Caliburn's lessons back on the Sweet Track…

All around her were the figures of the Witchsmeller and his Magic-hunters, with their armor frozen around them, stiff as statues.

And then, almost the very second that the thought came into her head, the helmet of the nearest Magic-hunter began to untwist, as Wish's Magic made it move. She didn't even have to point her hand at it, all it took was a thought.

"Be careful what you wish for, Witch…" whispered Wish. *"You wanted Magic-that-works-on-IRON…and you…shall…have it!"*

The Kingwitch was halted abruptly, midair, by a flying iron helmet that hurtled through the sky and—CLANG!—attached itself to the Enchanted Sword, making the Witch's sword arm so heavy that his whole body lurched violently to the right.

The Kingwitch tried to shake off the helmet, but it was stuck fast, for the helmet had come into the orbit of the spell that the Kingwitch had cast to bind the sword into his hand, and it would…not…budge…however hard the Kingwitch shook it. CLANG! CLANG! Another helmet, and an iron glove soared through the air and stuck to the other side of the sword.

The Kingwitch said the words of the undoing, to take off the binding spell he had cast, and he had the first stirrings of unease.

"What is *that*?" the Kingwitch asked himself in a startled sort of way.

For as the Enchanted Sword sprang out of the Kingwitch's hand and dropped point first into the ground, the Magic-hunters' frozen armor had exploded apart, leaving the bewildered Witchsmeller and his soldiers standing in their underclothes, staring upward in astonishment while their armor rocketed toward the Kingwitch. Spears and helmets and chains and knives and swords and breastplates, not to mention an entire Witch-destroying weapon, the whole armory of iron that the Magic-hunters carried with them on Magic-hunting expeditions, were sailing through the air toward the Kingwitch as if they were arrows fired at a bird.

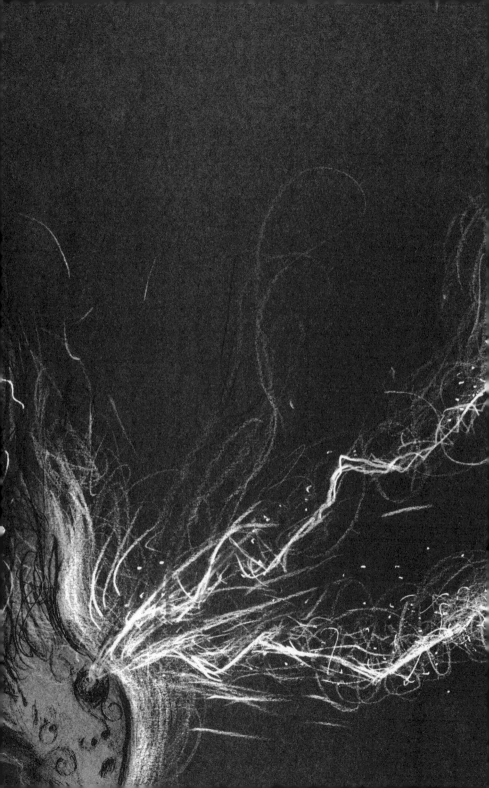

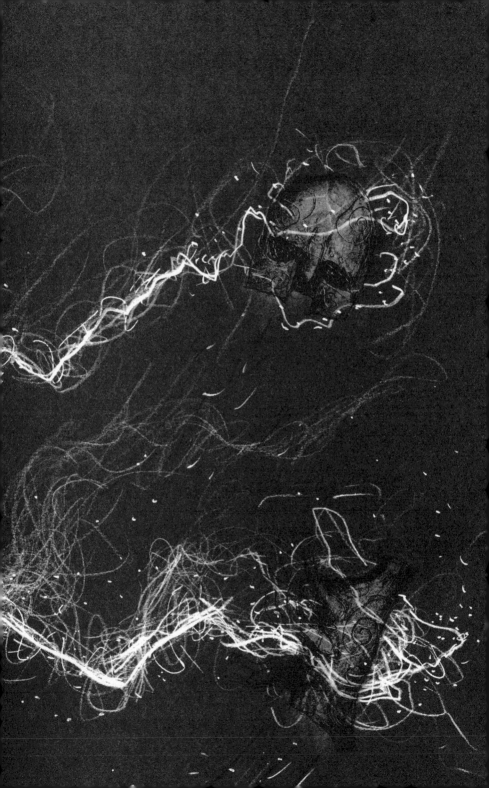

MORE *iron*, thought Wish, *more and more and
more*...

The army of iron attached itself to the Kingwitch as
if he were a magnet.

The Kingwitch tried to beat all the iron things
off, but they clogged up his wings, and the harder he
tried to fight them off, the harder they stuck fast, until
he became smothered in a thick ball of iron, iron that
melted around him as it met the green heat of his
Magic. It weighed the Kingwitch down, and he plunged
deeper and deeper in the air, and Wish added more and
more and more and more and more until he fell
to the earth like a stone.

Xar and Wish scrambled out of the way
over the heaving, tumbling earth as...

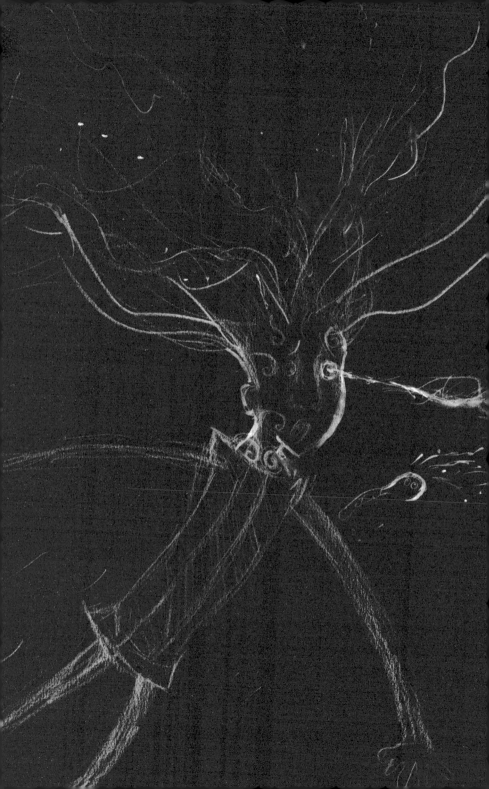

The Witch encased in iron landed with such force that he created a great crater in the courtyard of the ruined castle of Pentaglion. Just as the iron solidified in a final, enclosing ball, the Kingwitch shot one last blast of Magic from his five taloned fingers and…
REOOOOOW!

REOOW//

The Magic came screaming out and hit Wish on the chest and there was a mind-blowingly loud noise, and a blinding white light, and something exploded with such energy that Xar was knocked over.

The earth came to a shuddering halt at last, and great clouds of dust billowed and wafted across the shattered remains of the courtyard.

The ball of iron that encased the Kingwitch was, strange to say, exactly the shape of the stone that used to be Queen Sychorax's Stone-That-Takes-Away-Magic, maybe because it was a shape that Wish had seen before.

The clouds of Witches who had been hovering, waiting, watching for the outcome of this battle, shrieked across the sky, howling and raging against the defeat of their leader, before dispersing, flying away, who knows where?

The ball of iron rocked once, twice, on its pointed axis...and then it rolled to the edge of the battlements...and fell over the edge...and down, down into the ocean below, before disappearing under the waves.

The Wizards and the Warriors, the Witchsmeller, the Droods, and the Magic creatures staggered to their feet, coughing and choking, trying to work out exactly what had just gone on.

Queen Sychorax leaped up, and ran toward Xar,

Encanzo and Bodkin running by her side. The dust fell all around them like blue rain.

Xar picked up the Enchanted Sword, which had landed right in front of him.

The writing on the blade had gotten so scratched and rubbed away on both sides by the helmet and the other iron things, that it now just read:

Once...

"We did it! AGAIN!" grinned Xar as he put the sword into his scabbard. The two monarchs reached him where he stood, ragged and shaken, his quiff a little awry but still Xar-like in his jubilation.

"I TOLD you we could do it, Father! And did you see, Bodkin? Did you see, Caliburn?" he cried, punching the air in triumph. "I DID fight the Kingwitch! I TOLD you I could!"

"What on earth is the boy talking about?" snapped Queen Sychorax. *"Where is my daughter?"*

"There she is," said Xar, pointing at the great cloud of gentle, shimmering, bright blue dust falling around them.

Queen Sychorax was without words.

"She exploded," explained Xar.

Queen Sychorax's chest heaved as she looked around at the clouds of blue dust before...

"EXPLODED?" she said in horror.

"My daughter *EXPLODED*???

What do you mean she *exploded*? And why are you celebrating? The child *saved* you, you horrible boy! You're as bad as that Witch!"

My daughter EXPLODED?

If she hadn't been such a very great queen you might have thought that Sychorax staggered a little. She certainly turned deathly pale, and then she knelt down on the floor where the Enchanted Spoon and thirty iron pins lay quiet and cold and lifeless.

She reached out a trembling hand to touch them.

Squeezjoos whispered, "Don't you worrys, ice queen, don't you worrys...She'll be back," putting his little clawlike hands lovingly on the bewildered queen's cheek.

Queen Sychorax had given her heart away long ago.

But kneeling in the dust there, one, two, three tears dropped from her cold blue eyes.

"Outss of the way! Outsss of the way!" said the Once-sprite, swooping from nowhere, jumping from the back of the hovering falcon, and collecting the tears, one, two, three, as they dropped from the cheek of the mourning queen.

Encanzo stepped in hurriedly. "For shame, Xar, you have to explain! Your daughter will regenerate, Sychorax. She has a Magic eye, which makes her a very great Enchanter, and very great Enchanters have more than one life."

"Regenerate?" said Queen Sychorax, blinking blankly. "Magic eye? More than one life?"

She had forgotten how horribly confusing Magic people were.

They couldn't even obey the normal rules about life and death.

"*When? When* will she regenerate?" gabbled Sychorax.

"In a moment or two," said Encanzo soothingly. "It can take a while...In the meantime, we have to be careful not to step on any of this blue dust..."

"This blue dust is MY DAUGHTER???" said Queen Sychorax, looking around in astonishment and horror.

"What issss that man doing?" hissed Squeezjoos, eyes narrowing.

That man was the Drood Commander.

The Drood Commander was behaving in rather a peculiar manner.

He was working frantically, and as they looked more closely they could see he was actually *spelling* the blue dust with his spelling staff, collecting bright clouds of it and putting it in a gourd.

"Yes," said Encanzo, very puzzled, "what on earth are you doing, Drood Commander?"

"Didn't you see? The girl, the Enchanter, has Magic-mixed-with-iron, which makes her very, very dangerous!" said the Drood Commander. "Quick! We don't have much time! We must trap her in here and then she won't be able to regenerate!"

"Be careful there, Commander!" said Encanzo

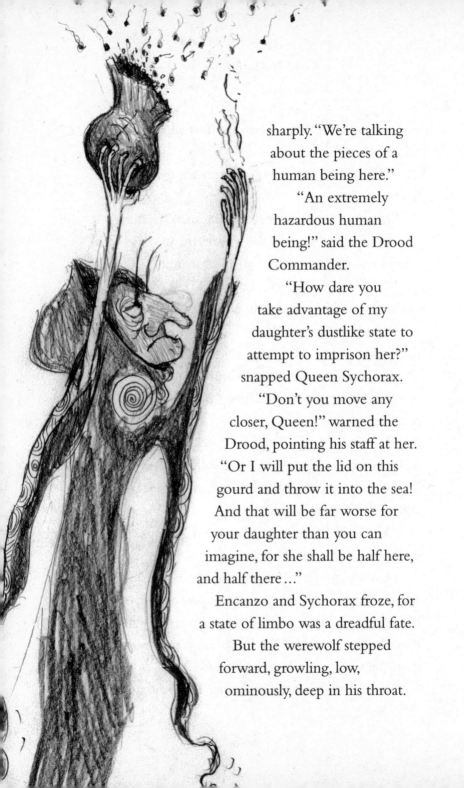

sharply. "We're talking about the pieces of a human being here."

"An extremely hazardous human being!" said the Drood Commander.

"How dare you take advantage of my daughter's dustlike state to attempt to imprison her?" snapped Queen Sychorax.

"Don't you move any closer, Queen!" warned the Drood, pointing his staff at her. "Or I will put the lid on this gourd and throw it into the sea! And that will be far worse for your daughter than you can imagine, for she shall be half here, and half there..."

Encanzo and Sychorax froze, for a state of limbo was a dreadful fate.

But the werewolf stepped forward, growling, low, ominously, deep in his throat.

"Get back!" ordered Encanzo. "That Drood is dangerous…"

The werewolf ignored him.

"What are you doing, werewolf?" screamed the Drood Commander, madly sweeping the blue dust into the gourd in great drifts. "Step back, you evil-bound beast! Halt, you loveless furball! I'm doing historically important work here!"

And then Xar had a brilliant idea…

And he did a Good Thing.

A really, *really* Good Thing.

Xar needed to get rid of those Witches. He knew that it was unlikely that the Kingwitch would have been defeated forever. His hand was still burning bright green. He needed all the ingredients in the spell to get rid of Witches, and they had just gone to considerable lengths to get hold of this one.

But for the first time in Xar's life, he cared about somebody else more than he did about himself.

So Xar undid the stopper on the collecting bottle he was carrying.

In a great glorious roar, the Giant's

Xar NEEDED what was inside this bottle…

BUT…

Last Breath blasted out of the collecting bottle into which it had been shrunk only an hour or so earlier.

"FORGIVE THEM!" roared the Giant's Last Breath.

"FORGIVE THEM!!!" at a decibel so loud that Sychorax and Encanzo and Xar and Bodkin had to put their hands over their ears.

"FORGIVE THEM."

18. Forgive Them

The released giant's breath was a roar so loud, and it made a wind so strong, that the bright pieces of blue dust that the Drood was trying to collect whirled up into the air in a flurry of excitement, and out of the Drood's reach.

The Drood gave a howl of frustration as up and into the wind they went, around and around, impossible to catch, and the Drood, arms flailing, dropped the gourd, which rolled on the floor, all the dust spilling out of it in great glorious swoops...

And the Drood himself lost his balance in the tremendous roar of the blast, and fell out and over the edge of the battlement that had been broken by the ball of iron that encased the Kingwitch only moments before, with a furious shriek.

Down the Drood fell, becoming smaller and smaller, and when he had nearly reached the ocean, his pin-prick of a body transformed into a gyrfalcon, before spreading wide his wings and flying out, out across the waves in the distant direction of the islands known as the Giants' Footsteps.

Just in time, for all around them the freed blue dust was singing...

Singing a beautiful sweet
song of life returning, as all the
whirling innumerable little pieces of
Wish came joyfully back to life again, and they
rushed around, those tiny fragments, in a confusing blur
of reshuffling Magic, whizzing back together in the
memory of where they were, the impossibly complicated
reality of a human body, forming the perfect sculpture of
what-once-was-Wish, until: Oh!

Bodkin would never tire of the heart-stopping
moment when up above, the small brown heart of Wish
re-formed in the air, and then down it plunged through
the chest, and Wish sat up and
took in that breath that was life
itself, in sweet, thirsty gulps.

Caliburn had found
Wish's eyepatch in the
rubble, and he hurriedly
handed it to her, before
the earth started trembling
again.

"Wish!" cried Queen Sychorax, extremely shaken, for it is not every day that you see your daughter blown into pieces, her heart flying through the air and her entire body reconstituting herself in front of your very eyes. "Are you all right? Is everything in the correct place?"

She held her daughter's hand and patted her down to check that she was real and alive and breathing and that all of her was there.

"I'm sorry, Mother!" said Wish, gasping for breath. "I know it's a bit unusual…but it seems that I have more than one life…I do hope you don't mind?"

"I do not mind," said the queen, in a definite tone of relief, "as long as you promise never to do

all this…all this *flying about in little pieces* in an untidy
fashion…all this…*making your heart go jumping through the
air*…ever EVER again…"

"You were *worried* about me, weren't you?" said Wish
shyly.

"Perhaps I was," admitted Queen Sychorax.

And then…

"The way you defeated the Kingwitch was, I have
to admit, *clever*. Queens have to think on their feet," said
Queen Sychorax.

The queen did not smile at her daughter very
often, but when she did, Wish's whole world lit up with
sunshine.

Wish smiled back delightedly.

And as Queen Sychorax smiled at Wish,
Encanzo embraced his son.

"You said you'd make me proud of you,
Xar," said Encanzo. "And I AM proud of you.
You resisted the power of the Kingwitch. I never
thought you could. I said 'be good' and you were.
You really are growing up."

Xar stuck out his chest in delight.

"It's all going to be fine!" said Wish, joyously,
holding out her arms. "Thank you, Lonesome! Thank
you, Squeezjoos!" she said, hugging the hairy
fairy.

The werewolf was so surprised he
actually let her hug him too.

*"URRRRR URRR URRRRR!
URRR URRR URRRRRR! URR
URR URRRRR!"* roared the
werewolf.

"URR URR URRRRR!"
shouted Xar. "Join in,
everyone! She's alive!"
Completely
forgetting themselves
in the excitement of
the moment, the
Wizards and the

Warriors responded to Xar's demand, and they also looked up to the sky above and echoed this wild cry:

"URRRRR URRR URRRRR! URRR URRR URRRRRR! URR URR URRRRR!"

Miracle on miracle.

What a sight it was, Wizards and Warriors howling at the sky alongside the most reviled, the most feared, the most despised beast in the wildwoods.

And then...

"WORRA WOORA REARRGH! WORRA WORRA CREAGGGGGLE!" screamed the werewolf, abruptly tilting his head downward, and fixing his savage gaze on the crowd with alarming intensity, foaming at the mouth, and making tearing-limb-from-limb motions with his arms, while gnashing his teeth. "GOORAGGOOGLE!"

And the crowd's happy supportive howling halted rather abruptly as they scrambled fearfully out of the way, pushing each other over and screaming a little, in case the teeth-gnashing and limb-tearing was intended for *them*.

This is the problem with werewolves, you see.

They're hard to love, even when you're on their side, because they're so...well...*scary*.

"Now it really IS all right!" said Wish, with a sigh of contentment.

It had been a terrible adventure, but it had all been worth it, thought Wish. She had been dreading the moment that her mother found out her secret, but now that she had, it was sort of a relief. Now could be the start of the Wizards and the Warriors finally working together to fight the Witches. Her mother would fall back in love with Encanzo, and they would stop this silly war between them. It was all going to be fine...

But now that she was over her initial relief, Queen Sychorax was no longer smiling.

She was standing, her immaculate hair covered in bits of brick dust and dripping wet. Her once-white dress dragged behind her in the dirt, streaked with mud and mess, torn by Witches' talons, and dripping in green Witchblood. She had made the unwelcome discovery (Sychorax may have suspected this already, but actual *proof* is always a bad moment) that she had an exploding daughter, with a Magic eye and a historically unfortunate Magic-mixed-with-iron component...It was all very irregular indeed.

"All right?" snapped Queen Sychorax. "*All right?* It most definitely is NOT all right! This is a disaster, and I am now going to take my daughter home, and I do not want to hear ONE WORD about this ever again."

She adjusted her disheveled hair, and brushed down her white dress briskly.

All of Wish's wonderful fantasies about this being a new start collapsed in an instant.

"But this adventure has been a lesson to all of us that things are going to have to change around here!" said Wish. "*People* are going to have to change, people like US. The Witches have returned to the wildwoods, and Wizards and Warriors have to join together, to fight them off, just like we did this evening."

"Never!" cried Encanzo.

"Not on your life!" spat Queen Sychorax. "Wizards are incapable of change!"

"As are Warriors!" said Encanzo, if anything, even angrier.

"No, no, don't say that!" said Caliburn. "*Everyone* is capable of change! What the children need is *education*…For the Witches are still out there, and when they come back, then this girl Wish is going to be tested, and she may be all that stands between us and oblivion…"

"Yes, and Caliburn's been giving us lessons while we were on the run!" said Wish. "He's a brilliant teacher, not just of Magic, but all the Warrior spelling-and-words-and-maths stuff, and when *Caliburn* is teaching me it seems to all make sense!"

"I am not going to have my child taught by a talking *bird*!" said Queen Sychorax. "I know perfectly well how to educate my own child, thank you very much.

"You have both been saved from the Kingwitch," she went on, "and now we must put things back to the way they were."

"But, Mother! You and Encanzo were in *love!*" said Wish, very distressed. "Remember the wolves? Every second Thursday!!! *It's the reason I am who I am!* The true love's kiss of a Wizard remained in your blood and it made me Magic even though I am a Warrior!"

Encanzo and Sychorax went very still.

Wish quailed before the look of utter horror in her mother's cold blue eyes.

"WOLVES? *THURSDAYS?*" said Queen Sychorax in arctic outrage. "Wizards and Warriors in *love?* Impossible!"

"Inconceivable," echoed Encanzo bitterly, in a voice hard as a diamond. "A queen like Sychorax was always going to marry some idiot Warrior with a thick neck and a big sword, so she could enjoy all these knickknacks, these golden plates, this Warrior jewelry trash around her neck... A queen like Sychorax would never be in love..."

"I had duties!" retorted Queen Sychorax. "Responsibilities! And *you* married one of your own kind, just as I did, Encanzo, for your disobedient son here must have had a mother once!"

"But the giant Proponderus told us the whole story ..." said Wish, now miserably muddled. They were talking

as if it had actually happened, while at the same time
denying it.

Grown-ups were so confusing.

Was it true or was it made up?

"The giant must have been listening to the fairies,"
said Queen Sychorax firmly. "Fairies are terrible liars.
This is *real life*, Wish, not a fairy story. Therefore, I repeat,
for the final time, Wish will return home with me, to the
safety of Warrior Castle, and as far as I am concerned,
this JUST ... NEVER ... HAPPENED."

At that moment, the Witchsmeller stepped forward.

It was difficult for the Witchsmeller to be quite as
scary as he had been only a couple of weeks before
when he'd left Queen Sychorax's iron fort in the full
screaming cry and splendor of the Magic-hunt.

He had his sniffing nose, of course, but even *that*
wasn't quite so alarming now that he and his Magic-
hunters had no armor, weapons, shields, spears, sprite-
catching equipment, anything. All of it had been used
by Wish's Magic to create the great grim iron prison
that now enclosed the Kingwitch. They were standing
there in that cold draughty castle, wearing mostly their
underclothes. Some of them had even had to cover
themselves with hastily arranged brambles (which make
rather prickly pants).

A person always feels at a disadvantage when they

are trying to address a queen while dressed in little more than their underwear, so the Witchsmeller spoke with less than his usual authority.

"Your Majesty!" he objected. "You can't possibly take this child Wish back to Warrior territories! This child here is, as I suspected, an extremely dangerous *Fule*."

A person feels at a disadvantage when they are only dressed in their underclothes and a few hastily arranged brambles.

He lowered his tone in horror. "And the Fule is MAGIC. There's no two ways about it…and when I say Magic, I mean…really, really *Magic*."

It was not wise to disagree with Queen Sychorax once she had decided something had JUST…NEVER…HAPPENED.

So now she turned on the Witchsmeller and fixed him with a stare that a Frost Giant would have been proud of and her voice dropped to about fifty degrees or so below freezing. "I hope you are not suggesting, pest controller, that *my* daughter, MY daughter, who is the product of nineteen lines of Warrior good breeding and is a direct descendant of Brutal the Giant-Killer himself on *both* sides of her family tree, is some kind of common CHANGELING?"

"Well…er…I don't know about that, but you have to admit something very odd has gone on…" spluttered the Witchsmeller, quailing under her stern gaze.

"Or perhaps," continued Queen Sychorax, in a voice so grim it could have shriveled a snail at fifty paces, "you are putting forward the notion that I, Queen Sychorax, exchanged a true love's kiss with a rascal of a Wizard and that that has in some way turned my impeccably pedigreed Warrior of a daughter treasonably and untidily *magical*?"

"But she was exploding all over the place! Into an enormous cloud of dust! Shooting spells out of her eye!

Making all the iron fly about like this!" babbled the Witchsmeller, waving his arms around energetically to re-create the moment. "We ALL saw her do it, right in front of us!"

Queen Sychorax's eyes narrowed to splinters. "So you *all* saw her do it, did you?"

She turned to the crowd and her voice was as brisk and as meaningful as a freshly sharpened knife. "Step forward, if you have seen *my* daughter explode like some sort of badly raised Wizardly firework! Put up your hand if you witnessed *my* daughter making spells with iron like some sort of ghastly Magic blacksmith!"

There was a dreadful silence.

Nobody put up their hand.

And then such was the force of Queen Sychorax's personality that everyone took a step *backward*, Wizards and Warriors alike, muttering things like: "Oh no, we saw nothing...nothing at all...It's difficult to see in this kind of light."

Queen Sychorax raised one splendid eyebrow and turned to the Witchsmeller. "It appears," she said, in a tone like a cat bite, "that *you* were the only one who witnessed this spectacle, pest controller...You and your Magic-hunters are dismissed, and don't expect me to offer you any references to the emperor."

The Witchsmeller trembled with indignation. "This

is an *outrage!*" he said. "I shall report this whole story to the Warrior emperor *myself*, and he shall remove your crown and bring the might of the Anti-Magic Commission down upon you and upon that Fule!"

"You're going to tell the emperor that *you* failed and that the Kingwitch was defeated by a couple of thirteen-year-olds?" said the queen, in a tone of gentle surprise. "But you're supposed to be his crack Magic-hunting troops! The emperor doesn't like *losers*, pest controller, and what *I* would do if I were you, is to take some of these Witch feathers lying about around here back with you to the capital, and make up some story about how it was YOU who destroyed the Kingwitch. And then maybe he will forgive you for losing all that expensive Magic-hunting equipment."

"*You* are the most appalling woman I have ever met in my entire life!" said the Witchsmeller bitterly.

Queen Sychorax gave a small smile.

I *think* she took that as a compliment.

The Witchsmeller drew himself up to his full height, and adjusted his underclothes. He and his Magic-hunters gathered up as many Witch feathers as they could find. And then they stalked out of the courtyard with as much dignity as they could manage considering they were half dressed and unarmed.

I'm afraid that the watching Wizards and Warriors

did not entirely hide their laughter, and the sprites certainly didn't.

"Very good. In which case, order can be restored," sniffed Queen Sychorax with satisfaction, for there was nothing that Queen Sychorax liked better than order being restored. "I will take Wish back to iron Warrior territory behind the Wall, so she will be safe if the Witches return."

"And as for *Xar...*" continued Encanzo, sorrowfully, "don't take this badly, Xar, but I do still have to take you back to Gormincrag."

"Why?" asked Xar, in shock.

He had never heard anything more unfair in his life.

"Let me explain," said Encanzo. "Gormincrag is not supposed to be a prison so much as a rehabilitation center..."

"They always say that!" yelled Xar in outrage. "But 'rehabilitation center' is just a fancy way of saying jail! *You* said you were proud of me! *You* said I was growing up! *You* said I did a great job at controlling the Witch-stain and being good! And now you're going to PUNISH me for it?"

"Look, I am impressed, Xar, with how you've been trying to be good, I really am," said Encanzo. "But here in real life you cannot wish away that Witch-stain, and it is only going to get worse. The Drood Commander was a bad lot, but I will go back to Gormincrag with you and make sure a new and kinder regime is installed, for that is where you will be safest until we can get rid of the Witch-stain entirely."

"That *isn't* what we need to do!" howled Xar. "We need to find the ingredients of this spell to get rid of Witches, which we found in my Spelling Book. Show him, Wish!"

Bodkin took out the Spelling Book and gave it to Wish, and she showed Encanzo and Sychorax the right page.

"Who wrote this spell?" asked Encanzo after a while.

"I did," said Wish. "With Caliburn's feather."

Encanzo sighed and gave the book back to Wish.

"This isn't a *real* spell. Wish just made it up," said Encanzo gently.

"What do you mean it isn't a real spell?" said Xar, very crestfallen indeed, for he had been pinning all his hopes on that spell.

"Look!" said Encanzo, "it's in the Write Your Own Story section, right next to a whole load of stories about Xar being the biggest hero the world has ever known. No one single spell could defeat the Witches on its own."

"Encanzo is right, and it is just as I said," said Queen Sychorax. "This is *real life*, Xar, not a fairy story. You have to be reasonable and do as you are told."

Wish stepped forward hurriedly.

They were all going to be there *forever* if they had to wait for Xar to be reasonable and do as he was told.

But at least she could finally say the words she had been intending to say all along, a couple of weeks back, on the Royal Stage in iron Warrior fort.

"You are wrong, Mother, wrong!" said Wish, defiantly holding up her fist.

Sychorax started in shock.

And then she gave Wish *That Look*, a Look of Deepest and most Furious Disappointment, the look that generally meant that all the words that Wish had been *intending* to say went completely out of her head.

But standing by her friends' sides, with Xar, Bodkin, the spoon, and all her enchanted objects, and the werewolf, the snowcats, and with two weeks of terrifying and challenging adventure behind her, Wish opened her mouth...

And carried on speaking despite That Look.

"You are wrong, Mother, wrong!" repeated Wish fiercely. "And so is King Encanzo! You HAVE to believe that the world can change, that the spells can work, that you can write your own story whatever the odds that are facing you! For it is surprising how often the universe depends on one...unlikely...chance!"

Queen Sychorax looked at her daughter.

A girl who ROARED...

That Look unfroze.

She remembered, once more, that she should not underestimate her peculiar little daughter.

Sychorax touched Wish on the shoulder.

"I'm sorry, Wish," said Queen Sychorax. "You'll understand when you're older."

Oh for goodness' sake! Why do they keep saying that? thought Wish angrily. The adults clearly weren't going to see sense *whatever* their children said.

You are WRONG, Mother, wrong!

The grown-ups had some growing up to do *themselves*.

So Wish turned with a sigh to Encanzo.

"All right then. I don't agree with you, but if I can persuade Xar to go back with you to Gormincrag without a fight, will you and my mother at least grant us one wish?" asked Wish.

"If you can persuade Xar to go back with me without a fight, that would be a miracle," said Encanzo. "I make you no promises about the wish, however."

Wish took Xar aside, and whispered something in his ear.

Xar looked thoughtful.

"All right," he said grumpily. "I'll go back."

"A miracle!" said Encanzo in amazement. "I must come to you, daughter of Sychorax, for Xar-training tips..."

"What is your one wish?" asked Sychorax suspiciously.

"I wish you would both grant us *just one night* of cease-fire," begged Wish. "One evening banquet, here, Wizards and Warriors sitting and eating together, one night to celebrate the ONE time that Wizards and Warriors fought together side by side and defeated the Witches, and when a werewolf and a Wizard saved a Warrior princess's life. One night, stolen out of time."

"Just this one night?" said Encanzo thoughtfully.

"And then we go back to real life," said Wish.

"It's a beautiful evening," she added persuasively. "And look! One of the giants is starting to dance!"

It was true. One of the larger giants was gently moving his long limbs in a slow dignified country dance, humming to himself and the moon above.

"And then in the morning I PROMISE I will go back to Gormincrag and even tell you how to turn my brother back from that creature into being Looter again," said Xar, gesturing at the furious form of the Creature-That-Once-Was-Looter, being held, rather gingerly at that moment, by one of the Droods.

Queen Sychorax gave a start.

"Have you no control over your repellently disobedient son?" she said to Encanzo. "He turned his brother into *that*?"

"Your own offspring is not exactly a perfect example of obedience herself," snapped Encanzo. "Do Warriors normally jaunt about the countryside in the company of Enchanted Spoons?"

This was unanswerable, and the two monarchs bonded silently for a moment over the problems of parenting.

And they were at least *considering* Wish's request.

"I will not dance myself," said Sychorax thoughtfully. "I never dance...but I would normally give my troops a little celebration after a battle like that one..."

"We in the Wizarding world would feast into the small hours," said Encanzo.

Everyone was tired.

Everyone was hungry.

If they went their different ways right now, they would have to climb down that mountain again, and nobody particularly wanted to do that after a long, exhausting fight against the Witches. It would be irregular...*most* irregular...but it would mark an irregular event. And it was, by chance, Midwinter's End Eve, the day before winter finally turned into spring.

Midwinter's End Eve was also known as "Fool's Day," and things that happened on that day did not really count.

"As long as you absolutely understand, Wish," said Sychorax sternly, "that it will be *just one night*, out of time. It will change nothing. We go back to war with the Wizards tomorrow morning. Both of you have to give your Wizard and Warrior words that you will come back with us tomorrow."

Wish blinked at her innocently.

"Oh yes, Mother, what you are saying makes total sense. It would just be one night, out of time. We give our word, don't we, Xar?"

"Absolutely," said Xar.

"Hmmmmmm..." said Encanzo.

"Hmmmmmm..." said Sychorax.

Quite by chance they were both thinking the exact same thing, which was that they would give in to their offsprings' request but they would not let them out of their sight for one single second.

We give our word...

but they both
had their fingers
crossed behind their
backs...

19. Midwinter's End Eve, Also Known as "Fool's Day," One Night Out of Time

S o Sychorax and Encanzo turned to their subjects and ordered one night out of time.

"WARRIORS!" cried Queen Sychorax. "For this one night, I decree a cease-fire between the Warriors and the Wizards, to celebrate a historic defeat of an ancient enemy, the Witches! Tomorrow we return to our battles…Tomorrow we carry on our war…but tonight, we FEAST!"

"ONE NIGHT OUT OF TIME!" cried King Encanzo.

The Warriors and Wizards gave wondering murmurs, for this was all most unusual. But the fight had been won, and the word "feast" acted on them all like a magical elixir.

"ONE NIGHT OUT OF TIME!" the Wizards and the Warriors cried back to their monarchs.

And so began one of the most extraordinary evenings in the history of the wildwoods.

A great bonfire was built in the center of the courtyard, and the flames burned red, yellow, and also eerie blues and purples, as the Droods and the sprites added Magic fire to encourage the real flames to burn higher, and hotter.

Warriors danced with giants, whooping around the

fire. The hairy fairies whizzed around in a state of high excitement, as everyone made music, Queen Sychorax's Warriors blasting out joyful horn noises, Encanzo's fiddles hanging in the air magically playing themselves, the giants humming happily, linking arms with each other, the sprites singing their high bright songs, of things too high for the human eye to see, sounds too low for the human ear to hear.

The giants sang their giant songs, which rolled out across the landscape:

"I need the space to run my fill
I need to jump from hill to hill

And if you take my woods from me
I'll wander out into the sea
And try to find another world

So I can live a GIANT life!"

The Warriors sang their own songs:
"*NO FEAR!* That's the Warrior's marching song! *NO FEAR!* We sing it as we march along! *NO FEAR!* 'Cause the Warriors' hearts are strong! Is a Warrior heart a-wailing, is a Warrior heart a-failing, is a Warrior heart a-railing? *NO FEAR!*"

And the songs of the Warriors mingled with the melancholy song of werewolf:

"I'm running for the moon
Up to the moon where I can be good
When all the world gives up on me
When everyone thinks bad about me
I still have the moon
It's me and the moon
Mostly it's me and the moon"

Every now and then the werewolf would break off to howl, *"Oooooww ooow OOOOOOOOWW!"*

The sprites rushed around, wildly overexcited, playing tricks on every one with naughty games like:

Hinkypunk cast a spell on one of the Warrior's bowls of stew, making it rise up into the air and land on his head in a sticky stewy mess. Tiffinstorm lobbed a softening spell onto some of the Warriors' knives and forks so they went all floppy in their hands and they couldn't lift their food up to their mouths...Bumbleboozle cast little "Stopping Time" Spells so that he could nip in and steal everyone's food while time stopped for a blink of a second...

And Caliburn flew around, very harassed, trying to stop all these things from happening.

Xar and Wish and Bodkin watched them all dancing.

"You see?" said Wish. "They *can* get on if they try."

"It won't last," said Bodkin gloomily. "Your mother said 'one night' and when your mother says something she means it...Tomorrow they're going to be quarreling and fighting all over again."

"Grown-ups are so annoying! They always think they know best. Why won't they listen?" said Wish.

Bodkin sighed. "Yes, but it probably IS for the best. You will be safer back in Warrior territories, Wish, and, Xar, I know it's uncomfortable at Gormincrag, but now the Chief Drood has gone, maybe they can find an antidote for the Witch-stain."

Both Xar and Wish looked at him as if he were crazy.

"Oh, Bodkin, we're not going back to Warrior territories, or to Gormincrag," said Wish casually.

"Wha-a-a-at? But you promised! You gave your Warrior and your Wizard words!" said Bodkin.

"A promise can be broken," said Xar piously, "in pursuit of a higher good. Anyway they lied to us, and so that promise doesn't count."

"What are you going to do?" squeaked Bodkin in alarm.

One of the many reasons Bodkin wanted to go home was that back in the Warrior fort, he had Wish all to himself, he and the spoon were her only friends. But out here, in the wildwoods with the wayward but undeniably charismatic Xar, Bodkin had to share her.

Bodkin told himself it was for Wish's own good, that all he was concerned about in his official capacity as a bodyguard was Wish's health and safety—but he knew really in his heart of hearts that he was ever so slightly jealous. Even though (and this made Bodkin very sad) out here in *real life*, an Assistant Bodyguard would *never* end up with a Warrior princess, not even a slightly odd one.

That was just in fairy stories.

"We're going to run away, while they're all busy celebrating," said Wish. "We have work to do. We have to find the rest of these ingredients for the spell to get rid of Witches."

"But Encanzo said that spell wouldn't work!" cried Bodkin. "Caliburn! Are you going to let them do this?"

The old bird flew hither and thither. "Yes, the

bodyguard is right!" said the bird in extreme agitation. "It's probably a really bad idea..."

However, Caliburn said this without total conviction because frankly he had not been looking forward to going back to Gormincrag. It was all very well for the bodyguard to speak. *He* hadn't been there, in those dripping gloomy depths.

"But then," said Caliburn, "the adults are making such an almighty mess of things maybe we have to put our faith in the children, crazy and unrealistic and reckless though they are...What did I say earlier?"

"You said, and actually I wrote it down because I thought it was rather good: 'I suppose this is all such a disaster that it doesn't really matter WHAT we do, as long as we're with our friends and we do it TOGETHER...'" said Wish, checking back in the Spelling Book.

There was a small scuttling sound from behind them, and the werewolf pounced, and when he straightened up, he was carrying in his mouth the Creature-That-Once-Was-Looter, who had broken away from the Drood holding him earlier, and had been spying on them. The Creature-That-Once-Was-Looter was now on its way to sound the alarm, and warn everyone that Xar and Wish were planning to run away, for the Creature-That-Once-Was-Looter was absolutely

The Spelling Book
Write Your Own Story

So Xar Boy of Destiny triumphs yet again against the evil Graxerturgleburkin!

THE EVIL GRAxerturgleburkin

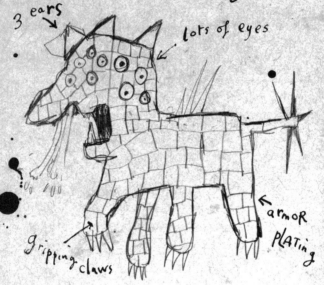

3 ears

lots of eyes

gripping claws

armor plating

<u>SPECial powers</u>:
Can drown you in RiVers of SNot
Bigger than a RoGreBBREath

page 3,284,631

determined that Xar should go back to Gormincrag, preferably indefinitely.

The bulging-eyed Unknown-Creature-That-Once-Was-Looter, swinging upside down by his four hind legs, looked so absolutely petrified to find himself actually in the JAWS of a werewolf, that he passed out for a second.

"Don't worry, Whatever-You-Are!" said Wish. "This is a very NICE werewolf, and he wouldn't bite you, would you, Lonesome?"

Lonesome shook his head, a little too vigorously, but stopped when the creature woke up with the shaking, and squeaked fearfully.

"Greeaggle Barg," apologized Lonesome.

And then he added, *"Greaggle Barg Rurgle"*—this time apologizing because Caliburn had told him that he shouldn't speak with his mouth full.

"Xar, you promised you would tell Encanzo what that creature is, so he can turn him back into Looter," urged Caliburn. "And remember what the giant said: You're supposed to be forgiving your enemies…"

Xar sighed. "He's going to be hopping mad when he gets back to being Looter. Trust me, he's never going to forgive me back."

But Wish passed him the Spelling Book, and Xar tore out the page where it said what Looter was. It was in a section of the book where Xar had been making up

mythical beasts, just beside that section where Xar had
made up a whole load of stories about "The Exploits
and Superdeeds of Xar, Boy of Destiny," and what
Looter was, apparently, was a Graxerturgleburkin.

No wonder they'd never guessed what he was, for
Xar had made that up. Xar had drawn a rather marvelous
picture of the Graxerturgleburkin, and they all admired
it, for it really was very like the Graxerturgleburkin himself,
slowly turning a deep purple as he hung upside down,
dripping from the werewolf's mouth.

With a flourish, Xar showed the picture of the
Graxerturgleburkin to Looter. "You actually got away
pretty lightly, Looter," said Xar. "You've only been
a Graxerturgleburkin for one month. I was stuck in
Gormincrag for over *two months!*"

The Graxerturgleburkin didn't look like he was
looking on the bright side of things.

Wish wrote a message to her mother on the bottom
of the piece of paper, and the message read:

"I'm sorry we lied to you, Mother. But the ends
justify the means…A fine outcome excuses a bad
method…You'll understand when you're older."

Xar wrote beside it, a message to his father: "I'll be
good, Father, I promise."

And then, carefully, Xar put the torn piece of

paper on the ground and got the werewolf to put the Graxerturgleburkin on top of it.

"Now he can't move," said Xar with satisfaction. "Because it's a windy night, and if he moves that piece of paper will fly away, and then Father won't know what to change him back from again…"

The Graxerturgleburkin's eyes bulged with fury, but also alarm. His many little talons gripped that piece of paper for dear life. He squeaked, as loud as he could, curses and insults in the Graxerturgleburkin language, but no one understood that language or would hear that squeaking above the sound of merrymaking and dancing.

He was stuck there now, to that piece of paper, and he did not dare scuttle or sludge away to sound the alarm.

But Xar was right.

There was a look in that Graxerturgleburkin's eye that said Looter wasn't going to be forgiving Xar anytime in the immediate future.

"We'll never get away," said Bodkin, in a last-ditch attempt to change their minds. "Encanzo and Sychorax are watching you both like hawks…"

Encanzo and Sychorax were indeed clever enough to know not to trust the children's words, so they had been keeping a sharp eye on those little rebels.

Sychorax was sitting on a rock, ramrod straight, her face a lofty regal mask, to show she was above such common things as dancing or celebrating. But every minute or so her eyes snapped across to check that her daughter was there, and that she wasn't escaping with any bad influences. (And maybe the very TIP of her toe was tapping in time to the music. She *was* human, after all.)

And Encanzo was prowling in the shadows, his face bleak as a midwinter cliff, great storm clouds billowing from his head, muttering under his breath: "I can't go back to that dark place…I can never go back…" while gripping tight to his Wizard's staff. "Never again… never more…" (And what he meant by that I have no idea.) But every now and then he cast a Magic glance over to check that his rascal of a son wasn't running away with Queen Sychorax's dangerous little daughter.

Xar told Crusher that he could join them later, at an agreed meeting place, because a Longstepper High-Walker giant was a little visible for a stealthy escape. But in the meantime he said the Once-sprite, perched like a little nightingale on Crusher's shoulder, should start up a song.

Wish suggested the song choice, and it was an unusual one.

It was a song that had not been heard in the wildwoods for many a long year, a song that began like this:

"I am young, I am poor, I can offer you nothing,
All that I have is this bright pair of wings,
This air that I eat, these winds that I sleep on,
This star path I dance in, where the moon sings…"

As soon as Sychorax heard the opening words, she turned white as a spirit, and Encanzo stopped still and lifted his head.

Sychorax marched right up to the giant and shouted up to the Once-sprite. "Stop singing that song!"

But Encanzo heaved a great sigh as if he could no longer bear it, stepped forward out of the shadows and said, "Wait a moment, Sychorax!"

And then Encanzo gave her a look that was a question, and he said:

"Just one night…one night out of time…for old time's sake…"

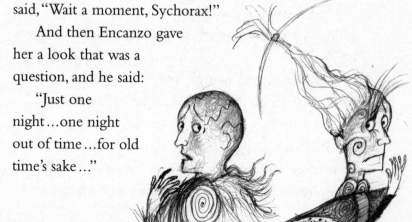

And he held out his hand toward her, and Sychorax paused as the sweet haunting words floated on the midnight air, for the Once-sprite had not listened to her, and he was singing on regardless.

It was Sychorax's own fault really, for it was *she* who had created that voice, in her dungeons at Warrior Castle, when she removed the Once-sprite's Magic. Beautiful things can be created out of loss and out of pain, and the Once-sprite's voice, which had always been sweet, now conveyed such a yearning sense of longing for the Magic that had been lost, the love-that-might-have-been, that it seemed like he was no longer a mere mortal, but a supernatural ghost of a sprite, blown in like a white winter leaf from the underworld, singing the past into the present with such pure intensity that it could even pierce the iron breastplate of the frozen queen herself.

"See the swifts soar, they live well on nothing,
You are young, you are strong, if you'll give me your
  hand…
We'll leave earth entirely and never go back there
We'll sleep on the breezes and never touch land…"

"It IS true, the giant's story about Encanzo and my mother, whatever she may say!" whispered Wish triumphantly, looking at her mother's white face, which was unfreezing just a tiny, tiny fraction as she listened to the music. "I knew it! Otherwise it would not affect her like this..."

"I promise you gales and a merry adventure
We'll fly on forever and never will part...
I am young, I am poor, I can offer you nothing
Nothing but love and the beat of my heart..."

...sang the voice of the Once-sprite. He sang with a little less melancholy than he had before, in Queen Sychorax's dungeons, because the Once-sprite had found a new life as a spell-raider, but there was still an overpowering bittersweetness to his song that was hauntingly seductive.

Sychorax, diamond-hard Sychorax, could not resist.

It *was* Midwinter's End Eve, after all.

And what happened on Midwinter's End Eve did not really count. Even a *queen* can be a fool on Midwinter's End Eve.

Queen Sychorax reached out her own hand, touched Encanzo's.

For old time's sake.

They both bowed, very regal, very courtly, very stiff.

And they began to dance.

They danced a little more stiffly than they might have done, once. Time had tempered them, just as bendy

little saplings harden into immovable tree trunks. Fine lines had traced their way across their faces.

But their eyes were the same eyes that had gazed out on the world a couple of decades before. One pair a fierce blue. The other a wild gray.

The two of them danced, and they were lost in the music for one fatal moment.

The song took them up into the air like the swifts, out of time, where there were no rules...

And in that fatal moment the children left, tiptoeing out of the courtyard. Crusher gave them the broken door, which he had kept in his pocket. So engrossed were the adults in their dancing and their merrymaking and eating and singing, that nobody noticed the broken door soaring off quietly into the night.

It was Midwinter's End Eve, ages long ago.

In a British Isles so old it did not know it was the British Isles yet.

A broken door, soaring through the quietness of the midnight sky, like a small flying carpet. Three children, all thirteen years old, poised in that moment between childhood and adulthood, lying on their backs, looking up at the stars. A talking raven, perched on Wish's foot. A spoon, lying fast asleep on her heart. The sprites, joyously swooping and diving, and buzzing around them. Down below them three snowcats, a werewolf, a bear, and a pack of wolves running, softly, quietly, their footsteps disappearing magically as they ran, in a spell cast by Ariel.

After a while of peaceful contemplation, Wish sat up and peered over the edge of the door.

"All right, we couldn't persuade our parents to join us, but let's not forget that we're doing really *well*!" said Wish. "The werewolf has learned some manners...The Once-sprite is happier now he's a spell-raider...and Xar is making definite progress in being good..."

"He still has some way to go," said Caliburn, a trifle gloomily, for only Encanzo had the power to set Caliburn and Ariel free.***

"And we do have ABSOLUTELY NO IDEA where we are going NOW," Bodkin pointed out.

Xar's arm was burning, and it gave him an idea. He sat up and opened the Spelling Book onto the page with the spell to get rid of Witches. And then he gave Wish Caliburn's feather. "Write!" urged Xar. "Write down the next ingredient! Think as hard as you can, and write!"

"Oh, that won't work," said Wish, dipping the feather in the ink. "I've tried that so many times before and it just won't—*oh!*"

***When Xar grew into a wise and thoughtful adult—and helping Xar run away from his own parent may have put Caliburn's moment of freedom back a bit.

To her astonishment, the feather, warm in her hands, began to write, almost as if by itself.

"Four scales of the Nuckalavee from the Western Whirlpools..." read Bodkin, in growing horror, "and five tears of the Drood from the Labyrinth of the Lake of the Lost..."

"Is there any more?" asked Xar.

"No, that seems to be it," said Wish, for whatever had animated the feather had run out, and all she was making now were a series of unintelligible blotches.

"I knew it! I knew it! We have the last ingredients in our quest!" said Xar, punching the air in his excitement. "Key!" he said to the key, who was steering them from the lock of the Punishment Cupboard. "Turn due southeast! Next stop... *THE LAKE OF THE LOST!*"

"Wha-a-a-a-a-a-t?" cried Bodkin, waving his arms around in horror. "But the Lake of the Lost is the DROOD STRONGHOLD! We can't go there! It's a suicide mission! Didn't you learn anything AT ALL from the Giant's Last Breath story? Pentaglion just took TWO tears of the Drood and those scary Droods came and destroyed his whole castle and his giant, and we're thinking of taking *FIVE*...? They're not listening to me are they, Caliburn?"

"No." Caliburn sighed. "They're not listening." Trying

to control the uncontrollable little princess was bad enough, but trying to control both her and Xar together...well...

"It's impossible," moaned Bodkin, lying back on the door and putting his helmet over his head.

But Xar and Wish were not paying attention to such gloomy thinking. They were excitedly surveying the spell to get rid of Witches.

"We'll get rid of those Witches in *no time* at this rate!" said Wish, with great enthusiasm. "Let's put a tick against the ingredients we've already *got* to make us feel like we're progressing. We've got the tears of the queen, and the Witch feathers..."

"Yes, but I'm annoyed that we've lost our first and most important ingredient in the spell to get rid of Witches by using it on the Drood," said Xar.

"The *moral* of that is worrying me," said Caliburn. "The giant's last words were about forgiveness, but it was the breath of forgiveness that actually *got rid of* the Drood in the end. So how does that work?"

This is the problem with stories.

Stories always mean something. The question is...

What exactly *do* they mean?

"It means we're going to have to start all over again finding ANOTHER Giant's Last Breath before we can find anything else!" said Xar. "It's very annoying."

Squeezjoos hovered joyfully above them.

"Yous don't have to start again!" said Squeezjoos. "*I hass a secret that I's hassn't told anybody! I's saved the day without anybody realizing!*"

"Nonsssense…" hissed Tiffinstorm. "An insignificant little hairy fairy like you could never save the day."

"But I has!" said Squeezjoos triumphantly. He paused for effect.

"*There'sss a tiny little bit of the breath left in the collecting bottle!* I sssaved it! I's put the sstopper back in just in time!"

Xar got out the collecting bottle, and there was the very, very faint whisper of green smoke in the center of it.

The last remains of the Giant's Last Breath.

"You see! I may's be sssmall but I is mighty! I is NOT too tiny to be a spell-raider after all!" crowed Squeezjoos.

"You most certainly are not," said Xar heartily. "That was extremely quick thinking of you. For this, Squeezjoos, I make you not only an official spell-raider, but the *Chief* Spell-Raider of our entire team!" said Xar, and the little hairy fairy was so overcome with excitement that he blew up like a puffer fish and turned three cartwheels in a row, and collapsed panting on Wish's shoulder. The spoon, who had woken up, gave him a celebratory bow.

"And look!" said Wish. "I can now tick off THREE of the ingredients! And there are only two more to collect!"

Wish lay back down on the door with a sigh of satisfaction and went back to dreamily surveying the stars.

"The universe is sending us a sign," she said. "Look! I'm sure that star up there is winking at us!"

And indeed, one of the stars did seem to be blinking on and off at them.

"Is it winking in a friendly way, though, or in a laughing-at-us way?" worried Caliburn. "Is it a good sign or bad sign? Are we really only being led by Xar's Witch-stain in escaping from your parents for the second time? Look! The Witch-stain is worse than ever! How can we know if Xar is EVER going to be able to control or get rid of it?"

Xar's hand was indeed still burning green in the moonlight.

"We just have to believe and hope that he can," said Wish simply. "If we believe in Xar hard enough, then we'll find our way to a happy ending."

"But you only think that because you're young and don't know any better!" agonized Caliburn. "When you're young you think that love conquers everything... You don't know the problems it can cause... You haven't seen the times where the Witches triumph, there is no second life, and the werewolf dies!"

"Well, I never want to grow up, then," said Wish. "I want to stay young forever. You know I'm right anyway,

Caliburn. It's why you came with us and didn't betray us to our parents..."

"And if you want to *stay* with us, Caliburn, you have to stop being so negative!" said Xar. "Wish is right. It's a good sign. It's a sign that everything will be all right in the end."

Caliburn sighed.

Some of his thoughts he kept to himself.

About LOVE, for example.

For as they lay on the door, the key, swiveling happily in the lock, was looking longingly at the spoon, and the fork was lookingly longingly at the key, and it was not so very different from the longing way Bodkin looked at Wish sometimes, and the longing way Wish looked at Xar.

There may be trouble ahead...thought Caliburn.

Who knows if Wish and Xar were right, on that midnight long ago?

For there would be storms tomorrow, there is no doubt.

But if we worry too much about tomorrow, how can we enjoy today?

So let us leave our heroes there, in the happiness of NOW, soaring gloriously through the sky, in the triumph and satisfaction of a quest completed, and in that blink of a moment before another quest begins.

And let us leave the grown-ups dancing.

In a while they will discover their children gone, the birds have flown, and then there will be tears and rending of clothes and wringing of hands, and Warriors blaming Wizards, and Wizards cursing Warriors, and their war and their worrying will begin again anew.

But for now they are *dancing*, in a moment out of time.

So let us enjoy that moment, lost in the music, a small sweet bittersweet smile on Queen Sychorax's face, for she knows this is a stolen time.

In that moment Sychorax and Encanzo are young again, free from all parental and regal responsibilities of being mothers, fathers, monarchs. In that moment they have no tribes to run, worlds to conquer, countries to rule, traditions to uphold.

They have earned those moments, the poor parents, just a few minutes to go back into the past, and unbend, relax, for an eyeblink or two, to be once more a young Warrior princess, who has just met a Wizard in the wood.

The Once-sprite is singing a different song now, another forbidden one.

"Once we were Wizards,
Wandering free
In roads of sky and paths of sea...

And in that timeless long-gone hour,
Words of nonsense still had power.

Doors still flew and birds still talked,
Witches grinned and giants walked…

We had Magic wands and Magic wings
And we lost our hearts to impossible things
Unbelievable thoughts! Unsensible ends!
For Wizards and Warriors might be friends.

In a world where impossible things are true
I don't know why we forgot the spell
When we lost the way, how the forest fell.
But now we are old, we can vanish too.

And I see once more the invisible track
That will lead us home and take us back…
So find your wands and spread your wings
I'll sing our love of impossible things
And when you take my vanished hand
We'll both go back to that Magic land
Where we lost our hearts…
Several lifetimes ago…
When we were Wizards
Once."

Dance on, Sychorax.

Fly on, door, through the quiet night.

With the three young heroes, lying on their backs, looking up at the stars.

And a very pleased-with-himself little hairy fairy, buzzing on Xar's chest, with his ear to the collecting bottle in Xar's breast pocket, whispering to himself.

"*I's* saved the day! ME, Squeezjoos! The smallest of them all has saved the day!"

For it was definitely the final fragments of the Giant's Last Breath in there.

There was no doubt about it.

If you held the bottle up to your ear, extremely close, you could still hear it, very, very faintly like an echo.

"Forgive them," the echo whispered.

"Forgive them."

Epilogue 1

wo weeks later…

Many fathoms down, far farther than five, for the ocean was terribly deep at the bottom of the Cliffs of Eternity, lay the Ball-of-Iron-That-Enclosed-the-Kingwitch on a bed of coral.

The ball of iron was silent, still.

But then from within it, there came a faint, muffled scraping, as of talons against something metal.

And the ball of iron began to move…

Softly, at first, and then a little faster.

The Kingwitch hadn't died.

He was in there.

He would keep scratching.

He had a little Magic-that-works-on-iron and he would keep using that Magic to break out of his iron prison.

The Kingwitch was nothing if not patient.

In the meantime he rolled over the watery landscape of the bottom of the ocean steadily, gradually, like a dark malignant glacier, or a slow but certain fate.

Epilogue 2

So that was the story of...

A word that froze, a heart that soared,
A boy who flew, a girl who ROARED.

Have you guessed which of the characters in the story I am yet?

I could be any of them, Wish or Xar, or Caliburn, the-raven-who-has-lived-many-lifetimes, or Bodkin the Assistant-Bodyguard-who-wished-he-was-a-hero, or Crusher, the-dreamy-Longstepper-High-Walker-giant, or one of the sprites, or the hairy fairies, ANY of the characters at all. (Not Eleanor Rose or the werewolf—I couldn't be either of THEM, because they weren't in the first book, so that would be cheating, and the narrator can be tricky but should not actually cheat, otherwise it's extremely annoying for the reader.)

I still cannot tell you who I am, I'm afraid, for as you can see, the story has not yet ended.

I can only tell you at the end...

but the end is getting closer.

Wish's and Xar's stars have crossed for the SECOND unlikely time, and for good, or for evil, their stars are now joined together and they are traveling in the same, very dangerous direction.

I left them, peacefully enjoying the present.

One of the reasons that looking into the future, or dwelling too much on the past, are such dangerous practices, is that what we see there might stop us enjoying the excitement and pleasures of the "now."

But pity me, for I have the curse of being able to see into the future, and although they do not know it yet...that door our heroes are lying on so peacefully is headed toward the Lake of the Lost, which, as Bodkin pointed out, is the Drood stronghold, and Droods are unrelenting, unforgiving, and the greatest Wizards in the wildwoods, and they will want to obliterate anyone who has Magic-mixed-with-iron.

The emperor of Warriors will be told by the Witchsmeller about Sychorax's daughter, and he too will want to eliminate the threat posed to the Warrior world by Magic-mixed-with-iron...

Encanzo and Sychorax will be chasing Xar and Wish, but Encanzo is in trouble with the Droods himself. And Sychorax is in trouble with the emperor of Warriors...and everyone will be chasing everyone else.

The forces of darkness will be closing in on our young heroes.

But WORST OF ALL...

The Kingwitch will be after them both. And he will not rest until he gets them. And he has a single piece of tiny blue dust that he thinks he may find helpful.

Can Wish and Xar break out of the sad circles of the history of the wildwoods?

They are young, they are hopeful.

Can they really write their own story?

Is that even possible?

Keep hoping...

Keep guessing...

Keep dreaming...

The Unknown Narrator

Never and Forever (Tor's Song)

Don't blame the wolves, for winter is bitter,
Don't blame the wolves, for wolves need to eat,
The winter has chased all the game from the forest,
The wolf cubs are hungry, and I would taste sweet...

I don't want to die before I have children,
I don't want to die when the world is so young,
I don't want to die on this glorious midnight
With words not-yet-said and songs not-yet-sung...

I am young, I am poor, I can offer you nothing,
All that I have is this bright pair of wings,
This air that I eat, these winds that I sleep on,
This star path I dance in, where the moon sings...

See the swifts soar, they live well on nothing,
You are young, you are strong, if you'll give me your hand,
We'll leave earth entirely and never go back there,
We'll sleep on the breezes and never touch land...

I promise you gales and a merry adventure,
We'll fly on forever and never will part...
I am young, I am poor, I can offer you nothing,
Nothing but love and the beat of my heart.

See the swifts soar,
They live well on nothing,
You are young, you are strong,
 if you'll give me your hand.

We'll leave earth entirely
 and never go back there,
We'll sleep on the breezes
 and never touch land...

ACKNOWLEDGMENTS
(THANK YOU)

A whole team of people have
helped me write this book.

Thank you to my wonderful editor,
Anne McNeil, and my magnificent agent,
Caroline Walsh.

A special big thanks to Samuel Perrett,
Polly Lyall Grant, and Rebecca Logan.

And to everyone else at Hachette Children's Group,
Hilary Murray Hill, Andrew Sharp,
Valentina Fazio, Lucy Upton, Louise Grieve,
Kelly Llewellyn, Nicola Goode, Katherine Fox, Alison
Padley, Rebecca Livingstone.

Thanks to all at Little, Brown,
Megan Tingley, Jackie Engel, Lisa Yoskowitz,
Kristina Pisciotta, Jessica Shoffel.

Thank you to Eleanor Rose and her Mum for
donating money to the National Literacy Trust
for her name to appear in this book.
Find out more about the vital work the
NLT does here: literacytrust.org.uk

And most important of all,
Maisie, Clemmie, Xanny.

And SIMON for his
excellent advice
on absolutely everything.

I couldn't do it
without you.

Turn the page for a sneak peek at Wish and Xar's next heart-pounding adventure!

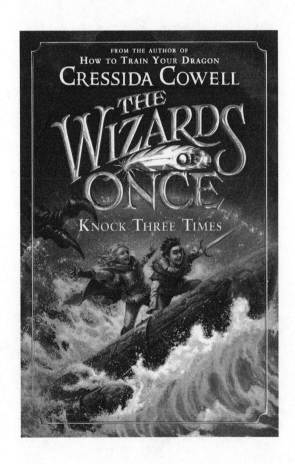

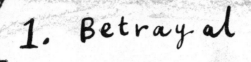

1. Betrayal

hree thousand years ago, at the end of the
era that would later be known as the Bronze
Age, the whole British Isles were covered in
wildwoods.

Good things lived in the wildwoods, animals and
Magic creatures and humans who minded their own
business, but bad things lived there at that time too, some
very bad things.

Two of these bad things were flying above the forest
even now. The bad things were presently invisible, but
if human eyes could have seen them they would have
noticed that they had soft black wings like the wings
of crows, and fingers that ended in talons like a bird
of prey, and noses a little like a beak. In fact, they were
WITCHES, not good Witches,
but very *bad* Witches indeed,
and they were flying high,
just below the clouds,
and as they flew they
were watching something
down below.

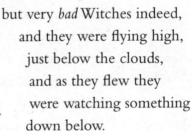

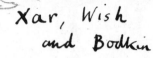
← Xar, Wish and Bodkin

The *something* was
a door, but instead of
being where a door
really ought to be,
vertically opening and
shutting between rooms
that are safely on the ground
in an orderly kind of way,
this particular door was flying
through the air, flat on its front like
a carpet, just above the treetops.

It was the little moving speck of
the flying door that had first attracted the
Witches' attention as they flew, with lazy
wingbeats in the strong currents of air high above
the trees, on their way back to their nests in the
Lachrymose Mountains. But it wasn't the door *itself* that
was now holding their scrutiny.

There were three children lying on their stomachs
on top of the flying door.

The invisible Witches looked down at the children.

And the children looked down over the edge of the
flying door, looking for something in the forest.

The Witches were hungry, so hungry that long dribbles
of black saliva were dripping from their lips. They hadn't
seen anything so delicious as these children in weeks, no,

perhaps years (and that will give you an idea why people didn't really *like* Witches, either in the Bronze Age, or any other age that the Witches happened to turn up in).

But something was making those Witches pause before swooping on the tasty, unaware little morsels below and fastening their claws into them.

"Thaw si ti gniod tou ereh?" whined Breakneck, waggling her nose from side to side. "Yhw si ydobon gnitcetorp ti? Od uoy kniht ti dluoc eb a part?"*

Ripgrizzle was pausing too, although the smell of the blood of the human children (which to a Witch is as delicious as that of a cake baking in the oven) was wafting up to him and making him drool like a dog. He was desperate to snatch the treats from under Breakneck's waggling nose and fly back to his nest to feed on the tender darlings all by himself.

But he too was cautious. Before the return of the Witches to the wildwoods, the air would have been full of flying things—birds and sprites and cockatrices, dragons, pixie, all manner of glorious magical creatures. But now, this early in the morning, which was too close to the night hours of the Witching-time, the forest was as quiet as death, and the Warrior humans kept their babies locked up safe in their castles, and the Wizard

---

* Witches speak the same language as we do, but each individual word is back to front. This means "What is it doing out here? Why is nobody protecting it? Do you think it could be a trap?"

humans kept their babies safe in their treehouse forts. So what were *these* human babies doing, then, flying cool as you like, on the back of a magical flying door, miles and miles away from any human habitation? Perhaps Breakneck was right. Maybe it was a trap.

The children were talking to one another, and one of them was singing rather shakily, with false bravery: "*NO FEAR!* That's the Warriors' marching song! *NO FEAR!* We sing it as we march along!"

Ripgrizzle's gigantic ears curled up at the edges, swiveling and tilting toward the child in order to catch the sound. The eye in the middle of his forehead opened up sleepily. The two Witches flew, unseen, lower, lower, to listen to the children's conversation.

The first young person was a Wizard boy called Xar, the second was a Warrior princess called Wish, and the third was a Warrior boy called Bodkin.

The three children were looking rather more ragged and sad than they had been two weeks earlier when they had run away from Wish's and Xar's parents. They had started out joyously, in the way that these journeys often begin. Running away had seemed like it would be an exciting adventure, but now they were hungry and tired and frightened, for they knew they were being hunted by the Warriors and the Wizards and the Witches, and that they must never be caught. If the *Warriors* caught them,

Sychorax would lock up Wish in iron Warrior fort, where the Witches could not get hold of her. If the *Wizards* caught them, Encanzo would lock up Xar in the prison of Gormincrag, where his Witch-stain could be treated. And if the *Witches* caught them…well, that was such a scary idea our heroes were trying their hardest not to think about it.

So for the past two days they had been looking for the house of the sister of Caliburn, Xar's talking raven, where they hoped to be able to hide.

"I KNOW my sister lives somewhere around here," said Caliburn for the umpteenth time. "She moved here a while ago, back when I was still a human…

"I know that my sister has one of the ingredients we need for the spell to get rid of Witches, the tears of the Drood, and maybe we can persuade her to give it to us," said Caliburn. "And she'll give us a bed for the night and a good meal, and she'll protect us for a while…"

None of them were feeling very strong at all, and the idea of a bed for a night and a good meal was even more attractive than the idea that Caliburn's sister might give them one of the ingredients they needed for their quest. In fact, it brought tears to Bodkin's eyes.

"What does your sister's house look like, Caliburn?" asked Bodkin.

Caliburn looked a little shifty. "Oh, you know, just

like any other old human habitation. I haven't been there in years. I'll know it when I see it."

"Your sister must have a very big house," said Wish doubtfully. "Look how many of us there are! Are you quite sure she'll want to have all of us to stay?"

Caliburn gave an airy wave of his wing. "Oh, my sister has loads of room! Of course she'll have us all to stay..."

"Even though we're a bit, well...ODD?" said Wish wistfully. "I can't believe that your sister won't mind about us being Wizards and Warriors working together, Caliburn—everyone else hates that. And some people even might say we were sort of... *cursed*."

Her armour was dented, she hadn't eaten in three days, and her face and hands and legs were deeply scratched from a terrible battle they had a week ago when they were ambushed by wyverns (a type of dragon very common in the Bronze Age).

With all her heart Wish wanted to believe that Caliburn had a sister who would welcome them, even though they were outlaws, disobeying the laws of the wildwood universe...but deep down she had a hollow feeling that this was very unlikely.

"Let's face it, Caliburn," said Wish, trying to be practical and not mind too much, "we don't really fit in anywhere. No one is going to want us."

"My sister isn't as prejudiced as everyone else," said

Caliburn. "There are kind people in the world. You just have to find them."

"You're quite sure your sister hasn't died and come back as a raven too, and the reason we can't find her house is that she's now living in some sort of NEST?" said Bodkin suspiciously.

"No, no," said Caliburn. And then, less certainly, "Probably not…"

Bodkin didn't quite know how to say this without hurting Caliburn's feelings, but they had been searching for Caliburn's sister's house for quite a while now without finding any sign of it. "Are you quite sure that you've got this right, Caliburn?" said Bodkin. "You've only just remembered that you HAVE a sister."

"Living many lifetimes is difficult," said Caliburn,

No one is going to want us..

rather flustered. "It takes a while to remember what happened in the previous ones. But now that my memory has been jogged, I know I have a sister, and she's down in that forest somewhere..."

"Well, I think we should give up looking for your sister and march right into that Drood stronghold on the Lake of the Lost and just take their tears from them," said Xar, who was not a patient person.

"You don't understand!" said Caliburn. "The Droods are unrelenting, unforgiving, and the greatest Wizards in the wildwoods, and they really don't like having their tears taken! They'll kill us if they catch us... Much easier for my sister just to GIVE them to us..."

And then Wish spotted something that wasn't the welcoming fires of Caliburn's sister's house, but something much more sinister.

"Some people are following us down there in the forest," whispered Wish, putting up her eyepatch a smidgeon because she could see better through her Magic eye. Sure enough, down in the tangle of green woods below them, way in the distance, there were the little flickering lights of many, many torches coming through the trees in their direction.

"Do you think it could be your sister, Caliburn?" Xar whispered hopefully, his tummy giving the most gigantic rumble. Only Xar could mistake the ominous torches of what was clearly a hunting party for a welcoming greeting from Caliburn's sister. But then, Xar was an optimistic sort of person, who hoped for the best at all times.

He had a deep cut over his right temple from where a wyvern had earlier tried to take his eye out, and an old bit of shirt wrapped around his leg covering a wound from a boggart bite that was going septic, but he wasn't going to let little things like these get him down. Xar was a happy-go-lucky sort of boy, with a wide-awake look in his eyes that suggested that he was determined to enjoy life despite unimportant details like infected boggart bites and wyvern injuries.

As Xar was also a boy of considerable charm and charisma, he had a lot of companions, and flying with the door were six of his sprites and three hairy fairies. These tiny little insect-y creatures, so paper-thin you could see their hearts, were buzzing around in a state of such alarm that blue electric sparks were coming out of their ears.

"Beware..." they hissed. "Beware beware beware..."

"No, it's definitely not my sister," said Caliburn, shading a wing over one of his eyes and squinting so he could see better. "They're banging war drums. My sister wouldn't bang war drums, unless she's changed a very good deal in the last twenty years."

"Don't worry, sprites," said Xar soothingly, for although Xar often led his companions into difficulty, he did take his responsibilities as the leader of his band very seriously. "I'll look after you..."

"Of coursse you will, Masster!" squeaked Squeezjoos, one of the smallest and most enthusiastic of the hairy fairies. "You iss the most brilliantastic leader in the whole world ever, and you woulds never leads us into any trouble!"

"But I don't understand it..." said Wish, bewildered. "Nobody knows which way we went—the sprites have dimmed their lights, we're flying so close to the tops of the trees that nobody can see us from below, so how can they be following us?"

"Maybe they picked up the scent of Crusher and the snowcats," Bodkin suggested.

Xar had other companions too, and they were down on the ground. A giant called Crusher, three beautiful snowcats, some wolves, a bear, and a werewolf called Lonesome were following on foot, way below on the forest floor.

"Impossible!" Xar whispered back. "I'm unbeatable at running away and so are my companions! We're completely untrackable..."

you woulds
never leads us
into any trouble...

As well as being just a *trifle* conceited, Xar was indeed very good at running away. He was the most disobedient boy in the Wizard kingdom, always getting into trouble for doing things like:

Getting his sprites to charm his older brother Looter's spelling staffs so that every time Looter tried to use them, they spanked him on the bottom ... Painting spots on the Magic mirror in the main hall so everyone who looked in it thought they were coming down with something infectious ... Pouring animation potion on the trousers of Ranter, his least favorite teacher, so whenever Ranter tried to put them on, the trousers skipped out of reach.

As a result, Xar had spent his entire short life running away from the wrath of his father, his teachers, and the other Wizards, so he had become something of a running away *expert*.

"Maybe someone'ssss betrayed us," hissed Tiffinstorm, one of Xar's larger sprites, eyes narrowing jealously. "Probably that werewolf. Never trust a werewolf who you met in a prison. That's good advice, kids."

"Don't you dare accuse the werewolf just because he's a werewolf!" said Xar fierily.

Wish agreed with Xar.

"Nobody's betrayed us," said Wish, soothingly, "we're on the same side now, Tiffinstorm. We're all outlaws together, remember?

"But who is chasing us down there in the forest?" worried Wish.

Caliburn began to list their enemies. "Well, it could be the Droods…or Xar's father…or Wish's mother…And what about the Witchsmeller? *He* hates you…Or the Warrior emperor? He'll want to get rid of Magic-that-works-on-iron at all costs…"

Squeezjoos bared his little teeth and squeaked, "*I'sll gets them for you, Master! I'sll bites great chunks out of their iron bottoms! I'sll makes their noses drip for a week and ties knots in their sandwiches! I'sll makes holes in theys socks so theys keep puttings theys big toes throughs it in a REALLY ANNOYING way! I'sll put itching powder in theys underwear and I'sll leave little fluffballs in theys tummy buttons and theys will NEVERS KNOW where the fluff is coming from!*"

As Squeezjoos was not a great deal bigger than a dormouse, and the threat of fluff in the tummy button was not exactly life-threatening, none of this was likely to be terribly worrying to a Drood or a heavily armed iron Warrior, but Xar thanked him solemnly and said, "Yes, of course you can, Squeezjoos, just as soon as I give the order."

The one enemy that Caliburn did not mention was *Witches*. Which, given that there were two very large Witches hovering right above their heads at that very moment, was a tiny bit ironic.

Find out more about
the wonderful world of

CRESSIDA COWELL

www.cressidacowell.com

Where you can find out all about
her books and events, play games...
and lots more!

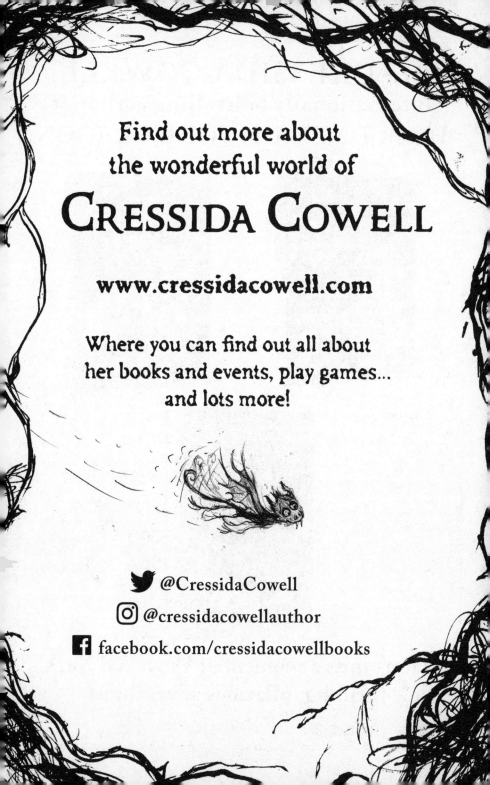

🐦 @CressidaCowell

📷 @cressidacowellauthor

f facebook.com/cressidacowellbooks

From CRESSIDA COWELL,
internationally bestselling author of
HOW TO TRAIN YOUR DRAGON

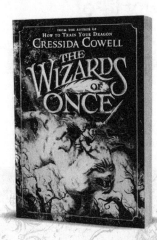

Don't miss a moment of Wish and Xar's thrilling, hilarious adventures!

LITTLE, BROWN AND COMPANY
BOOKS FOR YOUNG READERS

#WizardsofOnce

BOB919

SEE WHERE IT ALL BEGAN!

Find more adventures and play interactive games at
HowToTrainYourDragonSeries.com

 LITTLE, BROWN AND COMPANY
BOOKS FOR YOUNG READERS

BOB740

Step boldly into Morrigan Crow's Wundrous world!

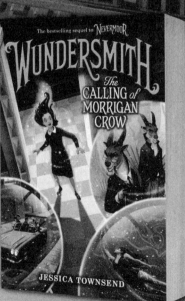

lbyr.com

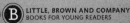 LITTLE, BROWN AND COMPANY
BOOKS FOR YOUNG READERS

#Nevermoor